Saving Lady Noan

Avi Ornstein

2026, TWB Press
https://www.twbpress.com

Dedication

To my grandson, Otis.

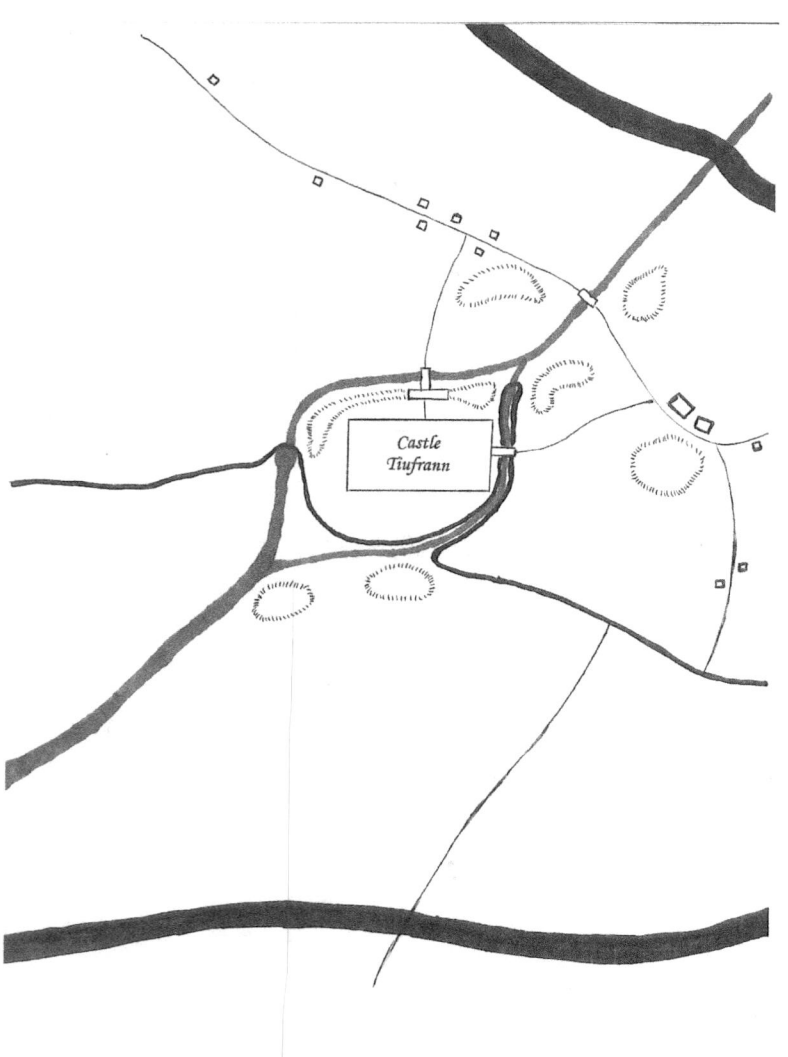

PROLOGUE

L ord Pitar and Lady Nimina stood atop the balcony of Castle Vork, looking upon their daughter with pride. Noan had flourished as she had grown, following the model of gender equality set centuries ago by Sonia. She had drawn upon her own physical abilities and, while quite beautiful, she had trained in armed battle, being proficient in both sword and bow. The few scars she had gained blended in with her bronzed skin and dark brown shoulder-length hair.

While her mind was sharp, her other attributes were stronger. She enjoyed mental challenges, but she had learned to be respectful of all others and interacted well with all the citizens of the barony. Lord Pitar especially appreciated how well his daughter got along with her grandfather and even more how she charmed her granduncle, King Linoan. Lord Pitar hoped that this would prove beneficial for himself and for the future of Glawynia.

Despite being only fifteen years old, she reflected her confidence quite well as she joked with the guards and ladies-in-waiting as they prepared to depart for another visit to the king. She waved happily as they got in order and began their roadway travel. Her parents waved back in return and Lady Nimina blew her a kiss

***

After a wonderful week with her granduncle, King Linoan, Lady Noan departed to return home. She road in a carriage with her nurse and two handmaidens and eight guards accompanied them, four before the carriage and four following behind.

The weather was cool and cloudy and a light snowfall began as they rode through the forest. Then a shower of arrows came from both sides, hitting the coachman and three of the guards.

"Protect Lady Noan!" one guard called out as more arrows continued to come from the darkened snowfall. None could see where the assailants were. Other guards fell from their horses as they were struck, spilling blood from the fatal blows. Their foes appeared to have a sense of infra-vision.

Lady Noan wished that she had a weapon, but such was not the case. The others in the carriage tried to see what was happening outside as the coach came to a stop. Noan was grabbed roughly as the other three were pulled out screaming. Unable to fight the opposing strength, her arms were bound behind her.

She closed her eyes as the clothes were torn from the other women. She could avoid seeing what was happening, but she was unable to seal her ears. She clearly heard their pain as each was ravaged, calling for salvation until they were slain. Silence followed, except for grunts from the raiding party as they ransacked the bodies and collected the guards' steeds. Noan was forced back into the carriage. Opening her eyes, she saw the bloody bodies strewn around the sight.

As they departed, Noan silently made two vows. "I will seek revenge on these barbarians, and I will never again travel unarmed!"

***

A few days later, a royal horseman arrived, drenched with sweat. He had ridden as fast as he was able, having nearly killed his steed with his incessant stress. He insisted on speaking with the baron's majordomo, Tobba. His message for Lord Pitar spread quickly through the court.

Lady Noan's party had been found slain – brutally. All were dead except for Lady Noan, missing and assumed kidnapped!

1 – MERCENARIES

Clouds continued to gather above them as the dwarves rode along, and they both sensed an unexpected chill in the air.

"Can't you get that mule to move any faster?" Anndimfoss asked.

"Be happy that it's moving at a steady pace," her husband answered. "We'll get there in less than an hour, and the time of day wasn't specified, was it?"

"No, dear, it wasn't."

The farmers they passed stopped harvesting the rye and glared at them. They could hear that some comments were exchanged, but they were unable to catch the words. They had no trouble, however, in catching the negative, derogatory tone. This strong sense of dislike had been growing for the past few hours, matching the negative change in the weather.

"You know," Ginderbar muttered, "I just wish we knew what it was we are getting ourselves into. It would also be useful to know whether the aversion the natives are displaying is due to our race, our armaments, the current political unrest here in Glawynia, a combination of all of them, or something else. The humans' animosity makes me tense, and my hackles are up." One hand stayed on the pommel of his sword.

Anndimfoss noted this and became aware that she had pushed her cloak back so that it was not in the way of her weapons. Like her husband, she wore a short sword and had one hand ax ready. Her morning star was also easily available. Ginderbar's crossbow lay across his back, as it would only be used for a foe at some distance.

All they had seen thus far were farmers, and nothing more threatening than scythes had been observed. That was not to say that a scythe could not inflict harm, nor was it discounting its long reach. But she was confident that they would, if necessary, have no difficulty in facing such opposition. The problem was that they had taken on a new profession, and they were clearly green, having had no true experience. The fact that this was also her first separation from Elmdimder also gnawed at her conscience, adding to the uneasiness.

The flat terrain rolled outward in all directions, as far as they were able to see from the back of their mounts. The minimal number of trees and especially the absence of mountains seemed totally unnatural to the two dwarves as they urged their ponies onward. Anndimfoss wanted to race through this region, but the mule her husband had tethered to his saddle acted as an anchor. The mule was a necessary evil, however, as the ponies could only bear so much weight. True to their race, they each had a solid, stocky build, though Ginderbar was actually on the lean side, towering a full seven inches over her while only exceeding her by perhaps six pounds.

As the road rounded a farmhouse backed by a small copse, an unimposing town came into view. They crossed a wooden bridge spanning a rather minor river that meandered through the farmland and approached the cluster of buildings. A notable number were two stories high, but the massive size of the doors stood out more than anything else. Ginderbar and Anndimfoss had interacted with humans all of their lives, but seeing every structure built on this larger-than-life scale was still difficult to ignore.

The stone structure of Castle Vork, while still a bit away, was visible over the roofs of these houses. The scowls directed toward them by the town's residents were even more visible. Two children playing in the street looked up and froze as if transformed to stone. Anndimfoss gauged that they matched her in height, as she was two inches short of four feet, but even combined together, the children probably wouldn't equal her in weight.

One suddenly discovered his vocal cords. "Dwarves!"

As if a trance was broken, they both scampered into a nearby alley, leaving a trail of dust behind that slowly began to settle toward the dirt road.

"Well," Ginderbar murmured, "that answers part of the question. I know that no dwarves live in this town, but why do they hate or fear our kind?"

"Hush, husband. We'll be finding out soon enough."

At this time, they were crossing the market square. All of the people moved out of their way as if they were lepers. Some spat at the ground as they passed. Quite a few uttered oaths or curses, and there was little effort to hide either.

The portcullis was raised at the castle wall, and an armed guard was standing at either side, each dressed in armor and bearing a sizable halberd. The dwarves dismounted and approached but stopped several feet away so that looking directly up toward their faces was not too awkward.

After glancing down at them, the guards resumed staring straight ahead, apparently attempting to totally ignore their presence.

"Pardon me," Ginderbar stated in a clear, level voice, "but we are here to see Tobba, Lord Pitar's majordomo."

Looking down, the guard to the left said, "It ain't court day."

Reaching slowly into his belt pouch, the dwarf produced a clearly stamped iron disk. He held it out on his open palm.

"Stalif said we should show this."

The other guard's eyes darted in the direction of the disk and then opened wide.

"We wuz tole two dwarfs'd be cummin', Tarz. Is'n it a strange lot what's bin showin' up this day?"

Tarz signaled them to enter as he eyed his partner to be quiet.

"Take yer steeds to the stable. Show the disk an' they'll say where to go next."

Anndimfoss smiled sweetly at each guard as they walked their ponies through the gateway. She felt a smile would do more to disarm them than any verbal response, and she was probably right.

Once inside, they looked around, quickly sighting the stable. Like everything else, it was oversized as far as they were concerned. They led the ponies and mule to the stalls, noting how activity once more came to a halt. Everyone was watching them.

Ginderbar selected the youngest stable hand, still a full head taller than him, and approached the boy with an air of confidence. He held up the iron disk, not saying anything.

The youth's scornful expression was instantly transformed. "Yes, sir. Yes, ma'am." The attitude was evident in the tone of his voice. "Right this way, if it pleases you."

He took the reins and led the animals to the stalls at the end of the stable. As he removed the saddles and blankets, the dwarves looked around. Ginderbar nudged his wife and pointed to another pony two stalls over. Perhaps another of the smaller folk was present. Equipment was present with several of the other steeds, so the dwarves didn't object as their load was lowered off the mule and placed at the end of the stall.

"This way, please," the boy said in a deferential tone.

He escorted them to a servant standing by the entrance to the castle. The gray and green livery that he wore bore the same coat of arms as had been worn by the guards, silver with a green chevron.

Ginderbar held up the disk to confirm the statement as his spouse thanked the lad. They were silently led into the building, turned to the right and walked down a long hallway. After passing several closed doors, all accentuating their smaller stature, they came to one that was open. The servant gestured for them to enter.

It was an antechamber, and a guard was present. "May I see yer passpiece, please?"

A variety of weapons lay spread on a table and bench.

Nodding to the servant once it was shown, he turned back to the dwarves.

"Please leave yer arms 'ere. I'll keep an eye on 'em."

The servant exited as Ginderbar and Anndimfoss removed all their weapons, placing them at the vacant end of the bench. The guard then opened the doorway at the other end of the room.

"Join th'others inside, an' 'elp yerselves to what's left o' the meal. Tobba should be 'ere soon."

The room they entered had arrow-slit windows, but too high in the wall for them to see anything other than the sky. Bread, meat and fruit, plus pitchers of one or more beverages, were on the table, and six other people were in the room. The aromas were appealing after the long day's ride.

"Welcome, friends," a thin woman said. She appeared to be a crossbreed, part elf and part human, with a dark complexion and short-cropped, black hair. "My name is Fitessa. The food's decent, but the wine is definitely cheap. Not worthy of anything other than rinsing dust from your mouth."

"Thanks for the advice," Anndimfoss said as they approached the table. She looked at the other guests.

A wood elf and a gnome sat at a small table, rolling a pair of dice and talking together quietly. Three young humans occupied another table. Two sat while the other stood. No, he also sat, towering like a small tree.

The door on the far side of the room opened with a squeal and got everyone's immediate attention. A servant held the door as a man with a more austere stance entered, also wearing the castle's coat of arms.

"Tobba, Majordomo of Vork," the servant announced. She then closed the door as soon as the majordomo stepped clear.

Tobba was nearly six feet tall and obviously weighed over two hundred pounds. Silver out-striped brown in both his hair and beard, matching the color of both his eyes and the coat of arms. He exuded a sense of serious confidence as he surveyed each person in the room as carefully as he himself was being studied.

"I will not waste time asking your background nor what you can offer to this effort, as I fully trust the judgment of Stalif. You do not yet know the specifics of why you are here, so let me first try to remove that haze and clarify why your assistance is being sought.

"I assume that even those of you from other kingdoms have heard that King Linoan is growing old and senile and his health is failing. It is also common knowledge that there is no clear heir to the throne. You are all aware of these facts?"

Seeing that everyone was nodding, he continued talking in the same flat tone.

"While the king has neither children nor siblings, his wife's brother, Lord Kistun, did sire two sons. Lord Pitar, ruling here at Castle Vork, was born to a human mother. Lord Blavin, ruling to the north at Castle Tiufrann, was born to a dwarf mother. Lord Kistun was married to neither of the women, but he acknowledged both as his sons.

"It has been recognized that they are the only two accepted contenders for the throne. The problem is that they were both born on the same night, and it is not known which is the elder, thereby being the rightful successor.

"Lord Blavin's lands include the mountain homelands

of a sizable portion of the dwarves in Glawynia. While each of the brothers has been fair to his people, the fraternal animosity runs deep. Each sees himself as the next king, and a fear of civil war is spreading throughout the kingdom."

"Now I understand the treatment we received," Anndimfoss whispered to her husband. She noticed that others were similarly exchanging quiet comments, though she was unable to hear what they were actually saying to one another.

"Let me assure you that you are not being asked to resolve this controversy," Tobba said, "though what you will be doing may influence the outcome.

"A bit over an eightday ago, Lord Pitar's daughter, Lady Noan, was returning from a court visit to her granduncle, the King. While only fifteen, she is Lord Pitar's pride and joy, and the fact is well known that she is loved dearly by King Linoan. Lord Pitar had hoped that she might affect the king's thoughts in one of his more lucid moments, swaying his awaited decision in favor of Lord Pitar. She never made it back!"

Tobba paused to take in a deep breath and compose himself. Exhaling slowly, he continued. "The entire party, other than Lady Noan, was found dead and looted. Her handmaidens and nurse had been raped, and evidence showed that it had been done viciously. The people are understandably in an uproar. Since Lord Pitar has not received any ransom note, he feels certain that forces loyal to his half-brother carried out this transgression, and that Lady Noan is being held prisoner in Castle Tiufrann.

"This castle sits atop an island formed where the Tiufrann River spills over the cliff edge of the highlands that mark the boundary of the dwarven mountains. A siege would be difficult, and it would endanger Lady Noan. Lord Pitar therefore had Lord Stalif, his wife's brother and his most trusted advisor, seek out a band of unknown mercenaries to rescue her by stealth. You are the ones that he found.

"Lord Pitar wants to avoid a war, if it is possible. He wants to reclaim his daughter and he hopes to keep the kingdom at peace. History tells of other times where nations were destroyed by such conflict. This is something he wants not to be recorded for Glawynia.

"The Vernal Equinox is five days hence. Castle Tiufrann and its guards, human and dwarf alike, are almost certain to be drunk, giving the effort a better chance to succeed. Should you each swear an oath of fealty by your patron deity, pledging to try, to the best of your ability, to rescue Lady Noan and return her to him safely, Lord Pitar will offer you a reward of 2,000 gold pieces. You will each be given 50 gold pieces in advance, that you might be able to cover any needed expenses. The remainder will be given to those who return with Lady Noan.

"Are there any questions?"

"How shall we recognize her?" the gnome asked.

"On the wall in the courtroom is a portrait that was commissioned last year. It is an excellent likeness of her."

"I have previously been to the market of Castle Tiufrann," the half-elf said. "Do you have any specifics of the castle itself?"

"We have available a map of the region and a layout of the first floor of the castle. Is that what you desire?"

"It would be better to know all of the floors."

Several others chuckled at that comment.

"Are there any other questions at this time?"

Faces were drawn in pensive thought, but no queries were forthcoming.

"I will then give you time to talk with one another. I will return within the hour to learn of your decisions."

As the majordomo departed, the eight individuals looked upon one another, contemplating the offer and whether they would benefit from this effort.

2 -- FITESSA

E llina had a plush life for the working class. The world had been at peace for over a century. Major plagues dated further into history, going back five or six generations. Only those of a few other races told firsthand of the horrors they had lived through. Her brother, Menod, owned the Norgard Tavern and also had sole marketing agreements with a fine dwarven brewery. Being in this border town in Glawynia meant that there was a constant flow of business, both with the kingdom of Blengar to the north and with the centaurs to the west.

Serving as a barmaid at the tavern allowed her to meet all the interesting people who traveled on this major thoroughfare. At least that was Ellina's perception of this well-packed dirt road that went south all the way to the capital. The royal guards stationed at the barracks in Norgard also added to the flavor of the tavern clientele. The tales others would tell in the tavern created a fascinating, rosy image of the world for her.

She was all of eighteen years old and at the prime of her beauty. Her pale, rounded face was framed by her fiery red hair and was highlighted by her sparkling green eyes. She felt her body had all the correct curves, and she wore a tight, low-cut bodice to display it to everyone else. Her brother often bantered with her about this, and he only hoped she found a decent husband before she got into trouble.

Such was not to be her luck.

Plonet was an elven minstrel who stopped at the tavern one cool autumn evening. He was thin, handsome, and rather tall for an elf, with smooth, tan skin, sandy hair and a pointed beard. He had a soothing, lilting voice, and he sang sad ballads, telling his audience of things he had supposedly seen and survived.

He told of the Great Quake that had occurred 181 years ago. It had so reshaped the world that it was now used as the reference for recording years. He also sang of the wars and the three great pestilences that had ravaged the lands in the four decades that followed.

When he finished his series of songs, Ellina found that tears were unabashedly flowing over her cheeks. He motioned for her to join him. As the hour was late and there were no other customers left, she willingly did so. She sat beside him, and he put his arm around her, consoling her and reassuring her that these were all things of the past.

As they talked, his second arm joined the first in a hug, followed by a kiss. Things progressed rather rapidly, and Ellina wound up accompanying him to his room for the night.

She never saw Plonet again, but the effects of that single night became all too evident shortly thereafter.

***

Ellina was very unhappy during the last period of her pregnancy. She got a lot of attention, but it was not what she wanted. She greatly preferred compliments, ribaldry and flirtation. She was also displeased with the distortion of what she had thought was a perfect figure. The fact that Menod talked to her with an "I told you so" tone only sunk her deeper into the doldrums. She ate more food more frequently, multiplying her remorse by increasing the rate at which she gained weight.

She thought nothing could worsen her depression as she entered her final month, but once again she was wrong.

Menod announced that he was going to marry Inicia.

Inicia was Ellina's childhood friend and the only girl who had given her any true competition in turning a man's head. The problem was that there was no longer any competition, and this winsome girl was now going to displace her position in Menod's household.

Surprisingly, their friendship survived, but Ellina resigned herself to being overweight, thereby making it a certainty. She also felt she was ugly, and her lowered self-esteem made her interpret any compliment as a twisted barb, making her cynical towards all men. The effect was cyclical, and both dress and manner wound up matching her image of herself.

***

Inicia served as the midwife when Ellina went into labor and helped bring forth her daughter on a hot summer afternoon. Ellina was sweating profusely and was totally exhausted when Fitessa finally made her entrance. Her elfin ancestry was conspicuous, both in the darker pigment of her skin and in the distinctive shape of her ears. These factors daily reminded Ellina of the careless evening that had convoluted her future, forcing her onto a dead-end path. She raised her daughter, but the limited love and minimal affection that Fitessa received came almost solely from her aunt and uncle.

***

Once she could maneuver on her own, Fitessa avoided her mother as much as she was able. This was especially true when her mother had been drinking, as Ellina then usually vented her anger on the hapless child. Fitessa wound up developing a strong dislike for three things in her early years. One was a distaste for anything beyond social drinking; she preferred to avoid the tavern whenever possible. She also had no interest in music, and especially for singing. Finally, she distrusted men, with the exception of Uncle Menod and Starnifsen.

Starnifsen was the brew master who dealt with her uncle. She loved the story of how his name was chosen, and often had him retell it.

"Well, I do not recall this myself, of course, being a tad too young at the time, but my parents claim that I was born during the Great Quake. Crockery and glassware were falling and shattering all around, and a great crack opened in the wall. My parents wanted to flee to a safer spot, but being right in the midst of birthing, things were sort of out of their control.

"Somehow, neither they nor I were harmed by that catastrophe. My father felt the gods were smiling upon us, though he couldn't imagine why we merited it. My mother said that a lucky star must have been shining down on us, and that idea stuck. And it was wedged so strongly into her mind that there was no dislodging it. I therefore was pegged with it as my name."

***

Fitessa was pretty and charismatic, though a bit shorter and more solid than was the norm for half-elves. Her light brown hair had distinct red highlights, and there was always a gleam to her deep brown eyes. She had a quick mind and a knack for numbers that startled Menod. He was certain it was inherited from her father, as it was totally absent in her mother.

By the age of ten, she was keeping the inventory for both the tavern and brewery, and she took on the chore with a mature seriousness. She began to accumulate knowledge about all of the different beers, ales, wines and meads from the different realms, absorbing and retaining all that she learned.

At the age of twelve she was apprenticed to a trader,

financed by a mutual agreement between her uncle and the dwarf. They correctly foresaw her great potential for trading in alcoholic beverages, including marketing their beer far and wide, and she earned her journeyman status by the remarkably young age of fifteen, meaning she was ready to go into business on her own.

Her only shortcoming was physical. She stood only fifty-six inches in height, and she lacked any muscle to defend her sharp tongue. When she began business, backed by her two benefactors, they added two bodyguards. A strong dwarf with experience in fighting was hired to drive the cart and a man-at-arms rode along. Their role was to protect against thieves on the road and to support Fitessa as needed when she bought and sold in towns and cities.

This wound up working out fairly well. She first traveled only in Glawynia and Blengar, including developing a degree of professional friendship with the wine master at King Algar's castle in the city of Gara. As her experience increased, she expanded her market to include Indrose. She became the sole dealer with the centaurs to the west and she also got a trade agreement with the gnomes far to the south. By the time she was twenty, she had made some excursions far to the east into both Ilyia and Eslardia.

The success of the trade unfortunately attracted the occasional attention of bandits and brigands, but she was smart enough to recognize when her entourage was outnumbered. It clearly cut into the profits, but they wound up being able to still operate in the black. During those five years, Fitessa also became competent with the broadsword and dagger, though she rarely applied that proficiency. Nonetheless, having that skill played an important role in enabling her to maintain her confidence, and that was critical in dealing with others in the liquor business.

***

A major change occurred shortly after her twentieth birthday. She was just finishing her meal at an eatery in Reslow, the capital of Ilyia, when she was approached by a small old man, his age predominantly made visible by the thinning of his hair. He wore nondescript clothes and had no marking features that caught her attention. He stood still with his cap in his hand, waiting for her convenience.

Uncertain of what he wanted or whom he represented, she placed her dining cloth on the table and turned to squarely face him. "Might I be able to help you?"

"You be the Tradeswoman Fitessa, be that not so?"

"Yes."

"I come from one who wishes to offer you a proposition."

"And who might that be?"

"She wishes that not be made public. Mayhap you'll come with me that you and she might meet and talk together?"

Fitessa glanced at the nearby table where her two guards were seated.

The old man followed her eyes.

"Nay. I swear by the gods that it be safe. You need not their aid, and the one I serve wishes to meet with you alone."

The little man slowly drew his dagger, hilt first, and offered it to her.

"I offer mine own life as a promise of this pledge, should you question it."

Recognizing that there could still be great danger, despite this interesting offer of faith, she accepted the dagger and decided to follow him. Her curiosity was certainly piqued. As they passed the guards' table, she motioned them to sit back down, though she left her pouch with them for safekeeping.

The stranger donned his cap and led Fitessa to a section of the city with which she was unfamiliar. Stopping at a doorway on a dark byway, he glanced to both sides. Seeing no one else around, he rapped firmly on the oaken portal. A mumbled exchange followed with the person within, but the half-elf was unable to catch the actual words, despite her better than normal hearing ability.

The door opened and she was hurried in. It then closed firmly behind her. She saw that the doorman was an elf, and he silently slipped a bolt back into place, securing the room.

"Please follow me," he said.

Fitessa noted that her escort had again removed his cap. She and the little man followed the elf as he strode down the hallway and stepped into a dimly lit sitting room. A veiled woman sat in a cushioned chair on one side of a small glass table. Some exquisite desserts and two crystal goblets filled with an amber liquor were before her. The elf silently motioned for Fitessa to take the other seat.

"The two of you can leave us for now," the woman said in a quiet but authoritative voice. "I will call should either of us desire anything."

As they exited, the doors were closed firmly behind them.

"Pardon the secrecy, but it is necessary in my profession."

"And what might that be?" Fitessa asked.

"In due time. Let me first discuss some particulars...and help yourself to the food and drink. I assure you that they are both safe." So saying, the hostess ate a canapé and sipped from one goblet.

"No, thank you. Business first."

"Fine. I like that attitude."

Fitessa was certain she could discern a smile beneath the veil.

"You have a profitable business, Tradeswoman Fitessa. However, it is possible to increase your profits. You pay two or three guards to accompany you, and loss to thieves takes away from what you get to bring home. Would it not be advantageous if these business expenses were decreased?"

"That is obvious and unquestionable. You certainly have my attention."

"You have developed a broader range of travel than most in your profession, due in part to the select wares you market. My guild is in need of a trusted courier to deliver messages between various points. We believe that you could fill that need.

"In return, we would take over supplying your guards, at no expense to you. We would also greatly decrease the interference you experience, though it might be necessary to sometimes stage a mock raid so as not to draw any attention, if you understand?"

"I believe I do, but I have some questions regarding what I am nearly certain is your guild, that I might separate rumor from reality."

"Ask, and then I will decide whether I will answer."

"I take it that you belong to the Thieves' Guild. What is your rank?"

"I am the Master of the guild here in Ilyia. That is why I cannot let you know who I am, at least not at this time."

"Understood. If I accept this offer, does it mean that I will be a member of the guild? If so, what are my responsibilities?"

"You will be a member of the guilds in Ilyia, Indrose, Glawynia, Blengar and Eslardia. I speak on behalf of my counterparts in each of the other kingdoms, with their total approval. The role you will be playing was worked out to meet all of our needs. Should you take on this mantle, the responsibilities would entail a lifetime membership. Your dues to each guild would be forgiven, unless you elect to expand beyond your duty of serving as our messenger.

"You will know the signals and passwords that will

allow you to recognize those who will send or receive messages, and you will also be taught the skills of our trade, as they may be needed in the future. Should you so desire, we will supply a system to cache your increased profits so that you don't have to explain them to anyone else. In addition, since you won't actually be stealing, nor will you be transporting stolen goods, you should not have to worry about dealing with the unpleasantries that careless members of our guild must unfortunately face.

"Are you interested?"

Fitessa found that she was tense. She eased herself back into the seat and contemplated the offer. It was very appealing, but it also carried some risks. The penalty for thieves in Glawynia was a long dungeon term, but others were far worse. In Blengar, a first offender lost a hand, followed by losing your head if you were caught again. In Indrose, the sequence was a branding of your hand with a hanging as the sequel. She wasn't sure what it was in other kingdoms, but that wasn't important if she wasn't going to be "at risk", or so she was being told.

However, if her role was learned, she could easily become a target for officials in any kingdom. In addition, an upheaval within any guild could be expensive. How real were these hazards? Did they outweigh the immediate financial benefits that were being offered? She was certain that this was a one-time offer; she had to decide now. Also, if she declined, might they decide to guarantee her silence permanently?

"What about the two guards I have currently employed?"

"You would complete their contract with them. We certainly want nothing to draw attention to any change in your system."

"And how often would I be expected to deliver messages?"

"It would be rather infrequent. I guess not more than a

few times a year. It would only be an alternate to existing channels, and we wouldn't expect you to change your normal trade routes. We therefore do not envision giving you any priority notes with a set time limitation for delivery."

"Hmm," she mumbled, thereby allowing a bit longer to consider this important decision. She figured that the infrequent need for her services probably meant that they already had other such messengers operating for them, even though she had never heard of any. That in itself was clearly a positive factor.

"One last question needs to be raised. You mentioned that I would be a member of the guild for life. What happens when I retire from trading?"

"At that point, independent of whether you do or do not decide to apply the other skills you have gained by then, you would have to start paying your dues. The cost would be based on your monetary status at that time, but the goal is not to sap our members, as that is counterproductive. We merely wish to make sure that we have the funds required to keep the system well-oiled and operating smoothly."

"Do you think Vegar would take great offense that some of my loyalty is deferred to Lulila?"

"No," she laughed. "He's an understanding god and has very close relations with his sister, despite the fact that many of her followers prey upon his. I take it that you are accepting the offer?"

"Yes, I guess that I am. So, what does this entail, and what do followers of the goddess of thieves, liars and gamblers offer her, anyway?"

"To answer your second question first, she is pleased when she is given a coin gained from another. It should be presented on the first Moonday of each month, either in a temple or, as is far more common, by 'losing' it in some place such as an uncultivated field or a sewer. In your case, setting aside a coin that you received as payment for a delivery would qualify.

"For your other question, all you need to do at this time is wear this on the ring finger of your left hand."

She produced a silver ring with some dark geometric markings on a disk region.

Fitessa took it and tried it on. It fit perfectly.

"As I told you, Fitessa, our machine is well-oiled. Once you get back to Glawynia, you will be contacted in a discrete manner. The ring is unique, and the other Guild Masters are aware of it. After our agents have begun serving as your guards, we will start your training and make use of you as a courier.

"For now, you will be taken back to the tavern where you are residing. Your guards are there, correct?"

"They better be."

"Fine. I don't know if you and I will ever meet again personally, but I wish to welcome you into the guild. If you need any help in the future, you can always turn to the guild, but be aware that services do carry expenses. Like traders, we are in the business to turn a profit."

The picture of the Master Thief's broad grin stayed in Fitessa's mind all the way back to the inn, and it lasted far longer than that, too.

***

Over the course of the next few years, Fitessa found that her margin of profit did expand handsomely. The guilds supplied guards and the number of robberies decreased markedly. Once in a while, a robbery was faked so that no special attention would be drawn to her unnatural luck, and she sometimes still had to operate with independent operators who were not members of any guild.

The only case that bothered Fitessa was when a robbery was acted out as an excuse to kill a thief who had broken some guild rule. She never learned what his actual transgression had been. He had been assigned as one of her guards and was joking about the "robbers" who had "attacked" them when the other guard stepped up behind him and slipped a dagger between his ribs and into his heart. It was then made to look like part of the robbery.

This had happened less than a year after she had joined the guild. It taught her to never fully trust the thieves. She also refrained from developing any ties of friendship with her guards, as the future for individuals in this profession was always questionable.

Fitessa found that the guild responsibilities were light. She was occasionally given an item to deliver, with directions of who was supposed to receive it. The actual items varied and the passwords changed frequently, but that was no problem. Once it appeared to be a bottle of cheap wine. Another time it was a dagger. On one occasion it was a book of lewd drawings. She didn't know where or how the messages were hidden, and she found that she was not curious to learn. It seemed that ignorance served as another layer of protection for herself.

The one part of the arrangement that did get her full attention was the training in thieving skills. The guild members who traveled with her would pass the time between towns teaching her what they knew. This included both time in the cart and at the campsites.

She obtained a nice set of thieves' tools and kept it hidden in a hollowed spot in the underside of the cart seat. It consisted of a set of wires and both straight and hooked tin metal rods for picking locks and testing for trap mechanisms. She made a point of never carrying the kit on her body, because it would be incriminating evidence that could lead to a conviction, in and of itself, in some kingdoms and baronies.

Some of the thieves lectured her on the use of the tools. Others taught by example, picking the locks on the chests in her cart. As she mastered a particular lock, she replaced it with a different variety. This gave her the material to expand her expertise under a legal umbrella. She also learned that the more expensive locks were by no means necessarily safer.

She also liked the lessons in picking pockets, though she doubted if she would ever risk applying them. It was a challenging use of her manual dexterity. She found that it required a mixture of deft movement of her hands, careful timing and distraction. The distraction could either be created purposefully or occurring happenstance, but it was a most critical factor. The only targets used to test this skill were her guards. They were usually quite experienced themselves, so the successful ventures were cherished, watching their faces as she returned the purloined pouch or item. They, in turn, pulled the same prank on her, and she was glad that it steadily became harder for them to succeed.

At the campsites, she also gained lessons and practice in hiding, moving quietly and listening attentively. Testing for traps and backstabbing were discussed on occasion, but she deferred from testing her ability in either skill. She hoped that neither would ever be necessary. However, she did improve her use of the dagger and also gained an adequate proficiency with throwing knives. These did get tested a few times in aiding her guards in dealing with inexperienced, would-be bandits, and Fitessa had no question of her advancements.

***

One eventful thing occurred during Fitessa's thirtieth year, though it didn't cause any major change in her lifestyle. It dealt more with the past than the future. It occurred as she was finishing the sale of three legs of dwarven beer at a tavern in western Ilyia. The deal included room and board for herself and her guards.

"You'll find dinner most pleasin' tonight," the innkeeper commented, "as we's havin' th' pleasure o' th' finest voice I's ever heard. It's been nearly two decades since last 'e was by this way."

"Actually, if you're having a minstrel perform, I think I'll either eat early or, if that's not convenient, I'll have my meal up in my room."

"But this's the great Plonet what's gonna be singin'."

"Did you say his name is Plonet?"

"Aye."

"Is he an elf?"

"Be there any other great balladeer by th' same name?"

"I don't know. Can you describe him?"

"Well, he looks like an elf...but that's as is expected, right? What more can I say? They all looks 'bout th' same, if'n you knows what I mean."

"Do you know his age?"

"Can't say as I do, but he's over a couple centuries, at least, as 'e was 'round when th' Quake came 'bout. Why's you got so many questions all o' a sudden?"

"Never mind...but I think I will eat downstairs. Thank you for your help."

***

Fitessa found herself walking aimlessly around the town, deeply mulling over what she expected to face later that evening. This had to be her father, an elven minstrel named Plonet with a sweet voice who sang sorrowful tales of the Great Quake and the terrors that followed it. One part of her wanted to see him while another part told her to stay away. She was somewhat surprised by the level of emotions that ran through her mind.

What was to be gained by this meeting? Why had he left her mother, destroying her? Why had he never visited?

Did he care about the damage he had done? Was it the subject of another of his lamentations? Would she even have the courage to confront him? Returning to her original question, what was to be gained?

It was a relatively small town, and she was only half aware that she was retracing the same route over and over again or that her guards followed a short distance behind her. Nonetheless, she couldn't find meaningful answers to any of her questions. She had often sought Vegar's advice on business, and that had helped instill a degree of confidence that allowed her to reach a conclusion and follow it through, but this was clearly not his domain. Nor did she want advice from Lulila. Lies were not what she sought, nor did she want to base her actions on mere chance.

This issue did not really fall within the realm of any particular god or goddess, at least not of those she knew. Perhaps there was an elven deity who could answer her prayers, but she was unfamiliar with that half of her heritage, so she knew not toward whom the prayer should be directed.

Looking up, she saw that she was standing in front of Perical's Tavern. It was time for the evening meal, as dusk was settling in. Perhaps there was nothing better than just gambling that the outcome would make the venture worthwhile. With a brief prayer to Lulila, she straightened her shoulders and walked into the dining room.

***

The meal tasted rather good, but her nervousness kept her from truly appreciating it. She told her guards that she would be staying up for the entertainment, but they should go to bed when they were tired. They would all be leaving early in the morning, as was previously scheduled, and it was important that they were well rested and ready to fulfill their obligations.

Plonet was introduced just after Fitessa had begun her dessert. The serving girls tried to meet their clients' needs without disturbing the minstrel's songs. From the first ballad, Fitessa found that there was no longer any question. This was her father. The songs matched the stories she had been told, and she saw the effect they were having on the others present. Somehow, though, they washed over her without penetrating her at all in an emotional sense.

The songs continued, and his voice did not falter. He did not seem to direct his songs of melancholy to anyone. Instead, he sang to himself, with his eyes closed most of the time. The audience slowly dwindled until only Fitessa remained. Then he suddenly changed his style, in that he stared straight into her eyes as his voice relayed a story of unrequited love.

As the verses progressed, he moved across the room until he was sitting at her table. With the last line, he smiled at her and lifted her hand in his.

"Is this what you do every night?" she asked.

"Pardon me, miss?"

"I asked if this is the system you regularly use to find a starry-eyed nighttime partner to warm your bed?"

"You must misunderstand me—"

"No, I don't think I do," she said rather crisply as she pulled her hand free. "I stayed because I want to talk with you, but nothing more. Are you willing to talk?"

"Well, yes—"

"Good. Do you remember, about thirty-one years ago, a green-eyed, red-haired girl in Norgard Tavern in the town of the same name in Glawynia near the Blengar border?"

"Should I?"

"Think back. She was a barmaid there. You sang your songs to her, and you then invited her to your room for the night. She was young, and pretty, and impressionable, and she believed the words of your songs."

"There have been so many pretty girls. I can't remember each, especially from so long ago. Why do you ask me about this one?"

"Because she was enraptured by an elven minstrel named Plonet who sang the songs you sang, and he did it in the style you used this night."

"Then it was probably me. That was over three decades ago, and there have been thousands of nights of singing since then. Why does she matter to you?"

"Matter? Matter? I'll tell you why it matters!" Her voice had suddenly shifted to a shout as she vented years of anger. She pushed herself up from the table and stood before him. "Look at me! I am a result of that single night! You used my mother and tossed her aside! You never looked back, never even wrote to her! Do you even think about what effects you might leave behind you, what havoc you wreak in other people's lives?"

"To be honest, no. The past is just that. It is behind me. I share my songs and love with those who wish to share them, but there is no commitment, and I travel with the wind. I did not know of your birth. If it mattered to her, why didn't she let me know?"

Fitessa felt sheer disgust welling up within her. He was cold and callous, showing no remorse, no feeling of guilt. He hadn't even asked her name, and he clearly wasn't concerned about her at all. Perhaps he had impregnated her mother, but he was not her father.

Turning abruptly, she exited the tavern and retreated to her room. The only effects that this meeting had had were the closing of any interest in her mysterious father and a hardening of her dislike and distrust of men and minstrels, especially male minstrels.

***

It was a bit over a year later that Fitessa met Stalif. It

was the dusk of Starday. She had just reached Wosgard and planned on making some purchases on the morrow, as Sunday was recognized as market day in each and every kingdom. She was just leaving the stable when a confident man in fine clothing approached her.

"You are Trademaster Fitessa, are you not?" he asked in a quiet, even voice.

Her experience and professional skills played out with minimal effort. She sized him up and down. Clearly a member of nobility, he emanated a sense of authority. He was a gentleman, but his cloak could as easily be hiding a weapon as a purse of value.

"Yes, and you are..."

"My name is Stalif. I am an advisor to Lord Pitar of Castle Vork."

"Ah. Well, I will be making a regular visit there later this month. Do you have a special order that you wish me to fill?"

"Actually, I do, but not an order of wine or beer. Is there a private place you are willing to meet? I can offer the use of my room at the Silver Spur Inn, as long as the invitation is not misconstrued."

"That would be fine. I am always willing to lend an ear to a business proposition." Fitessa was careful to stress the word *business*. She was familiar with the Silver Spur Inn; it was very reputable and was in a good part of the capital city.

Signaling the guard to follow at a distance, she and Stalif exchanged meaningless chatter about the weather as they walked along, noting the mild summer and conjectures regarding what type of winter they would have to face.

When they reached his room, Stalif took the seat opposite her and held up a bottle of rather good wine.

She thanked him, but declined the offer. "What is this deal you were mentioning?"

"Right to the business, I see. You definitely match

your reputation."

"I take that to be a compliment."

"It is. I can only tell you a limited part of the undertaking at this time, but it should clearly be financially worthwhile. However, I must first verify a few points."

"Go on."

"You service Castle Tiufrann on a regular basis?"

"Yes."

"You usually are accompanied by two or three guards, and they change frequently, don't they?"

"Yes. I surmise that this has something to do with the growing tension between Pitar and Blavin."

"Indirectly. We need to have a party enter Castle Tiufrann. Since you regularly enter on business and are accompanied by guards who vary, your comings and goings would not be questioned, nor would there be many questions about who is with you."

"Possibly..."

"Also, if some materials need to be brought in unnoticed, your cart could supply the means of transport."

"Again, possibly... I need a bit more in the way of details."

"All I am free to say at this time is that we wish to form a small band of mercenaries to carry out a desired errand, and it needs to be done covertly."

"Do these plans include unlawful acts?"

"Not directly, but what results when plans unravel, which happens all too often, cannot be foretold."

"How large is this small band, and how much are you offering in payment?"

"Well, Trademaster, we would guess that the number will be less than ten. How much you earn will depend upon the role you play. We figure that you could escort two or three members, plus perhaps some equipment. If that were the case, we would pay you thirty gold pieces. If you were willing to play an active part, the payment would, of course, be noticeably greater.

"Are you interested?"

Fitessa didn't require much time to reach a decision. In her better business deals, she had perhaps made that much in profits in her best month of trading, and that was only with the padded margin resulting from her relations with the Thieves' Guild.

"Whether I will take part in a capacity beyond that of escort will depend upon learning more details. However, you can count me in for at least that minimal position. When and where do you want me and my cart?"

"Be at Castle Vork one eightday from today. This stamped disk will gain you entry. Ask for me."

Standing up, he placed a small piece of metal in her hand. They then shook hands to seal the deal, and Fitessa left to return to her room in the inn where she was staying, which was only a short walk from the Silver Spur Inn.

As she walked, she considered the necessary changes in her schedule and the possible contingencies that might come up. One thing was certain. She would have to contact the guild to make arrangements should she decide to go for the larger purse.

3 – UHU

P anasi is the name of a tribe of wood elves living in the wilderness to the northwest of Blengar. It is also the name of their live oak. Wood elves can draw strength from their gods through live oaks, so their tribes are always found around these rare trees, which they care for with an intense reverence.

The deep brown color of their skin matches that of the tree's bark, and the green-brown tones of their hair reflect the color of the leaves. The garments they wear are almost always in shades of green and brown, which helps explain why they can seemingly vanish in the forest by simply standing still.

The grassy region beneath Panasi's canopy is treated as hallowed ground. If danger threatens the tribe, this is where they gather, drawing upon the tree to increase their strength that they might face their foe. Once a wood elf is halfway between the outer rim of the canopy and the bole of the tree, his or her strength is doubled. At one third of the distance from the trunk, the strength is trebled. This relation continues as the wood of the tree is neared. In theory, a wood elf has limitless strength when touching the tree's bole. However, the strength is cut into a proportional fraction afterwards for an extended period of time, meaning that if it was doubled, it later drops to half the normal level, returning the balance of force to the tree. Therefore, wood elves only draw upon this force when it is truly needed.

All in all, wood elves have a closer affinity to nature than any of the other humanoid races. They are frequently able to speak with the animals and only take what they need, serving as role models for druids. Each clan has a particular animal as its totem and cares for this conduit to the gods. Five clans are represented in the tribe of Panasi. The most powerful is the clan of the pegasi. The other four, in descending order, are the lynx, the boar, the owl and the deer. Animals representing each clan are usually present, having close bonds with individual wood elves from the appropriate clan. This is common in all wood elf tribes in all parts of the world.

***

Uhu belonged to the clan of the owl. Even though he was stronger than his peers, he never seemed to stand out when there was a crowd. His face was plain and he lacked charisma. His only friend, Vahors, belonged to the clan of the pegasi and unfortunately reminded Uhu all too often of the difference in their rank. Thus, Uhu tended to spend much of his time by himself. At the age of ten, youths rarely recognize how much the barbs they inflict upon others can hurt.

He sometimes got into a fight with other youngsters, but he had the wisdom to try to avoid brawls. Though he usually won, Uhu saw that it didn't resolve his problems. He was fortunate that he veered away from relying on his muscles, as that kept him from becoming a bully.

At that young age – remember that elves can live for a millennium or more – the only responsibility outside of the family was to attend classes. He learned to speak in the language of the animals of all five clans, in addition to elven and the "common tongue" of other humanoids. His only other lessons at this stage in his life dealt with an awareness and understanding of the animals and plants that surrounded them, expanding in both breadth and depth on a regular basis.

The free time was devoted to exploring the woods, swimming in the stream near the tree of the tribe and listening to the world that surrounded them. Elves have a natural ear for music and appreciate the songs of nature. Uhu definitely found this music to be pleasurable. Listening carefully also wound up making the class sessions easier.

As is common for young wood elves, he would sing or whistle along with whatever music he found to be familiar and to his liking, whether it was at Panasi or in the wilderness. He also made frequent attempts at using the two instruments preferred by his elders: pipes and drums. Uhu never displayed the natural knack that sometimes appeared among his race, but neither did his efforts cause discomfort to anyone's ears.

At an early age, he had been able to master the crow's whistle. Placing a blade of grass in the gap that appears when his two thumbs were positioned side-by-side, he found that it acted as a reed, vibrating when air was blown past it. He could make a wide range of loud or soft whistles by varying the pressure exerted on the grass and how hard he blew. He quickly learned how to avoid producing the undesired cacophony that often came when a crow's whistle was used by the inexperienced.

He also experimented at making pipes from reeds or soft-cored pieces of wood. They displayed that he was an amateur, but they also showed a steady pattern of improvement. He never envisioned himself as becoming a tribal musician, but he enjoyed the results of his efforts, and he had the time available at this stage in his life, so he indulged in these endeavors for long periods of time.

***

On one outing shortly before his eleventh birthday, Uhu found a hollow wing bone of a large owl. He took that as a good omen and used his dagger to carefully cut the holes for a pipe. He found that the notes produced were pleasing and serene, and he created tunes when he was out by himself. He was also surprised to find that they carried for far greater distances than notes produced by a normal pipe and they often caught the curiosity of various animals.

This was how he met his first clan bond, a small owlet that was awakened by Uhu's notes. Dusk was approaching and Uhu was piping a sweet, repetitive tune as he made his way home when a young dwarf owl appeared on the branch he was about to duck under.

It fluttered its wings, steadying itself, and then asked, "What are you?"

"Me?" Uhu responded. "Why, I'm an elf."

"What's an elf?"

"Well, it's what I am."

"I don't understand!"

"Where are your parents? They can probably explain this better..."

"I don't know! Mother was hunting for food when I stepped out last night. I fell, and I can't really fly yet. I've been staying off the ground, but I don't know where our hole is, or our tree, or my family, or anything!"

"Have you eaten?"

"No! I'm hungry!" he pleaded in a high pitch, and he opened his mouth, begging to be fed.

Uhu couldn't see any mice, moles or shrews. And, even if he did, he didn't know how to catch them. He did see a fat sphinx caterpillar. He didn't know if the owls normally would eat them, but this young one needed to be fed.

He picked up the insect and placed it in the owlet's open mouth. It quickly swallowed the whole thing.

"That tasted strange!"

"Well, it's all I could find."

"I'm still hungry!"

"Here," Uhu said as he pushed an out-stretched finger against the front of the little bird's body. This forced it to step up onto his finger as it didn't want to fall backwards. "Come home with me and I'll give you some real food."

"Good."

Uhu tucked his pipe under his belt and gently petted the owlet as he resumed his walk home. The sun was down, but he could see fine by the starlight, and the path was very familiar.

"My name is Uhu. What is yours?"

"Mother called me Brash."

"Well, Brash, you now belong to a new family!"

***

Brash caused a definite change in Uhu's life. He learned responsibility, as he had to feed his ward on a regular regimen and he also had to teach her how to hunt. He talked to the two other owls residing in their village and relayed this information to Brash.

He found that he also had to change his lifestyle to be compatible with the owl's nocturnal pattern. Instead of sleeping at night, he had two long naps. One was in the afternoon and the other was in the pre-dawn hours. This exposed him to an entirely different population that shared the same environment. He had heard of the animals of the nocturnal world, but he now expanded his knowledge on a firsthand basis.

A very different community of insects was out at night, as well as a variety of birds that fed upon them. The bats were very active, and porcupines, skunks, opossums and rodents were all easy to see shifting around in the trees and on the ground. Even the larger animals, including the boar and deer that lived in Panasi, preferred this time. The animals he always thought were lethargic had merely been resting during the daylight hours. He began to learn the importance of not making judgments on one's first impressions.

***

Brash was a fast learner, but Uhu found that her name was appropriate, as she often acted without thinking.

"Why did you attack that rabbit?"

"I like the taste of rabbit."

"I know, but that's when I've given it to you. You can't catch a rabbit yourself."

"Why not?"

"For starters, it's over double your size."

"So?"

"You just can't kill it. Even with your best efforts, you will only harm it. And it's not right to do that."

"Why?"

"Because it's just not right! You have to select prey that you can defeat and that you will eat."

"But why can't I try for other things?"

"For one thing, some of them may turn on you, making you the prey."

"Oh."

"You don't want to be hurt, do you?"

"No."

"So, trust me. Now, do you see that mouse over near that log?"

"Oh, yes! I'll get it."

"Hold on, Brash! Wait until it's in the open where you have clear maneuvering space. A little patience is all you need... Now, get ready... Go!"

***

As the years progressed, Uhu slowly matured (as is normal for elves), but he was still very much a loner. He learned from his parents how to set nets properly in the streams and thus catch fish. When cooked properly, they had a delectable taste that appealed to most of the tribe. They thereby earned an adequate living, feeding themselves and trading for other goods that they needed.

On occasion, Uhu would travel to the river that was farther to the east. Setting a net there was a bit trickier, but it often yielded larger fish, making it worthwhile. He would be accompanied by Brash, now full-grown, and he found that she seemed to fill the gap left by the lack of close friends. He still spent time with Vahors when he was home, but Uhu found that he didn't fit in with the tribe the way his friends did.

One spring day, just as he reached the river, intent on setting up his net, he heard some loud noises in the brush behind him. It was very gruff, and it was an unfamiliar language, so he quickly retreated to the thick growth surrounding some trees a bit downstream. While running, he was careful to not harm Brash, who was sleeping in a pouch positioned over his chest.

It was late morning, but his rapid movement woke her. Blinking her eyes, she quickly once more shut them tightly.

"Why do you disturb me in the middle of the day, Uhu?"

"Hush, Brash," he whispered. "Danger may be approaching."

Her curiosity got the better of her. Opening her eyes to allow in just a slit of light, she got out of the pouch and moved onto a neighboring branch.

At this point, two large bears appeared and ambled down to the river's edge. They were a darker shade of brown than Uhu and their body length was greater than his height. Uhu and Brash watched as they waded into the water. Standing upright on their hind legs, they intently studied the water before them. Their claws were a few inches long and they occasionally swiped into the water before them. After a while, one captured a large fish and brought it ashore to dine. Another bear came out of the forest on the far side and also entered the water.

The wood elf and owl watched as the bears continued in like manner until each sated its hunger. While they watched, one had left, but it had been replaced by yet another. Uhu had heard how the bears would feast during the spring spawning, but he had never previously witnessed it himself. He was fascinated.

"You know, friend," he said, "I bet that there must be some way we could work with the bears to help one another."

"How?"

"I don't know that yet, but I'm going to work on it."

"When?"

"Oh, I'll start now, but I'm sure it will take some time to come up with something. It will require patience."

***

After watching these great fishers for another couple of hours, he decided that conditions made this an unsafe time to try to set his net. He therefore carefully headed back to the west, watching out for any other bears that might be converging on the river and its bounty.

Obviously, the first step in his plan would be to learn how to talk bear. Vahors' mother had come from the clan of the bear in another tribe. He would have to ask her to teach him the language. If he couldn't talk to the bears, no plan would ever work.

Other animals that caught and ate fish were the otter, the eagle, the kingfisher and the heron. His grandaunt was from the clan of the eagle, so he could learn that language from her. While he didn't yet know what he planned to do, a broader range of options would have to be better. It would take some time to learn two more languages, but nothing was pressing.

***

During the following year, Uhu became a very serious student. He was unable to give any clear answer when asked why he was expanding his skills, but both women were happy to teach him. He also suddenly had a desire to learn to use weapons that he had previously given only minimal attention. He viewed it as another way to add to his potential.

He had been decent at using a staff or handling a dagger, but he had never gained any accuracy in throwing the dagger or using the bow and arrow. Both points were remedied, and he also started to learn how to use a long sword, though he didn't own one himself. This increased his standing with his peers, but he didn't noticeably change his level of social interaction.

He learned that bears liked the taste of fish, but they were only able to catch them in quantity when they spawned in the spring, crowding the river in their multitude. He reasoned that a bear might be very interested in joining in an effort that could make fish available at other times of the year. The eagles, thanks to their excellent vision and the benefit of their aerial vantage point, could know where the fish were, but they could only catch the fish when they were near the surface.

Over the winter, an idea developed that pooled the eagle's vision, the bear's size and prowess and his nets. If he could interest the other animals, it might actually work! As he waited until the bears would awaken from hibernation, he increased his effort at mastering the two new tongues. He also learned how to approach each animal in a manner that would be interpreted as non-threatening that was critical if he wanted to get a chance to present his idea.

***

Getting an eagle to agree to try out his proposal

proved to be easier than he had expected. The eagle quickly perceived how it would benefit from this arrangement. Now he only needed to get a bear to join the effort. His friend's mother had repeatedly warned him to wait until the bears had fed well, as they would be too ravenous when they first appeared in the spring after the long hibernation. Rational thought would be close to impossible at that time!

Uhu decided that a fitting time might be when a bear had sated itself on fish during the spawning. It would be in a good mood and it certainly would not be very hungry. Thus, he found himself at the same site a year after his plan had first unfolded. However, this time he waited away from the river until he saw one bear spread out in the sun to rest after gorging itself on fish. Two others were still catching food a bit farther away, upwind from the resting bear.

He had Brash stay on an upper branch and then shook some bushes before stepping out. He had specifically been warned to not startle a bear by appearing silently.

"I come as a friend," he called out as the bear turned in his direction. He stopped a few feet out, once he could be seen clearly. If necessary, he was ready to bolt back into the forest. "May I talk with you?"

"What do you want to talk about?"

"Fish."

"They are good, and they are plentiful. But this is our site. If you wish to catch fish, find another spot. Is that what you wanted to know?"

"No. It is true that the fish are many now, but would you like to have fish throughout the summer?"

"Perhaps. I can listen."

"It is easy for you to catch the fish now, but it is harder later on. I have an idea of a way to catch them when we want them."

"The 'we' is the two of us?"

"You, me and also an eagle."

"An eagle?" the bear asked, looking skyward.

"Yes. I have a net, an object that can catch the fish. The eagle has great eyes. He can tell us where the fish are and when they are over the net. You can scare the fish into the net by charging into the water and making great splashes."

"By splashing water, I can catch fish?"

"Yes, when my net is there."

"That sounds very interesting. Let me sleep upon it, as I am not hungry now."

"My name is Uhu. What is yours, and when and where should I seek you out?"

"I am Grunall. I will meet you here when again the moon is a full circle. Now let me sleep."

"Thank you, Grunall. I will return."

***

At the scheduled time, nearly a full month later, Uhu met with Grunall and Kriikee, the eagle. The first attempt netted two fish, which Uhu wisely gave to his partners. It was a good investment and sold them on the process, even though the next three tries failed. When the net yielded four large fish on the fifth attempt, the partnership was secure.

After repeated modifications, the system got to a stage where it proved to be very worthwhile. A session would stop when Uhu had all he could carry and the others were sated. It fell into a pattern where they met every two or three eightdays, adjusting for weather conditions.

Kriikee would scan the river until he found a school with enough fish of sufficient size to justify the effort. Grunall would then get in position while Uhu would set up his net. On the eagle's call, the bear would charge forward, driving the fish into the net, which Uhu quickly pulled shut before many had a chance to escape.

He was careful to avoid over-fishing any one site, changing the region they fished each time. He always also allowed smaller fish to go free to replenish the river. They continued this through the summer months and into the fall. As the days grew cooler, Grunall began to grow lethargic, as he soon would be hibernating, so the fishing business closed down.

However, it recommenced the next year and then became an annual effort. As the decades progressed, Uhu's partners varied, but he saw no reason to stop a winning system. He also became very fluent in both languages and also developed a strong bond of friendship with both the bears and the eagles. The bears and eagles in his region knew him as a trusted ally, with ties just as close as those he developed with the owls.

The distinct notes of his owl bone pipe became his calling card, signaling either friendship or a call for help. And the others knew they could depend on him on the rare occasion that they might need help. The accuracy of his bow twice saved endangered cubs.

***

For some reason, despite his ease at developing ties with various animals, Uhu continued to have difficulty in relating to his own kind. This eventually led to his undoing. It began when he was one hundred thirty-one years old.

In events that occurred every five to ten years, different tribes would gather so that those who were of age might be able to find mates, as the custom was to marry someone from a different tribe. The limited number of eligible selections meant that one's mate was usually from a different clan, but that was not considered to be a problem.

Uhu normally avoided these gatherings, but this year it was held at Panasi. While visiting tribes brought some food, the host tribe had to supply the major share, and all families were expected to contribute. Uhu was therefore unable to simply take off into the wilderness.

His desire to be somewhere else changed when his eyes fell upon Ursina. He believed that she was the most beautiful thing he had ever seen, and the beauty was not just how she looked, though he couldn't find any faults there. Her hair fell to her waist, tied back in the pattern of a thick vine. It had bright green highlights that were matched by her sparkling eyes. He was fascinated by the curves in her body and was enraptured with the way it undulated when she walked. Similarly, her voice, her interests and her views all blended to totally enchant him.

She came from the same tribe as his grandaunt, who was a distant cousin of Ursina's father. Her mother was from the same clan as Vahors' mother. Thus, she and he had ties to the same animals, even if his relations were adopted. He gave her his full attention, including taking her to meet some of his bear friends, hoping to compensate for his weaker social skills.

The problem was that Vahors was also interested in Ursina. She saw things she liked in each, so she played one against the other, encouraging each to outdo the other's efforts.

In his favor, Uhu was friends with bears. He was renowned as one of the most successful net fishers in this region of the world. He was an expert bowman and could play beautiful music. On the negative side, he was from a lower clan and was socially naive. He also did not have many elven friends.

Vahors, on the other hand, belonged to the tribe's most powerful clan. He also was a priest, serving the gods and adept at healing the sick. He was a central member of the Panasi community and got along with everyone.

The deciding factor was that Vahors took Ursina for a ride on a pegasus. Uhu had been able to describe the beauty of the world as seen by the owls and eagles, but now she was able to see that first-hand. After that flight, nothing

Uhu could offer was good enough to regain her interest.

He discovered that he had lost her, and he simultaneously found that his ties to his only friend had been severed. Uhu experienced feelings of pain and agony whenever he saw Ursina and the emotions of anger and spite toward Vahors grew stronger and deeper.

He therefore more frequently spent longer periods away from the tribe. He learned of all the caves in the region from the bears and he began using some of the smaller, uninhabited ones as homes away from home.

***

This was actually not a sudden change. This had been a gradual but steady progression of the pattern Uhu had been following all of his life. The alienation continued for nearly two decades, with him becoming a stranger in his own tribe. Then three things occurred in rapid succession that brought everything to a head.

The first was that Vahors and Ursina had a daughter, whom they named Flame. She permanently erased any dreams that Uhu had of Ursina leaving Vahors. He accepted that with finality.

He left on an extended excursion into the wilderness, avoiding any interaction with other elves. When he returned almost a month later with a new partner named Swoop, he found that the second event had occurred: his parents, the only true remaining ties to the tribe, were both dead.

Their bodies had been found near a large stream where they frequently went fishing. One of several owls sent searching for them in the dusk when they had not returned had discovered them. As the evidence had later been pieced together, it appeared that a large cat had attacked and killed his mother. It had broken her neck and his father had died in a fight attempting to save her. The news was hard to take and it brought on a flood of guilt, though no one suggested there was anything he could have done had he been there.

The final factor involved a wood elf gathering that was to occur that summer. In a desperate move to try to fill the new void, Uhu decided that he was going to find a mate. However, a distorted image filled his mind.

He was impressed with the power, wingspan and intelligence of Swoop, but he could not see these traits attracting a mate for him. Ignoring the fact that many other members of the clan of owls succeeded in finding partners, he felt that only a pegasus could win a worthy wife, as it had been the deciding point in his competition with Vahors. He therefore believed that he had to obtain a pegasus for himself!

After visiting his parents' grave, he left Panasi to figure out how he could achieve this goal.

***

Uhu wound up following the best plan he could conceive. It took two days for an eagle he knew he could trust to find an appropriate family of pegasi. They were moving back toward the herd's summer grazing range, but they were progressing slowly. Two large, male bears agreed to help Uhu, as he had done them favors in the past.

He selected a point the pegasi should be reaching in two days, as it was near a large beehive that the bears visited on occasion. Their presence would therefore not seem unnatural. The eagle monitored the selected target by day and Swoop checked by night while Uhu and the bears settled in to await their arrival.

On the evening of the second day, the pegasi reached a very small clearing that was nearby and stopped for the night. It was surrounded by thick brush, which would allow Uhu to move in very close without being seen. The bears could follow an often-used forest path that cut past the clearing's edge. The eagle had noted that, while the colt still nursed a bit, grazing supplied the bulk of its diet. To top everything off, the sky was covered with a thick blanket of clouds, so it would be especially dark at night. This was obviously the optimal condition.

***

After the sun's last rays had vanished and Swoop had assured him that the winged horses were all asleep, Uhu told the bears to give him a few minutes to get into position before starting down the path. A strong breeze rustled the leaves and branches, making it easier to move without being heard. He quickly advanced to the bushes close to where they were bedded down.

His elven infravision made it easy for Uhu to pick out the pegasi. He also could notice Swoop silently flying overhead, and he then caught sight of the approaching bears.

As they came near, the stallion woke and raised his head, but he didn't do anything else. The bears suddenly crashed into the clearing and roared as they reared up to stand at their full height. The pegasi quickly got to their feet, but the network of overhanging branches made flight impossible and the bears kept the colt's parents cornered so that neither was able to do anything without risking being mauled by one of the bears.

Following Uhu's plans, they succeeded in separating the colt from its parents. Before he would whinny for help, which might agitate his parents into illogical action, Uhu raced forth and placed one hand over its mouth. He stroked its neck with his other hand, attempting to calm it.

"Come with me," he said quietly into its ear. "I will find a safe place and will protect you."

The colt was scared and worried, but it responded to

his reassuring voice. Glancing wide-eyed at the large, barely-discernible dark bodies of the bears that were threatening his parents, he turned and trotted off with Uhu, following the direction implied by the pressure of the elf's hands.

The pace slowed down so as not to over-exert the colt, but Uhu kept moving for a couple of hours until they reached a small cave. It was dry and quiet inside, with a small pond of cold water that dripped from a stalactite overhead. Uhu had prepared a supply of fresh-cut grass early this morning. He had the colt eat a little and then go back to sleep. Once it was breathing calmly and steadily, he went quietly out and scanned the sky for Swoop.

As his friend landed on the stump of a fallen red pine, Uhu ran over and questioned him.

"How did things go? Are the bears safely away? What are the colt's parents doing?"

"Hush," Swoop said. "The bears worried them long enough and then took off in two different directions, one going east while the other headed south. The adults were searching for their colt, calling out as they roamed through the forest. I would guess that they simply suppose that he fled in the darkness, and they can't really see anything.

"Once the sun rises, I expect that they will take to the air and continue their search. However, they will most likely be too distraught to follow an organized pattern. If your supposition is correct, it will be a while before they seek assistance.

"Now you get some sleep while I catch a meal. We will have to move on tomorrow night, and you will have to spend the day caring for your new ward."

Agreeing with this, Uhu returned to the cave and curled up just within its mouth to rest, far enough inside so that he couldn't be seen from the air, but making it impossible for the colt to pass by.

***

He had expected things to improve as they moved north, but this was far from the case. No bonding developed with the colt. During the day, it complained about staying in a cave and instead wanted to run and play in the sunlight or fly the short distances it had recently mastered. Moving on at night proved to be very difficult, as the colt was tired and desired to sleep. It wanted to be with its parents and even balked at eating.

The herd of the pegasi and the wood elf tribe organized a very structured search, doing ever-expanding aerial scans. Swoop let him know that some elves were tracking, using lynxes and boars. They had picked up his trail, even getting past his first lengthy walk in a stream. In addition, owls had been called upon to search at night.

Only two days had passed, but Uhu had hoped the colt would have been assumed dead. He hadn't imagined such difficulties. He felt that a trap was closing around him, and he considered deserting the colt. But this would mean that he had given up everything with nothing to show for it, so he discarded that option.

Heavy rainfall began in the afternoon. Uhu took this as a good omen, as it would prevent aerial inspection while also washing the scent and clearing the track from the trail.

"We will head farther north," he told Swoop, who rested within the coverage of a large conifer. "Join us when the rain stops."

"Or the next night, should the rain continue throughout this one," Swoop muttered.

Pulling his cloak tight, the elf awakened the colt and, with objections, got it to leave the dry cave and move through the pelting rain. The pace was even slower, and Uhu noted that his ward was lethargic. He wondered how a cold was identified in pegasi and what the proper treatment was.

The rain varied in intensity, but it kept up until well past midnight. Uhu finally reached an acceptable cave shortly thereafter. When they got inside, there was no question that the colt was shivering. A raspy cough and sneezing had developed by morning, and the elf decided he had to take the poor beast out in the sun to warm it up and fight this ailment. He hoped that it would suffice.

While he did not see the pegasus that soared by overhead, the opposite was not true. A group of pegasi and elves arrived in the early afternoon, and Uhu was taken prisoner. He felt that his world was closing in on him in a suffocating manner, but he did have the slight consolation of knowing that the colt would now be cared for and cured.

Silently and sullenly, he was escorted back to Panasi.

***

Uhu was very uncertain of what to expect as punishment. His crime was unprecedented, as far as he knew, but at least he had not caused any permanent harm. He was resigned to accept whatever was meted out, as he viewed his future as dismal and meaningless anyway.

Vahors was chosen to decide his fate, which Uhu took as the final insult. He silently swore that he was going to leave Panasi and never return. He also would find new gods to follow, as these had never served him well.

As the tribe gathered in a circle at midday, Vahors stepped forward.

"Your actions are hard to comprehend, Uhu," he began. "We don't know why you did this, nor do we wish to hear your explanation. We fear that you are a threat to the stability of our tribe, though you have contributed well in the past.

"The decision that I have reached is that you are to be exiled from Panasi. You may take what you own that you can carry by yourself, but you are never to return.

"Is that understood?"

Vahors expected Uhu to be dejected and to plead for a lesser punishment. He couldn't know of his recent silent oath, so he now couldn't understand why his former friend was smiling at him.

"Yes," Uhu said. "How soon do you expect me to leave?"

"Before sunset."

"I will be gone within the hour!"

With that, he turned his back on Vahors. The tribe parted as he returned for a final time to the home of his parents.

Taking out the better backpack, he sorted out the items he would take. First, he selected the two best nets and a spare set of clothes. He gathered a tinderbox and five spare strings for his bow. Two water skins and a quiver containing a score of fine arrows were set on the side.

His sword and one dagger were already attached to his belt. Two additional daggers were placed in the backpack, as was his bone pipe, carefully wrapped in a protective layer of cloth. He then made a package of smoked fish and got a length of rope from the wall. Going into his parents' room, he took the few pieces of jewelry that had belonged to his mother, not wanting to leave them for whatever vultures would come in after he left. These were placed in his belt pouch.

Packing most of the items, he put on his cloak and swung the load onto his back, fastening the quiver to his belt. He pushed the spare strings into his pouch and slipped the unstrung bow into a pair of loops in the backpack. Picking up his staff, worn smooth by years of handling, he glanced around before exiting. While he felt that he wouldn't miss Panasi, he did have fond memories of his parents and this home. They would travel with him, recorded in his mind.

Stepping outside, he let the door close behind him.

It was dark outside, as ominous, thick gray clouds blocked out the sun's rays. He wondered whether it portended misfortune for him or Panasi as he began to walk in a southeasterly direction.

Swoop flew down.

"Why are you headed in this direction?"

"Why not? I have heard that there are supposedly civilized nations of other races there. I mean to investigate."

"May I come with you?"

"Most assuredly. I know that the clan would welcome you to stay, but you are the one friend I have and can trust."

"Then we will travel together to discover this new world that awaits us."

A fine drizzle began to descend as they took a turn in the path. Glancing over his shoulder, Uhu took a final glance at the great live oak.

***

For several months, Uhu and Swoop journeyed through southern Blengar. They survived by what means were available. At times they lived off the land, even selling fish when the catch was plentiful. On other occasions, Uhu was paid for his knowledge and experience with the forest or merely for the exertion of his muscles. Sometimes he earned a few coins for playing his pipe. When things went well, he saved a bit of money. If they weren't so good, he sold a piece of jewelry.

Unfortunately, the scales more often tipped in the wrong direction. When winter arrived, things would become difficult if he couldn't find either steady work or something that paid very well.

In addition, he felt out of place everywhere that they went, as wood elves generally avoided "civilized" regions. He only met two others of his own kind, and neither even wanted to talk to him. The void he experienced as an outcast was more painful than he had envisioned.

People paid if he toiled for them, but no one wanted him to stay around. He found that he was starving for friendship, even though he hadn't been aware of it in Panasi. He simply needed to talk with others, even if the topics were unimportant. If not for Swoop, he was certain that he would go insane.

***

Such were the morose thoughts meandering through his mind as he trudged southward on a cool, cloudy day. He was following the main road toward Indrose when a horseman pulled up beside him.

"You're unquestionably far from your home. Might I ask where you're headed?"

Uhu looked up. He could see Swoop resting on a branch above the road and discretely signaled him to stay there.

"You can ask, but I'm not certain of the answer."

"Might you be looking for work?"

The man now had his full attention.

"Perhaps. What do you need?"

"Are you proficient with your sword and bow?"

"Not to boast, but I think I'm decent with the first and good with the latter."

"Can you show me how good you are?"

Uhu glanced around. A small orange and yellow butterfly was flitting around eighty feet away.

"Look at that brightly winged insect. How might you rate that as a target?"

"I'd say it would be an understatement to call it difficult."

Without speaking, Uhu strung his bow, notched an arrow and drew it back. Following the motions, he waited until it was in front of the trunk of a large maple. He let the arrow fly and it pinned the butterfly by one wing. The insect broke away and fluttered to the ground, unable to fly any further.

"I'm duly impressed!" the man said, dismounting. "There is no question of your proficiency with the bow!"

Uhu remained silent as he retrieved his arrow and put the butterfly out of its misery. He had meant to hit the butterfly in its body, killing it instantly, but he knew enough to keep his thoughts to himself.

When he got back to the road, the man was offering him an open hand.

"My name is Stalif. As I understand it, your kind can speak with animals . . ."

"To some degree. I know the tongue of a few."

"That can also help. I am looking for a band of adventurers. They will be paid well, but I am not free to divulge further information at this time. Might you be interested in such employment?"

"It sounds worth investigating. My name is Uhu."

"Today is Sunday. Can you be at Castle Vork on Starday, seven days from now?"

"I don't know. Where is it?"

"It's in central Glawynia, southwest of here, though you'll have to swing either south or west to get around the mountains."

"Is it well enough known by those who live in these parts? Will they be able to point the proper direction, should I ask?"

"There should be no problem, as long as you maintain a steady pace."

"Then I think I can make it."

"Here. This disk will get you into the castle. The guards will know where to direct you. Let me also advance you five gold pieces to cover expenses for going out of your way."

"Not to belittle the offer, but why do you trust me? Why do you feel I won't just take this and go my own way?"

"In the first place, you didn't try to rob me, despite your fine ability as a bowman. In the second case, I think you would want to earn more than that, even if there may be a risk involved. Am I right?"

The wood elf was impressed by the candor of this stranger. It was something that had been missing for months.

"You're right," Uhu chuckled. "I'll be there."

"Good. I'm sure we can use your help!"

Saying this, Stalif remounted and rode south, waving as he departed.

When the horse and man were out of sight, the elf turned and looked up at the owl.

"We're going to Glawynia!" he called out.

4 – THE TRIO

K ilgali is a small barony in the western reaches of Indrose, ruled benevolently by Baron Exox in a very personable manner. Its domain surrounds two fresh streams that feed into a moderately sized river. The baronial manor abuts the edge of the river's flood plain. While almost self-sufficient, the community is dependent upon the river and rainfall, so it is not surprising that they worship Waliwal, who rules over that element.

A group of five youths had grown up together and had developed close friendships. They referred to themselves as "the pack" and freely roamed the village, having visited almost every home and played hide-and-seek throughout the manor. They were also welcome in the temple of old Irok, the druid who served Waliwal and also was the teacher of the youths in Kilgali. They reflected the potential of this close-knit community.

The eldest member of this group was Sind, the only son of Exox and therefore the future ruler of Kilgali. Based on seniority and social rank, this sandy-haired youth of ten commanded the others. Stefan, who was two months and several inches Sind's minor, was considered to be the second-in-command, though he always willingly deferred to his friend. He was smart, strong and agile, with a wiry body and an auburn mane. Stefan's father, Chat, served as captain of the baronial guard. Thus, these youths reflected the relation of their fathers.

The next eldest member of the group was Jienna, the cute, dark-haired daughter of the head forester. Her deep brown eyes could still either of the ten-year-olds, even though she was a year younger. Her closest friend was

Esne, a charming beauty with flowing blond hair, ebon eyes and a sweet voice. She was Stefan's sister. Though she was only nine, she had already begun flirting with the older boys in the village.

The last member was Jienna's brother, Reph, who was a bit more than a year younger than Esne. He was rather plain and a bit slow, but the others all loved him. Reph was very friendly and always trailed after them. In addition, despite his young age, he already showed his father's solid build and was stronger than either Sind or Stefan. While he perhaps had difficulty in learning the druid's lessons or in articulating clearly the ideas that crossed his mind, he had a sharp eye and an unquestioning perception of what occurred around him.

They were an unstoppable force. Reinforcing one another's confidence, they felt that nothing was beyond them. With their free reign of the manor, they visited the guards' barracks and the armory, joking with the guards when they were off duty. They liked the raucous, noisy banter and the flash of metal as the guards went through their daily practice. Reph was especially fascinated with the weapons.

A fair amount of time was also spent at the other two homes. There they found pleasure in the soothing, steady sounds that accompanied the daily toil. Stefan's mother was a weaver, and they watched intently as the shuttle moved back and forth through her loom, transforming yarn into brightly colored cloth. When the others visited Jienna and Reph, the sound was different, but it had a similar effect. Their mother milled grain to make bread, grinding it in her small quern, made of aged oak.

Listening to sounds became a common pastime. They learned to identify birds and insects in the fields and woods. Closing their eyes, they marveled at the way the babble of the water racing over the stones in the stream was ever varying but yet the same. Stefan became adept at creating a set of pipes from reeds, memorizing the various tunes he liked out of those that resulted from simple experimentation.

On sunny days, they often went to the spit where the stream emptied into the river. They would search for flat stones, wanting them to be thin and smooth. They then debated over which of two skills to attempt. One was to skip the rocks as far as they were able, trying to go all the way across the river. The alternative was to throw them into the air with a fast spin, where the goal was to have them come slicing down into the water with almost no splash and a pleasing, quiet "chunk" sound. Each excelled at both and who performed best on any day was unable to be predicted beforehand.

This idyllic life was forced to take a sharp turn at the end of the summer. Jienna and Reph were startled when a rogue wolf unexpectedly took the life of their mother. The pain they experienced was close to unbearable. The other three felt it almost as sharply and they strove to console their friends. Death had not had a direct impact on any of them before this, and they all found it hard to accept. The fact that the wolf was hunted down and slain did little to console them, though it did keep them from fearing the forest.

Through the fall and winter months, they started discussing what they wanted to do with their lives, instead of simply living the here and now. Sind's role had always been known, but the others had never really thought about it, though they had similarly simply assumed that they would do what their parents did.

Jienna resolved that she wanted to be a forester, and she got her father to promise to start teaching her the necessary skills. Reph felt that he wanted to be a hunter, where he could use his growing strength. He especially wanted to hunt down creatures such as the wolf that had slain their mother.

Esne had favored the steady sound of the quern over the clickety-clack of the loom and wanted to help fill the void left in her friends' home. Stefan, however, was unable to come up with an answer, no matter how much the other four pestered him. Nothing seemed to be appropriate.

He was sure that he didn't want to be a man-at-arms. He enjoyed watching his father, but he felt nothing register inside him, and he was seeking that spark. His friends suggested one trade after another, but they were all turned down. He didn't want to farm or fish. He liked Irok, but he didn't want to be a druid. Neither did he want to be an innkeeper, carpenter, forester, miner or smith, nor any of the other ideas that were suggested and discussed.

While he enjoyed playing music, he couldn't picture that as a career. He liked to read and was mentally more alert than any of the others, but he didn't want to be a scribe, which he thought would be boring. He felt that he wanted to use his mind, but he was unaware of any other career that depended directly upon that ability.

Sind finally asked his father what else might be open for Stefan to consider. Exox suggested that he consider being a spellcaster. The idea captured all of their minds, as they had learned of the power of magic in stories they had heard or read. They began talking of the great things Stefan would be able to do, and he at last felt the spark he had been seeking. The marvelous ability to change the world that surrounded his was a fascinating goal, simulating the unlimited skills that they had heard in one tale after another.

None of them had ever seen a spellcaster, so there were no bounds to their fantasies. Exox finally promised that he would have a member of that guild visit Kilgali. The possibility of Stefan being apprenticed was mentioned, but that would still be several years in the future.

***

The expectation of seeing real magic was an incessant undertone of the winter's discussions. At times they wondered if their parents weren't teasing them, but it held their interest nonetheless. Their imagination was strongest when harsh weather kept them indoors.

"If you can become a conjuror or sorcerer," his sister pointed out, "think of the wondrous things you could do!"

"He could make me as pretty as you," Jienna interjected.

"You could give the horses wings," Sind suggested.

"Why not make *us* fly?" Stefan asked.

"Gee, could ya'?" questioned Reph, his wide eyes reflecting his mind's vision.

"I don't know," Stefan answered. "The sorcerer can fly in the stories of Nista, remember?"

"Yeah, that's right."

"I'd like you to stop the snow storm and make summer come early," their leader stated.

"And then I'd make it stay for some extra months."

"I wonder," mused Jienna, "can spellcasters make magic rings?"

"I don't know."

Stefan turned back to Sind.

"Did your father say when we'd get to see magic?"

"No. But he gave his word, so you know we'll see it.

***

When the warm weather returned, this was pushed to the back of their minds, as the magic of the actual world again unfolded. They resumed their explorations, adventures and escapades, including an independent outing to Alf's Village, a freeman's town a mere mile downstream from Kilgali, but on the opposite shore at a site where a bridge spanned the flowing water.

The three fathers sat them down and explained that

they were not to go off that far on their own again. There were unkind and evil people and forces in the world. While they could consider themselves safe within Kilgali, such was not necessarily true elsewhere. The seriousness of the lecture rang true, remembering the wolf that had killed Jienna's and Reph's mother, and they all promised to stay in the barony. Even so, it also sparked their curiosity of just how different the rest of the world might be.

An eightday after that lecture, Exox told Sind that a wizard called "Gray Eyes" would be visiting in the fall.

"That's 'is real name?" Reph asked.

"No, Reph," Esne responded. "Magicians never tell their real names. They always go by something else."

"Why?"

"Maybe they get power from the name," she offered.

"No," Stefan countered. "Some of the tales tell how they do it to protect themselves."

"So," his sister said, "you'll have to get a new name if you become a spellcaster?"

"I guess so."

"How will you pick it?" Sind queried.

"I don't know."

"What about 'Number Two'?" Jienna asked. "You know, the way you always agree with Sind."

"Or 'Smart'," Reph suggested.

"Let's wait until the wizard comes, and we can ask him," Stefan offered.

The discussion then changed to considering and debating what marvels they would see.

***

Fall finally arrived. The morning of the expectant day, Exox gathered a select portion of the barony populace in his courtroom.

"The wizard will be arriving soon. Gray Eyes is to be

treated with utmost respect, which he deserves. He has been here before, though not for many, many years. I believe I was your age, Reph, when last he honored this manor. He was, as I understand it, a good friend of my father."

A few people in the room murmured quiet comments. Reph's mouth began to open, but his sister hushed him.

Exox resumed speaking when it was quiet, saying, "I don't know just when our honored guest will arrive, nor do I know just what he will do, but be appreciative of whatever is offered.

"In the meantime, some tidbits will be served, but I must ask that you remain seated and stay away from the center of this room. Those are the wizard's specific instructions."

At the clap of his hands, servants began walking around with trays of various delicacies, but their avoidance of the barred region was very evident.

A little less than an hour later, a cloud of purple smoke suddenly formed in the middle of the room. As it dissipated, an aged man stood in its midst, coughing slightly. He was thin and gnarled, with a bald head and a long, white beard. He wore a rich, sapphire blue cloak, the color of Lamanna, the god of magic.

Waving the last wisps of smoke away with one hand, he coughed again.

"I don't know why I maintain the theatrics," he said to no one in particular. "I can't stand the odor and my throat doesn't seem to favor it, either."

Looking around, he saw the lord of the manor approaching. He stepped forward, holding out his arms.

"Ah, Exox," he exclaimed, grabbing the baron in a strong hug. "It is good to see you again, lad. I am happy to be back in Kilgali after all these years. It's been far, far too long since I made the point of visiting."

"You are most welcome, Gray Eyes. Is there anything

that you either desire or require?" Exox asked.

"Just some water, please." He glanced around at the attentive audience, pausing when his eyes fell upon the baroness.

"Bubo! You are just as beautiful as when I met you at King Ryal's coronation in Midsite nine years ago!"

"Thank you, m'lord," she responded, beaming at the compliment.

"Now, Exox, which of these youths is your son, and which of his cohorts is harboring an interest in the field of magic?"

The baron motioned Sind and Stefan to step forward.

"The one on the left is our son, Sind. The other is the son of the captain of my guard. His name is Stefan. I believe that his mind is sharp enough to join your guild, but that is something you will have to judge."

"Hmm... Come forward, boys. From the missives I received, you have three other cohorts who belong to your band. Is that correct?"

Stefan merely nodded, but Sind gathered the courage to speak.

"Yes, m'lord."

"Please have them stand."

Esne, Jienna and Reph complied.

They jumped forward as the wizard's voice came from the chairs behind them.

"It's nice to get a rest from supporting that weight. And it's also nice to let some air cool us down, as it was getting too hot!"

"The chairs's speakin'!" Reph shouted. "How come's they hasn't done that afore?"

"It's alright, Reph," his sister said. "Remember, we were told we'd see magic today."

"Oh...yeah!" His perplexed look was replaced with a broad smile.

"Thank you, children," Gray Eyes said. "You may sit

down again."

Reph hesitated as the girls repositioned themselves.

"It's safe?" he asked.

"Yes, child," the wizard answered. "It's quite safe."

Once everyone was looking at him, he held up a finger.

"Magic is the control of a special force."

As he said that, he moved his lips and a bright green flame sprang forth from the tip of his finger, looking like a lit candle.

People in the room gasped and stared.

"How do you feel, miss?" he asked as he pointed his finger at Esne. The flame disappeared.

"I guess I'm fine, m'lord," she said.

"Nothing out of the ordinary?"

"No, m'lord." She hesitantly shook her head.

His lips again moved as one hand went within his robe.

Unexpectedly, Esne was giggling as she grasped at her sides, as if she was trying unsuccessfully to protect her body.

"Oh, stop!" she called between her giggles.

Suddenly, she was once more sitting still, though her face was quite red.

Reaching into his pouch, the wizard withdrew some pebbles and offered them to Sind and Stefan.

"What have I given you?"

"Stones, m'lord," they answered in unison.

Taking them back into his hand, Gray Eyes moved his other hand over them while whispering something.

Returning them to the boys, he asked, "And now?"

"Why, they're gold, m'lord!" Stefan exclaimed.

"Do you agree, Sind?"

"Yes, m'lord."

"Well, you may keep them, though I must warn you that they will once more be plain pebbles in less than an hour.

"You may now sit down, lads."

He looked at the silent assembly.

"You have just seen some examples of minor magic. Our guild prefers to refrain from doing parlor tricks like this, but I was willing to make an exception, today.

"It is important that you understand that we learn to control this force for more meaningful purposes than mere entertainment. What you saw today were four simple spells. The first was Throwing Voice, by which I can make my voice appear to come from an inanimate object. The second and third were Flaming Finger and Tickle, which need no explanations. The last was Pyrite. Pyrite is a mineral that looks like gold but is not. This spell changes stone to actual gold, but only for a limited time.

"I have some serious business to take care of while I am here, but that will wait until after we have eaten. That is, if it is alright with you, Exox."

"But, of course, m'lord," the baron answered.

He then led the wizard into the dining hall, and everyone else followed.

There was diverse, active conversation among the adults during the meal, but the children spoke solely of the magic they had seen and what it implied. If this was minor magic, what might Stefan be able to do if he became a spellcaster?

***

After the meal was over, a private meeting was held with *the pack*, their parents and Gray Eyes. All were seated and Exox instructed the servants that they were not to be disturbed. Gray Eyes was comfortably seated and took a brief time to study each person in the room, giving special attention to Stefan. His brow was furrowed as he considered how to start the discussion. Everyone else waited in silence, though Esne and Reph fidgeted a bit in their chairs.

"Our guild finds it important to identify those youths who are interested in joining us and have the necessary potential. Interest is easy to recognize, but it is important that one also understands that mastering magic is a lifetime endeavor. The period of apprenticeship merely starts one on the path. How far one goes depends upon effort and attention to lifestyle.

"You have expressed the interest, Stefan. Do you understand what I have just said?"

"I think so, m'lord."

"Good. For now, that must suffice.

"The second factor is more difficult. Many people believe that they can easily recognize possible spellcasters by merely studying their face or the lines on their hands. Such is not the case. A central factor required of a spellcaster is a high level of intelligence, but it also requires a certain degree of internal integrity. Fortunately, there is a way that this can be resolved.

"Ages ago, a master wizard created the Potential Quotient Ring."

Gray Eyes paused to remove a dull black ring from a pouch that had been inside his robe.

"This ring draws upon the powers of Lamanna, and it is only able to operate once each eightday, on her day. That is why this meeting was scheduled for today, Starday. This ring measures one's potential for drawing upon her force."

Saying that, he put on the ring. It glowed with a blinding whiteness! He quietly removed it.

"Please come here, Stefan."

The boy stood and nervously walked across the room. It was a short distance, but it felt like it took an eternity to reach the wizard. He nervously held forward a hand, comprehending that this single test would decide whether he could become a spellcaster or if he would have to resume his search for a possible future for himself.

As it was fitted onto his finger, it magically adjusted to fit. It then began to glow, not nearly as brightly as when Gray Eyes wore it, but there was no question of the emitted light.

"Does this mean I can become a spellcaster, m'lord?"

"It unquestionably does, my boy. Your potential is evident, actually far more than just evident. However, you are still too young to start the apprenticeship. I shall return in a year. If you still desire to take up this trade, you will be welcome in."

The expression on Stefan's face had changed from uncertainty to unquestionable pride.

"Yes, m'lord!"

"And if you do, the title will then be *Master*, not *m'lord*."

"Might I ask a question?" Chat ventured.

"Of course. You are his father, so you have a vested concern," the wizard responded, turning to face the captain of the guard.

"My wife and I need to know the cost of the apprenticeship."

"Don't worry. It won't cost you anything. The guild covers the expenses."

"Thank you, m'lord!" Waka said. Her husband smiled at her and at Stefan.

"May I ask one other question?" Stefan directed this at the wizard.

"Yes."

"Do all spellcasters have to change their names?"

"No, but it is highly recommended. When others know your true name, they may be able to control you, and the same is true if you know theirs. You can start thinking of a possible moniker."

"A moniker, m'lord?"

"A name that people will call you."

"Oh!"

"That is enough for today. I have work awaiting me back in Midsite."

"I wish to thank you again, Gray Eyes," Exox said as he stood. Everyone else followed his example.

"The pleasure was mine. This lad has very great potential. He may be a great asset to the guild."

The wizard muttered a few words that no one understood, and then he wasn't there. He had disappeared, without any sound or even a puff of smoke!

***

The next year passed all too quickly. Stefan began to unexpectedly shoot upward in height, passing Sind. His mother said she could see him grow from day to day. They all saw this as the beginning of the break-up of "the pack". Esne was especially apprehensive of her brother's departure, but that was somewhat mollified by the arrival of a new brother, Weel. Her attention to the infant actually contributed to the group's fragmentation, speeding up the process.

As the summer waned, Sind began the formal training to prepare him to take on baronial responsibilities in the future. On the scheduled day, Stefan packed the few possessions he would be taking with him. The parting was not easy for any of them, but it was most difficult for Reph. As it had been hard for him to accept his mother's death, he couldn't picture this change in his personal world.

Sind stood by Exox to welcome Gray Eyes' arrival in the midmorning. It was a brief greeting. Chat and the wizard then signed formal apprenticeship papers and final farewells were said. Stefan promised his mother that he would write frequently, and then he and Gray Eyes were gone.

***

From Stefan's perspective, he had been standing by the wizard looking at those he held dear and then he was in very different surroundings, unlike anything he had ever seen before. Gray Eyes had mumbled a few syllables, and then the world suddenly changed. He hadn't felt any motion or vertigo, nor had he heard any sound, and there had been no flash of light. Somehow, he had expected more.

They stood in a stone room with a plush blue carpet. The walls were covered with fine tapestries of the most powerful beasts: dragons, griffins, manticores, unicorns and giants. Between the tapestries were three large, wooden doors. Glancing around, his eyes scanned over a fireplace and shelves that went all the way to the tall ceilings, filled with books, scrolls, bones, bottles and stoppered vials. Several small tables and a fair number of chairs were distributed around this very large room.

"If I may ask, where are we, m'lord?"

"This is the guild meeting room, in the Guildhall of Indrose, lad. It is next to King Ryal's castle in Midsite. And, as I mentioned a year ago, the title you are to use when addressing me or any other members of the guild is 'master'. This will apply for the full four years of your apprenticeship."

Stefan made a mental note. He had set the goal of doing the best he was able, and this was a simple rule that he would be certain to follow at all times.

"And how will I recognize the other guild masters, Master?"

"We will all be wearing the sapphire blue of Lamanna. Starting tonight, after your initiation, you will wear the apprentice's white tunic with the broad blue diagonal stripe. If you meet another apprentice and do not know his or her name, use the term 'novice'. Also, your given name will not be used here. Have you considered a moniker?"

"Yes, Master. I had liked Jienna's suggestion of Star, as Starday is Lamanna's day, but my sister said that the way I've gained height so rapidly, I should call myself Starspire. Would that be allowable?"

"If you are satisfied with it, then who am I to object? However, in most cases, you will find that I and the other members of the guild will simply refer to you as 'novice'.

"Another novice will now show you to the dorm and will inform you of the schedule of duties. The initiation ceremony will be at dusk."

With that, Gray Eyes clapped his hands. Two of the doors opened. A servant came to take the boy's pack. A young girl in apprentice tunic entered through the other door and walked up to him. She had a fair complexion and long brown hair that matched the color of her eyes that sparkled with an air of excitement.

"This is the new novice, Master?" she asked.

When Gray Eyes simply nodded, she turned to face Stefan.

"Hello. My moniker is Wyscan."

"Mine is Starspire."

"Come with me, and I'll show you to our room."

He followed her as she led him up a long spiral of stairs until they reached a rather bare tower room. There were six beds, six desks and chairs, straw matting on the floor, a trunk by each bed and one shelf of books, plus a worktable with a variety of oddities. There were two windows, looking out upon a city that exceeded the boy's imagination.

"One window faces sunrise," Wyscan commented. "The other lets us watch the sunset. Your bed is the one on which your pack was placed." She pointed it out.

"How many other apprentices are there?"

"Geas is in her final year. She is almost sixteen. Menton is in his third year. Astra has just begun her second year, and I have been here three months. You are now the greenhorn, Starspire, so I will at least be free of the most menial task."

"Does that mean I will have to empty the commodes?"

"No!" she laughed. "The servants handle that sort of thing. You will have to take care of the worktable. It will be your job to see that the needed components are present and you will have to clean it every evening before going to bed. The servants are not allowed to touch that."

"Oh," he paused. "I understand."

"We are expected to be up and dressed by sunrise and we are to be back in this room by sunset unless we are working with a guild master. At the meals, we are to be silent unless asked a question. Our responsibility is to catch the words of wisdom spilling from our masters' lips. Unfortunately, you will discover that most of the comments during the meals are most mundane. However, this is one of the rules.

"Let's see... We are also expected to follow any directions we receive from those in blue and we should inform them of anything we think they might want to know, and I mean anything, even if it may seem to be of only the slightest importance. The last rule is that all matters of the guild are not to be shared with anyone outside of the guild."

"That's it?"

"Well, you'll find that much effort and energy will go into your studies, and individual rules may arise, but that's it for the general rules. Among the novices, we do have some additions.

"First, sleep is important, that we might regain the manna we use, so we do not disturb one another's rest. Since we must all share this room, we agree that there will be no secrets between us regarding anything that is nonmagical, with the exception of our true names, nor will there be any modesty. You will learn that control of sexual desires and avoiding promiscuity increases one's manna, so we feel that we can help one another develop that strength by starting here. At least that's what the others tell me."

She giggled at this point.

"I don't know about you, but where I come from, we were raised to believe that it is normal to be more or less dressed in public after the age of eight."

He nodded his agreement.

"Well, it took me a few weeks to get used to dressing while Menton is present, but it seems to be harder for him. Not being seen, but trying to ignore us. And Geas especially seems to try to tempt him! She and Astra may start doing it to you, too, so watch out!"

She gave him a broad grin.

"Thanks, Myscan. What is this manna you mentioned?"

"It's the force we get from Lamanna. The greater your experience, the better your training and the purer your lifestyle, the more manna you will have. And manna is what you draw upon when you cast spells, so it decides how many spells you can cast and how powerful they can be."

"Oh. I guess it's really important then."

"You better believe that! Anyway, the masters will explain it better.

"Now you better rest, so you'll be ready for the initiation. I look forward to this, 'cause now I'll be able to watch it. That'll be different than when I was the one being initiated."

"What is it like?"

"Sorry. I can't discuss it with you until you're initiated, and by then you'll know. So just take a nap for now. No one will come in until then."

"When is supper?"

"Oh! I'm sorry!" She held her hands to her cheeks. "I forgot to tell you that you have to fast until tomorrow morning. You can only have water. Did you have a good breakfast?"

"No. I was too nervous to eat much."

"I wasn't warned either. I was afraid my stomach was going to growl and embarrass me!"

"Did it?"

"No, thank goodness!"

Once again, she smiled at him.

"Close your eyes and rest your body and mind, Starspire."

She quietly shut the door as she left the room.

***

Later in the afternoon, a servant brought Starspire a plain white tunic. He was instructed to change into only that single item of cloth, removing everything he was presently wearing. That was to be left behind on his bed.

As he stood barefoot, waiting in the dorm room, his stomach growled, drawing attention to his hunger pangs. He hoped that his stomach would refrain from making such noises during the initiation ceremony.

A female apprentice came to get him. Mentally estimating her age, he surmised that this was probably the one Myscan had referred to as Geas. She held a finger to her lips when Starspire was about to speak and then motioned for him to follow her.

Holding a single candle upright in her left hand, she proceeded serenely down the stairs and into a room that he gauged as being rather large, though compared to the scale of the meeting room, it was probably only medium-sized. It was painted bright blue, and everyone except for the other four novices wore blue robes. There were many lit candles and a large brazier was in the center of the room, next to a low, padded table, also blue in color. A bench with a variety of items was behind the brazier, and Gray Eyes stood on the other side of the table.

A gesture of his fingers called Starspire to step forward. With a degree of trepidation and a matching dose of excitement, he complied.

"We stand here tonight as witnesses, asking for your blessing, Lamanna, as we welcome this boy as an initiate into the Order of Enchantment. We ask you to show your acceptance of him in the formation of his birthmanna, as he will be reborn into a new life."

The wizard had been looking over the boy's head, facing the audience behind him. He now lowered his gaze and stared into Starspire's eyes.

"You have previously shown that you have the potential to be a spellcaster. You will now take the next step into the Order of Enchantment. It requires courage and pure thoughts, that Lamanna will accept you. Those of us who serve her in this order have pledged to use our magic to do good. 'Good' is actually self-defined, but each of us knows what it is and understands the importance of consistency.

"Are you ready?"

"Yes, Master."

He tried to say it with confidence, but he wasn't sure how it sounded. He was glad that he wasn't facing all the people who stood behind him. He tried to clear his mind of that, imagining that only he and Gray Eyes were in the room. That helped him calm down a bit, lessening the queasiness that had begun to swell up within him.

"Disrobe, neophyte, and lie upon this table."

He complied, finding hands from behind that accepted his tunic.

He watched as Gray Eyes placed a ceramic bowl upon the brazier. A silver disc was placed within it, and a smaller piece of gold was added. This was stirred with a ceramic rod, and herbs and bits of other materials were selected from the bench and added to the crucible. Words and hand motions continued throughout the process.

A bronze knife was heated in the flame and then held above the guild master. Starspire felt someone grab his left hand, but he didn't look to see whom that was. His full attention was on the glowing knife.

Gray Eyes brought it and a small glass to the table. With a deft movement, he made a small cut in Starspire's left thumb. The pain was minimal. The blood was collected in the glass. He sensed a cloth being pressed against the cut, but he watched with his full attention as the blood was added to the crucible.

An oily ointment was rubbed into the region of his navel. He glanced up and saw that two men in blue were over him. They stepped back as Gray Eyes brought the crucible from the brazier, holding it with tongs.

"You will now stay still as your birthmanna is created. If Lamanna will accept you, she will see that you feel no pain."

Somehow, this reassurance didn't prevent the tensing of all of his muscles. He gritted his teeth as the hot contents were poured onto his stomach. Closing his eyes, he silently pledged that he would not reveal the pain he was about to experience, no matter how intense it might prove to be.

But there was no pain! He heard a sizzling sound and smelled the odor of burning oil, but that was it. A silent but honest prayer of thanks went up to Lamanna.

Gray Eyes removed the silver disk from his navel and held it up for all to see.

"You are now a novice to the Order of Enchantment!" he declared.

The wizard removed a similar disk on a silver necklace from within his robes, holding it up next to the newly formed one. Both glowed brightly.

Starspire's peripheral vision then saw similar lights from behind him. Glancing around, he became aware that the others in the room were each holding up his or her birthmanna.

An awl was used to place a small hole near the edge of his birthmanna and it was placed on a silver necklace. It was then placed around his neck, and a novice's white tunic with the broad blue stripe was lowered over his head.

"Lessons will begin tomorrow. Introductions to the members of the Order will begin at breakfast. Many will depart on their own affairs after that. For now, novice, sleep soundly."

And that was it. Starspire was bursting with questions, but everyone was leaving the room. The other novices led him silently upstairs.

***

After Myscan introduced everyone to him, she asked Starspire what he had thought when his birthmanna was being made.

"In all honesty, I had never been so scared!"

"I know," she said. "It looked almost as scary from where I stood."

"I finally found the edge had worn off when you were initiated," Geas said. "I've become confident that they won't bring in a neophyte who Lamanna won't accept."

"I hope you're right," Astra commented. "I don't want to see a rejection."

Everyone nodded in firm agreement.

"So, this is my badge of membership in the Order?" Starspire asked.

"That, and much more," Geas offered. "We are not barred from sharing our knowledge with you. The amulet will glow when it is near you, and only you, as it contains your own blood. It is an unquestionable proof of being a spellcaster and should always be worn, but hidden within your clothes. It serves as the focus of your tie with Lamanna and will play a part in casting many spells, especially those that have mental effects upon others.

"In addition, as long as it touches your skin, you will be unable to be bound by non-magical means. Ropes and chains will simply slide free. And you will not be able to be poisoned. You may become sick, but nothing more. There may be other powers. If so, we guess that they are learned at the end of the apprenticeship."

The vision of the power of this silver amulet astounded him. All he could say was "Wow!"

"Now, get to sleep, everyone," Geas ordered.

***

Starspire found that he was in a totally new life, and he adjusted fairly quickly. His early lessons consisted of learning to identify components necessary for various spells, including gaining the knowledge of how to handle them and the appropriate quantities needed for various spells. He also had to learn the different hand motions and gestures that went into spellcasting, and the importance of being able to make them as unnoticeable as possible.

He was taught how to have restful, regenerative sleep that was necessary to replenish his manna and the variety of acceptable prayers that could be made to Lamanna before bedding down. He gained the understanding that contact with large amounts of metal, especially iron, interfered with the casting of most spells. Therefore, spellcasters preferred bronze daggers and utensils. This also contributed a cognizance of why spellcasters avoided the use of armor. This restriction even wound up applying to leather armor, since that restricted the freedom of motion and the free flow of air over the body. Tight clothes were generally shunned altogether.

No matter how carefully he listened, he never caught the words used in any spells, and he was unable to repeat what he had heard. Menton explained the process.

"Unless it is written in your own spellbook, you will always hear and forget, even if you are reading it from a scroll yourself. And that won't be possible until you have learned the Read Magic spell.

"My guess is that you will get your spellbook soon. You will then start to learn your first cantrip, which you will have to learn by memory, as you will be unable to read it. As a new novice, you will only be able to attempt casting it once or twice a day, as that will deplete your manna.

"Don't be discouraged. With practice, the execution of the cantrip will improve. Once you've got it down, the masters will find another you can manage, and with the use of spells, your manna will be able to increase."

"Will I be able to choose what spells I learn?"

"No. Remember that, to each of us, the spells we know are our stock and trade. If every spellcaster knew every spell, the supply would exceed the demand, and our guild would falter. The restriction of spells is what makes a wizard powerful. That will control what we are taught. If you freely give away what you know, you will find yourself out of business. That is one of the fundamental lessons of the apprenticeships, and it will be driven into you."

Starspire wound up finding this to be all too true.

A lot of his time also went into his chores, which included being at the beck and call of everyone above him, which included everyone except for the servants. Since the servants were kept out of certain rooms and also did not handle anything that was magical, it meant that a lot of the menial work was left to the novices, and the others could defer the tasks to him if he was not already busy.

Other lessons in reading, writing, mathematics, science and history were also included, as knowledge was the skeleton of magical power. While he had received a fundamental education in Kilgali when he was Stefan, he found that he was pushed far beyond that now. He also became aware that the spellcasters continued learning throughout their lives. He noted that point in his first letter home, also stressing the fact that his former name should be forgotten. Henceforth, all correspondence had to be to his new name.

***

A serious spellcaster with thick, raven eyebrows and fine, silky hair that was a shade lighter gave Starspire his spellbook. This guildsman's name was Tome.

The book was only four inches by six inches and was less than an inch thick. The pages were made of thin but firm parchment, and the only writing in it was his name, which was inscribed inside the front cover.

"This book," the guild master said, "is of importance only secondary to your amulet, Novice. Like the silver birthmanna, it should be kept close to your body. This is especially true for the next month, as it must absorb your sweat and feel the beating of your heart. It must be with you while you sleep and while awake, while you eat, while you toil and while you study. It will become one with you, and this will later enable you to draw forth spells from it, even if you haven't used them for decades.

"The entry of spells will in turn require the use of some of your blood, mingled with magic ink, and a Write Magic spell must be cast, requiring manna from both you and the one who writes in your book. However, you will then be able to cast the spell again and again without losing it. When a spell is merely read aloud from a scroll or some other book, it is invoked and then vanishes. Therefore, remember the importance of not vocalizing when you read spells from any other source unless you mean to do so."

Tome took out a vial of magic ink, a pen and a small knife. He pricked Starspire's finger and added several drops of blood to the vial, replaced the stopper, and then shook it well. "Starspire" had been printed neatly upon the vial.

"This is the ink that will be used for making entries into your spellbook. When it is used up, more will be prepared. I will now inscribe your first cantrip, and you will start learning it tomorrow, when your manna is replenished.

The boy watched as figures were carefully drawn. As he stared at them, the ink seemed to move around on the page so that he was unable to read anything.

"Rest your eyes, Novice. Without the proper spell, the words will not let you read them. It will only tire you."

"Thank you, Master."

After using some sand to be sure the ink had dried properly and none would smear, he closed the book and gave it to the boy.

"Place this within your tunic, Novice, and return to your chores and studies. Tomorrow will come when it is ready."

"Yes, Master."

**

The next day, Rouge called him into a small room. She was one of the two guild masters who taught most of the novice classes. She had bright red hair and matched it with red upon her lips and fingernails and a red scarf around her neck.

"I was informed that you were given your first cantrip yesterday, Novice. I am to help you learn it. It will have to be by rote memory at this time. I will state one word. Repeat it silently several times. When I give you the next, repeat both. We will repeat this until you have the entire phrase. You will then try to cast it once each day. After a full eightdays, I will observe and evaluate your performance. This is in addition to your normal work. Is that clearly understood?"

"Yes, Master."

"Good. Then please let me see your book."

She opened it and fitted a circular crystal monocle over one eye. Casting a brief spell, she inspected the entry. Rouge closed the book and looked at Starspire as she returned the book to him.

"I see that Tome made a good selection. Your first cantrip is Lamanna's Light. You must hold the palm of your hand open when invoking the spell. When you are successful, that palm will project a blue light that will enable you to see anything within a range of about three feet. It will last for at most fifteen minutes, but it will let you see in an otherwise dark area. Try to cast it before going to sleep.

"You will now start to learn the spell."

This session lasted for about half an hour.

The day could not go fast enough. Whenever possible, Starspire repeated the phrase again and again in his mind. He felt he had all of the pronunciations correct, but he wouldn't be certain until he got to actually test it.

Dusk finally arrived, and he quickly changed into a nightshirt. He was so focused on testing his first cantrip that he didn't notice that the others were watching him intently. He held up his palm and recited the spell. A faint blue light appeared in a small area, flickered, and then vanished.

He would have considered it a failure had it not been for the encouragement he received from the others.

"It worked, as the light was produced," Astra pointed out, "and this happened on your very first try!"

"It means you had every word correct," Myscan added.

"All you need to do is say it more clearly and with stronger confidence," Menton said.

"How did you all know I was learning my first cantrip today?" he asked.

"It was as evident as if you carried a banner," Geas laughed. "Remember, we each went through it ourselves. I was so unsure of myself that I got no results until my third day. I feared I had the words wrong, but the other novices gave me the support I needed. I learned that this is one of our duties, and that's why you were told to try it now."

"All I can say is thank you, to each and every one of you." His tone made it evident to all of them that his appreciation was sincere.

Starspire found that he was more tired than usual, but the night's sleep rejuvenated him, and the spell worked far better the next evening. By the time he performed for Rouge, it went so well that she let him know he had enough manna to carry out two cantrips each day!

***

Over the course of his first year, Starspire made steady progress in mastering his skill. He expanded his repertoire to a total of eight cantrips, and his manna level reached the point where he could either cast five cantrips or Read Magic and one cantrip in a single day. He had considered receiving his crystal monocle a milestone, as every spellcaster required one to be able to read magical script. He fully understood why this was the first actual spell that was taught to every spellcaster.

At this point, he was working on two new spells. One was Magic Script, which was actually a very marketable skill. Few in the trade succeeded in properly writing with magic ink, so there was always a demand for one who could clearly perform this spell. Tome was confident that Starspire had the necessary abilities. The other spell, Identification, had even broader applications. Casting this spell allowed one to tell what powers were contained in magical potions or items such as rings, wands and artifacts. If he mastered these and nothing else, he would at least have a career.

He had also developed strong friendships with the other novices. While he respected the magicians, the separation between master and novice prevented personal ties. Two ceremonies had occurred over these months. He had shared in the pride radiating through the hallway when Geas had been accepted into the guild. Personally, he had found even greater pleasure in Brown's initiation. He was glad when this boy displaced him in the lowest position, with the transfer of the more menial responsibilities.

The end of this year was marked by Sind's visit; he accompanied his father to attend King Ryal's wedding. They met during one of Starspire's brief free periods. Sind couldn't believe in the additional height that his friend had gained. He pointed out that perhaps his body was trying to fulfill his new name. Both also noted how the other was far more mature than when they had last been together, a result they agreed developed from now having true responsibilities.

The activities of the other members of "the pack" pretty well matched what Starspire had garnered from his letters. Jienna and Reph had started informal training with their father, as opposed to formal apprenticeships. Sind told him how Reph was also growing, both in size and strength. While he had difficulty in controlling projectiles, he showed a natural knack with hand-held weapons. And Esne continued to drive her mother crazy with her puppy love for almost every boy in the village!

***

The next three years seemed to fly by for Starspire, in part due to being so busy all of the time. Spare time did not exist, and the efforts in this profession made his need for sleep imperative. As he progressed, his responsibilities increased, which gave him less time to learn new spells.

Even so, he had excellent control of both Magic Script and Identification, plus four others. Detect Magic meshed nicely with Identification, as it enabled him to tell if an item was magical. The other three only had potential use if he went adventuring. That possibility had kept smoldering in the back of his mind for four years, but he was certain that he had far more yet to learn before that could be given any serious consideration.

By the time he was sixteen, he had passed six feet in height, already making him the tallest person in the hall, and he was still growing. The sapphire blue robe he received at his acceptance into the guild had extra cloth in the hems to allow for his continued growth. He was glad that he had time for a visit home before starting work as a guildsman, since this would fortuitously allow him to attend Esne's wedding.

He made the trip by horse, as he had no magical alternative. That proved to matter little, as his blue robe and tall height had a far greater impact on the residents of Kilgali than when Gray Eyes had appeared in his puff of smoke. He was just as startled by the changes he observed.

Reph was nearly six feet tall himself and far more solid in build, but Starspire was even more shocked when he looked at Esne and Jienna. The scrawny girls he had left behind were now young women! Esne had one year left as a miller's apprentice and Jienna was already employed. Exox had hired her as a forester to help meet the demands of his estate, actually serving both him and the entire community.

If his sister had been a charming beauty before, she was stunningly gorgeous now. Starspire was certain that this judgment was not only because she was his sister, nor because she was about to be wed. He had seen many beautiful women in Midsite, and he was confident of his appraisal.

Her blond tresses flowed down past her waist and her

bright green eyes sparkled. She was petite, but she had the right curves in exquisite proportions. Looking down upon her, he found it hard to believe that they were from the same family if it were not that Weel, now four, combined their individual features.

Her beau was Olaf, three years her elder. Though a few inches under six feet, he was a full foot taller than Esne. He was muscular, and Starspire remembered his easy-going, amiable attitude. Like his father, he was a carpenter, converting the forest wood into fine, useful items. He showed attention to detail in all he did, and this was an aspect that won over Esne in selecting him as her lifelong partner.

Irok held the wedding outside of Chat and Waka's house. The day was warm and cloudless, which was taken as a very good omen. Starspire slipped away while the celebration was going on and went to the carpenter shop and home that Esne and Olaf would share with his father. As part of his gift to the couple, he used a Clear cantrip several times, making the house and shop cleaner than either had ever been, perhaps even cleaner than when they were first built.

Back at the wedding, he gave them a vial containing a potion that had been concocted by Geas.

"If you ever reach a point where things are difficult and there is much stress, drink this together and it will make the problem pass."

"Will it truly work?" Weel asked.

"The spellcaster who prepared it promised that it would," he said as he lifted his little brother, tussling Weel's mop of hair.

"Thank you, Stef... Starspire," Olaf said, carefully placing it in a safe position among the other gifts.

The most valued gift, however, came from Rosin, Jienna and Reph. It was the quern that had been used to grind flour in their house. Tears flowed from Esne's face as she accepted it, actually hugging it as many memories surged through her mind.

Everyone found that the end of the visit came too soon, but Starspire had to return to the guildhall. He promised to continue writing, taking advantage of the rare occasions when someone was known to be coming this way. He also told the others that they should try to come to the capital and see the wonders of a city. He didn't know when he would next be able to visit, but he would return. Of that, he was certain!

***

Back in Midsite, he settled easily into his new role. He worked at the store that sold both clerical and magical supplies and items, situated between the guildhall and a druidic temple, a large portion of which was a wooded park. A hallway connected the rear workroom to the guildhall. There were always two large guards on duty in the shop, one of which was always positioned at the entrance during business hours.

Each craft had the responsibility of selecting one guard. The spellcasters had two who alternated shifts. One had been a bouncer at a high-class brothel. The other had served as a man-at-arms at a barony in Eslardia, coming with extremely good references from a wizard there. The druids had selected two berserkers. After noting their massive bodies and bulging muscles, anyone who came in was careful to not disturb whichever guards were on duty.

To limit business to serious customers, an entrance fee of a gold piece had to be paid at the door. If the purchase totaled less than ten gold pieces, a surcharge of an additional gold piece was added. This both covered the cost of having the guards and encouraged people wanting small items to take their business elsewhere. The primary purposes of the shop were to bring in sizable sums of money and to serve the needs of members of the two professions.

While the most common business consisted of selling components and potions, that was not the main source of income for the Order of Enchantment. Far more money was earned by buying and selling actual magical items and by identifying the powers of such items. There were also occasional requests for the writing of magical scrolls.

Starspire predominantly worked in the latter two roles. A representative example was when a wizened old woman brought in a particular item for identification and evaluation. She cautiously edged her way into the shop, a bit intimidated by the guards that towered over her. She carefully unwrapped a necklace that she possessed and believed to be magical. After a cursory inspection, he had her sit in a comfortable chair and offered her a cup of tea. Assuring her that he would return the original item to her, he then took it to the workroom and cast first a Detect Magic spell, and, as wound up being appropriate, an Identification spell. This actually took a bit less than an hour, though some items might take longer than that. It turned out to have the power to make the wearer feel that she was more beautiful, affecting her confidence and ability to interact well with others, even though it did not actually affect anyone else's perception of the one who wore it. As was the common practice, the potential market value of the item was then estimated, and he divided that value by three.

As was the general rule, the customer was offered that amount for the item. If a tenth of the determined value was paid, its powers were revealed. If the client decided to sell it, they received the difference between the two amounts. The source of funding to cover the guild's expenses was very clear. In that particular case, the woman had paid the fee and retained the necklace, knowing a granddaughter whom she was certain would benefit by wearing it.

This business, however, was sporadic, so it left

Starspire with quite a bit of spare time. Much time was used for his personal advancement, through reading and study, but some was devoted to training novices. His first such assignment was to teach Brown to properly cast the Identification spell. In addition, he found that it was easy to converse with the druids and guards. They found him to be more talkative than most spellcasters, and he thereby learned quite a bit about other parts of the world and their skills and profession.

***

Thus, the next three years went by. Starspire stopped growing at two inches short of seven feet! The original cloak had not been adequate for that. Esne and Olaf had had a daughter, Kuku, less than a year after the wedding, but he had still not been able to return to see her, nor had anyone from Kilgali come to visit him. That had begun to gnaw at him.

Based on his mental image, he had reached a point where he had eleven manna units available when he was well rested. A cantrip used about one such unit and the spells he knew each used about four. He had also added three more entries to his spellbook. Each of these could prove beneficial if he did decide to strike out on his own, and they therefore strengthened that idea. Even so, he still needed a nudge to overcome the inertia of complacency.

Shortly before his nineteenth birthday, he forced himself to visit his family. He was fascinated with his niece and found that Esne was even more beautiful than when he had last seen her. She and Olaf were doing well and the vial of potion had not been touched, which he interpreted in a positive manner.

Like him, the other members of "the pack" were still single. Sind had assumed a diplomatic role, visiting neighboring baronies to discuss their most pressing common interests, which were the threat of orcs in the mountains to the west and the lack of adequate action on the part of King Ryal.

"Two barons have daughters who are catching my attention," he confided in Starspire. "I don't see anything in the immediate future, but there are possibilities a few years hence. I hope that you can meet them and give me your advice, as I find the selection difficult."

"In that case, I advise you to wait a bit longer, until you feel that you don't need my advice."

The meeting with Rosin's children went differently.

"We's wonderin', Starspire," Reph said, "what's happen to th' plans we's had t'explore th' world?"

"Reph and I have been talking about it," Jienna explained. "This is my fourth year as a forester and his second as a hunter. We enjoy working with Dad, and things are comfortable here...but that's the problem; it's too comfortable.

"We hear the minstrels and what you tell in your letters, and we want to get out and see it ourselves. Esne and Sind are tied down, but we thought we could join you and go and do something exciting before we're old. I mean, look, I'm already eighteen!"

Starspire stifled a chuckle at that perception. Instead, he decided to share an idea that he had been mulling over for several weeks.

"To be honest, I've been thinking of doing some adventuring myself."

"Ya' tellin' th' truth?"

"Honest, Reph. But I think you two would have to gain some other skills."

"And what could we do now? Who would take us on as apprentices?" Jienna snorted.

"Well, I can think of a place where you could each fit in."

"Doing what?" she laughed.

"You, to start, could be a druid. They're not all like Irok, you know. Think of the druid who comes each spring and fall to bless the fields and crops. Druids accept aspirants at any age. With your background as a forester, you could take the calling to serve Sylvan."

"If you're joking with me, I'll find some way to get my revenge, because that really sounds appealing. But if I become a druid, what would Reph do?"

"I was thinking that he could be a berserker."

"What's a b'serker?"

"Berserkers are fighters who serve druids. It's a risky trade, but it has its advantages."

"I've heard that berserkers are fearsome," Jienna said. "Just being fearsome can't be accurate and now I want to know more details, as we're dealing with my brother."

"Fair enough. I know a few, so my sources are firsthand.

"Berserkers are trained to fight in special ways. They only use hand-held weapons, which I understand is Reph's strength. Once they start fighting, they are unable to stop unless they are unconscious or their opponents are either dead or have fled in fear. Only druids can overcome this bloodlust. When blood is drawn, their strength increases and they emit an aura that can cause foes to panic, dropping weapons and running away. That's the source of the fearsome quality you've heard about.

"Despite what I've said, they aren't agents of destruction, even though they do serve Kreva, the goddess of war and death. They are by no means invincible and they don't have to fight if it goes against their common sense. They are merely trying to help maintain a proper balance in the world.

"The training they undergo includes treatment with potions that harden their skin and remove their sense of fear. They wear minimal clothing, as they oppose anything that limits their movement and aren't bothered by cold.

They also paint their bodies in bright colors to be sure to attract the attention of any adversaries. Once a battle is over and the bloodlust ends, their body is clearly drained, and they must rest to recuperate."

"That's all rather remarkable," Jienna said. "Is there anything else to this cult?"

"I wouldn't call it a cult," he responded firmly. "While I'm not certain, I believe that berserkers learn the secret language of the druids, both spoken and written. I have also heard that they can call upon Kreva to cast at least some druidic spells, but I am not sure if that is true. I recall, too, that there seems to be a special bond of friendship between all berserkers; at least that was true whenever I saw a pair meet."

"Well, Reph, what do you think?" his sister queried.

"Soun's good, Ji. D'ya like it? Can we go wi' Star?"

"I know Dad won't be happy, but we do want to get out of this small village in this little corner of nowhere. Can you really get us accepted by the druids?"

"I can't promise that, but I can introduce you at the temple, and I'm willing to bet that they'll accept you!"

"Ya' don' bet, Star!"

"I know, Reph, but there's always the exception."

"Come on, Reph, let's talk to Dad."

The two took off, running pell-mell to their cottage.

***

Starspire found that it would have been a safe bet. The druids willingly accepted Jienna and Reph into their fold. Their training started the very first day, but they were able to meet frequently with their friend, especially when he was working in the shop.

Reph's body adapted well to the potions. By the end of one year, his skin was as tough as leather armor. While he had already been fairly proficient at handling both a long sword and a battle-axe, these skills were honed to an expert status, and he also learned how to use a halberd, a formidable weapon that consisted of a pole with an ax-like blade and a steel spike at one end. Jienna confided that, while Reph's teacher was unable to correct the sloppy normal speech that had been ingrained under Irok's tutelage, her brother was able to speak Druidic perfectly. He was even able to read it well!

Jienna also found that she was well attuned to serving the god of farm and forest, just as her friend had foreseen. Her father had helped her develop adequate ability with staff and short bow. The druids trained her to be adept with both scimitar and sling, which replaced her former weapons. She was also taught the skills of healing. These could easily prove to be life saving when they adventured.

She learned the religious skills required to perform the social roles of prayer, blessing and marriage. She was a sharp student and was strongly motivated, which her teachers repeatedly pointed out to younger aspirants. Jienna didn't let this go to her head, but she silently appreciated it. Her mentors considered this to be another positive attribute.

Lessons included the religion's philosophy, stressing the importance of nature and balance. Mistletoe and holly played an important part in communing with the gods, and Jienna learned how to properly harvest and store these components, drawing upon the grove within the temple park.

At the end of the year of training, Jienna considered the high point to be her successful concoction of a magical potion. Placing a turtle shell and two gallons of water in a cauldron, she had brought them to a boil. Powdered bone, caterpillar cocoons, dust from a bookshelf and powdered lime were then added, stirring as it all simmered for two hours. After removing the turtle shell, water that had been blessed by a more powerful druid was added and the cauldron was removed from the fire. Once it was cool, she used mistletoe to call upon Sylvan to ignite the liquid. When the flame died, Jienna succeeded in skimming an oily substance from the surface, which she placed in a vial and then stoppered firmly shut.

She now had a parchment salve that could be rubbed onto scrolls or parchment. Such treatment would protect them from natural aging and nonmagical flame!

**

This occurred in late summer, just as Starspire completed his on-going training session of a novice. They decided that it was time to go out into the world, while the weather was still reasonable. If nothing came of this effort, they could always return to Midsite for the winter.

Collecting the necessary gear, they set off for Mercenaries' Hall, a large bar on the eastern edge of Midsite. Legends told how great heroes had been hired there to carry out fantastic deeds.

As they rode through the city, their occupations were obvious. Starspire stood out, tall in the saddle, wearing the bright blue robe of a spellcaster. Jienna's cloak was just as clear in identifying her as a druid. Reph wore only a loincloth and boots, with his body painted in bright red and blue. He carried his pack over only one shoulder so it could be easily dropped if there was any need to fight. His three weapons were all very visible and there was no possibility of questioning his profession!

Reaching the Hall, they left their horses in the stable and settled down at a table. The young magician had water while the others sipped at mead. It was a warm, balmy day and wisps of clouds were visible drifting across the portion of the sky that could be seen through the open doorway.

"We's not 'the pack' no more," Reph said. "What's we gonna call us?"

"How about 'The Trio'?" Jienna suggested.

"As good as anything else," Starspire said. He was eying the other people in the large room. They looked like ordinary folk. While he had been in the city for eight years, he had never visited this place of business before, in part because he refrained from drinking. Somehow, he had expected to see the qualities described in the ballads. It just wasn't there.

"How long's we gonna hafta wait?"

"We don't know, Reph. We'll just have to be patient."

On saying this, Starspire took out his pipes and began to play them quietly. A few customers glanced over, but they then returned to their own business, which predominantly was drinking while talking quietly with one another.

Some small fights occurred as the hours dragged on, but the two bouncers quickly cleared them up. Reph's presence kept the disorderly individuals away from their area. While the boisterous clients might enjoy a scrap, they had enough sense to avoid a berserker, even if they were quite tipsy.

As evening approached, Starspire called over a barmaid. She was solidly built and older than his mother. Despite her long day, having been there before they arrived, she was still happy. There was an honest smile on her round face, and it seemed to belong there.

"Yes, m'lord?" she said.

"My curiosity has the better of me. Might I ask a few questions?"

"That 'pends on if they's too personal. Is you thinkin' o' getting' fresh?"

Reph joined in her light-hearted laughter.

"No. ma'am, I don't intend to be fresh."

"Ah, now, that's too bad!"

All four found they were getting into a jovial mood.

"So, what's ya' want to know?"

"Well...have you been working here long?"

"Since 'fore you's was born, an' then some!"

"How often do people come here to hire mercenaries?"

"I see! That's why you's all been a sittin' here this long day, jus' nursin' yer drinks. An' ya' wi' only water, too, m'lord! Ya' want's to go off an' be heroes so tha' minstrels'll sing o' yer glories, right?"

"Sure 'nuff," Reph answered. "We wants to slay dragons an' bring back treasures! We's 'Th' Trio'!"

"Perhaps we'll start with simpler tasks," Jienna ventured in a more subdued tone.

"Well, now. So you's 'Th' Trio', huh? I'll ha' to keep m'ears perked! Anyhow, as to yer question... This hall got its name more'n a century ago. Every now an' agin', someone comes in lookin' fer th' likes o' you's, but they's sure from elsewhere. You's th' first mercenaries what's come 'ere seekin' 'venture in a few years."

"That's what I was afraid you'd say," Starspire moaned.

"Wait," Jienna said. "You said we're not the only ones who believe the legends. Foreigners come here seeking people such as us. How often do they come?"

"Mebbe one or two times a month. They asks fer strong arms an' brave souls, an' us what's 'ere gets a good laugh out o' it!"

"Thank you for your help," the druid said, giving the barmaid a silver piece.

She curtsied and left, her smile even broader than when she had arrived.

"Look," Jienna said. "We have to give this at least an eightday. If no one comes by then, we will have had time to think of an alternative plan. We have a little bit of money left between us. Let's find a cheap tavern nearby. We can spend the nights there and the days here. What do you say?"

"Why not?" her brother said.

"Fine," Starspire agreed, "but we have to be careful with the money we have."

***

An inexpensive tavern shared an alley with the hall. They rented a room for a full eightday, paying one gold piece in advance. The room had three straw pallets, a table with chairs and a chamber pot, which they were informed would be emptied once a day. No meals were included.

Reph claimed the central pallet and had no difficulty in going right to sleep. The other two stayed up for quite a while, discussing how reality was so different from fantasy. Perhaps they were being rather stupid in directing their future according to ballads they had heard when they were younger, but no better method of seeking their fortune came up. They finally turned in when clouds blocked the limited moonlight that had been coming in through the room's small window. The single candle had not been tall, and it had gone out long ago.

***

Starspire was up at dawn. Despite how late he had gone to bed, his body was following years of habit. He knew he would be tired and would have to go to sleep earlier this evening.

Jienna was already up, kneeling in one corner. She was quietly supplicating her god. While the spellcaster didn't comprehend the words, he hoped they included a request for an answer to their problem. It then came to his mind that today was Sylvanday. No wonder Jienna was up so early!

When she was done, they woke Reph and repacked their gear. They weren't going to trust leaving it in this establishment. The fact that the room was already paid for gave them no assurance that they could trust the owner, nor was there any confidence that others might not enter the room in their absence. They bought hot meat pies from a street vendor as they went to check out their horses. Paying for another day's use of the stalls, including feed, they went into Mercenaries' Hall and claimed the same table.

The friendly barmaid greeted them when she came in a bit later in the day, offering them a wish of luck. Jienna assured her that the day was going to be fortuitous.

They watched the flow of clients in and out as the day progressed. Time went slowly. However, a bit after noon, their friend came running over. She was clearly excited.

"You's right 'bout t'day," she said to Jienna. "A man's right now talkin' wi' th' barkeep. He's lookin' for th' likes o' you's!"

"Please show him over!"

Jienna offered her another coin, but she refused it.

"Th' bit o' silver you's gave me las' night was good enow – but don't ferget me when you's is all rich!"

She left quickly and soon returned with a well-dressed man, though the dust on his trousers, cloak and boots showed that he had been traveling quite a distance. They stood when he reached their table.

He silently inspected each of them while the barmaid went back to her duties.

"A druid, a berserker and a magician. You might be just what I'm seeking. I was told you are looking for employment. Is that correct?"

He was looking up at Starspire, so he spoke for them.

"As long as its honest pay for honest work."

"That it is, though I'm not free to discuss it here and now. My name is Stalif. I am here on behalf of my brother-in-law, Pitar, who rules Castle Vork in Glawynia. Might I ask your names?"

"I am called Starspire, a member of the Order of Enchantment. Jienna is a servant of Sylvan and Reph is her brother."

"We's 'Th' Trio'," Reph added.

Stalif nodded to let the berserker know he had heard him.

Turning back to the spellcaster, he asked, "Do you think you could meet me at the castle five days from now? It will allow me time to find a few more to meet our needs. I will then be able to explain the job. All I ask is that you don't talk of this. Can you accept this proposal?"

Starspire glanced at Jienna. She gave a quick nod of her head.

"We'll be there. You understand that we can't commit ourselves until we learn more."

"Most assuredly," he said. "Here. Take this token. Give it and my name to the guards on duty when you reach the castle."

After giving them directions, Stalif left the hall.

"Seem's as we's on our way!" Reph said, beaming at the others.

5 – TINIKI

Tiniki's childhood had been all too normal. Her parents ran a bar that was the center of the village's social activities. She dutifully did her lessons and chores as they were assigned, either by her parents or her brother, Lesk, who was forty-two years her senior. During the day, her free time was spent with her friends. In the evening, however, she was fascinated by the miners who congregated in the bar. She could spend hours watching them gamble, especially when they played cards or word games. She was careful to avoid getting in their way, as that invariably meant that her parents would intervene and she would be sent to bed.

When playing with her friends, she was the butt of her share of practical jokes. She was proud, though, that she dished out more than she received, amusing their god by capitalizing on her agility. Firsh (commonly called "The Trickster") was only pleased by pranks pulled upon those you know, so she didn't have to worry about the strangers in the bar. This also discouraged her from becoming familiar with the adult clientele.

As the years passed, Tiniki and her friends matured. They eventually began to frequent the bar, where she started working as a barmaid when she was only forty. The protection of being a nondescript child accordingly vanished. She was thus unable to simply sit and watch the men and women play. This actually honed her skill at paying attention to detail. She developed an acute knack at correctly judging others by watching their faces and mannerisms. Within half an hour as a spectator, Tiniki could invariably have garnered enough information to be able to tell whether a card player had a strong or weak hand, and she almost always could discern when someone was bluffing.

In word games, the same unintended messages made it possible to figure whether answers were close to being correct or far from the mark. Dice games were different. All she could tell was whether the dice were honest or weighted. This contributed to the development of her intense dislike of games of pure chance.

Her ability of correctly reading faces wound up extending beyond the betting table. Tiniki found that she could similarly gauge a person's emotions. She could even tell if one was being truthful or lying when they were talking. This unfortunately contributed to her diminishing circle of friends.

Tiniki was rather comely, with long, dark brown hair that matched the color of her eyes and skin. But when she spoke, her raspy, masculine voice countered the visual appeal. She also was a bit taller than was normal for her race, measuring in at a full six inches over three feet.

Gatan, a miner like his parents, was the only one who saw solely her positive attributes. Only three years older than Tiniki, he had been her friend since infancy. His interest in her was now flowering, and she willingly returned it. She had a strong feeling that it was more than a mere infatuation on the part of either of them.

As was usual in the Gnomish Mountains, the village was a small, very close-knit community. Trading occurred frequently with other villages, but the gnomes normally spent their lives close to where they were born. Everyone knew what went on and there was a great degree of trust, which was validated by their general traits of being honest and fair in their interactions with one another, with the exception of trying to outdo one another's pranks.

With their long lives, they had a habit of not rushing things. Relations were allowed to develop slowly. Lesk had already been engaged to Soki for seventeen years, and their plans for marriage were still a decade or two away. Grandma Pali was three hundred and fifty-three years old and cooked most of the meals served at the bar. She repeatedly reminded Lesk and Tiniki that they had many, many years to look forward to, as long as there weren't any major disasters like the earthquake that took their grandfather's life one hundred and sixty-one years ago, when their mother was only eleven.

***

Gatan and Tiniki were sitting under a dense copse of red pines on a warm evening, watching the moon as it rose silently over a mountaintop.

"I know this is premature," Gatan said, "but might we marry some day?"

"I'm only forty, Gatan! How do you expect me to answer that now?"

"I'm not asking for a formal answer. I'm only asking if it might be possible..."

"Almost anything is possible," she said quietly, looking downward at the thick pile of needles that lay beneath them.

"Yes, but do you think about us being together in the future?"

Looking up, she found that his eyes told her that it was a serious question. She decided he deserved an honest answer.

"Often."

"Really?"

"Really. I'm not trying to please Firsh right now."

"Might I start dating you, such as taking you to the next Full Moon Dance?"

Tiniki felt a surge go through her body. She wished she had a sultry voice like Soki. It seemed to melt her brother whenever she talked to him, no matter what she actually said. Fortunately, she knew that Gatan accepted her as she was.

Smiling sweetly, she leaned close to him and said 'yes' with a kiss.

He returned the kiss and then sat upright, reaching for his pouch.

"I have a gift for you."

His hand went into the pouch and stayed there for a couple of minutes, fumbling around among the various items that lay within it. The motion suddenly stopped and his hand was still. Tiniki could tell he was grasping something, but he sat motionless and she felt the tension grow as she waited to see what he was holding.

Removing his hand, he opened his fist. A slender silver necklace was fitted with a pale blue gemstone. It emitted a strong blue light.

It was a moonstone, and it was a blue one! These stones, only found in the Gnomish Mountains, were highly valued, especially at the blue to purple end of the spectrum. They absorbed warmth and released it as visible light, which is why he had clasped it for several minutes before showing it to her. The light also had a magical property, muffling sound. She waited until he had fitted it around her neck and she had hidden it within the bodice of her dress. She didn't want to garble her praise of this beautiful gift!

"It is the most wonderful thing I have ever received, Gatan. I shall prize it always, and it will be worn forever!"

She placed her hand against where it sat, hidden between her breasts. Leaning forward, she gave him another, longer kiss.

"Where did you get it? How could you afford it?"

"I found it in the family mine ten days ago. It is my first moonstone. I had it mounted...and now it is yours."

The mild breeze rustled the needles of the pine trees above them and they saw a pair of moths flitting silently overhead. The world seemed to be at peace. Together they looked at the moon. Giving one of these stones under the light of the moon was considered an act of true love!

***

The critical turning point in Tiniki's life occurred almost ten years later. The village was holding the annual picnic to celebrate Long Day, one of the most important holidays for gnomes. No one worked. Instead, they spent the day in leisure activities, especially trying to please Firsh. After this day, the periods of sunshine would once again decrease until Short Day was reached.

Gatan and Tiniki had been openly engaged for two years, and the strength of their relation continued to increase. He was laughing heartily at the prank they had just carried out, as Soki was still sneezing from the powder that had been so liberally sprinkled in the bouquet of flowers Tiniki had offered her. It was at that moment that the ground suddenly began to tremble.

Soki, Tiniki and Lesk were thrown over by the violent quake. The other family members were seated, so it didn't affect them as strongly. A chasm in the ground suddenly opened as a mine beneath the field collapsed. Lesk caught Grandma Pali and saved her from sliding into the gaping hole. People were both crying out in pain and calling out one another's names as a cloud of dust exploded upward from the breach in the ground, obscuring everyone's vision.

Then an aftershock initiated a landslide. Tiniki watched in horror as the falling rock and dirt buried Gatan and her parents! When the ground was finally still, they were among the five gnomes who had perished. Many others were wounded. Tiniki was in a state of total shock, staring blankly at the strange, fearful world that surrounded her. Grandma Pali rocked her back and forth while Soki tried to console her, the tears flowing copiously from both of them. Lesk offered help to some of the other villagers, too shocked to know what to offer to his remaining family.

Tiniki was put to bed with her hand firmly grasping her moonstone. She was in a stupor for two days, repeating Gatan's name and only eating what was pushed into her mouth. She finally fell asleep, but she was breathing shallowly and fidgeted in her bed, frequently moaning or crying out. Lesk got a healer to visit their village, but she told him that there was little they could do. Tiniki was fighting an internal battle that only she could resolve.

Restful sleep finally came to her, and she slept for more than a full day. When she woke, she was gaunt, listless and morose. Lesk discussed this condition with their grandmother, and they hoped that she would somehow snap out of it soon. In the meantime, he had to tend to the bar, which now suddenly belonged to him.

Soki gave up her participation in her family's trade as cobblers and helped Lesk run the bar. The abrupt changes in their lives led them to set the date for their wedding at the twenty-seventh anniversary of their engagement, which was a bit more than a month away. Tiniki started coming out of her room for short periods of time, but her depressed mood and sulking made her poor company. The only time the fog seemed to lift at all was when she watched the evening players.

The merriment of her brother's wedding finally shook her free from her grief and mourning. While dancing with Lesk, she told him that she had to bury the past with their parents and Gatan, yet she found that she was unable to simply return to her previous life style in a setting seeping with so many memories, at least not for a while. She confided in him that she had decided to use her skills to try to make it as a gambler. She knew the odds of being truly successful were slim, but she hoped he would support her attempt.

He willingly agreed, as anything had to be better than

the recent past. He offered to bankroll her and reminded her that the door to the bar would always be open if she wanted to come back.

"I'm not leaving tonight!" she laughed. It was the first time she had laughed since that fateful day, and it had a cleansing effect on both of them.

He was silent, unable to tell his sister how happy he was to hear that sound again.

"I'll first try my hand here. If it doesn't work, I may never leave, but I'm honestly glad to know that I'll have a haven to turn to should I need it."

She then gave him a big, warm hug, which was returned in kind.

***

The next night, Tiniki watched the other players for a while and then joined the game. She bet conservatively at first, losing more than she won as she categorized how the others' mannerisms matched their hands of cards. Once she felt confident, she became more liberal with her bets.

She found that her judgment was good, and the coins began to shift to the pile before her. Carrying on meaningless, trivial patter between hands helped keep her opponents off guard. It also helped her avoid disclosing anything about her own hands, as it stayed at a consistent level throughout the game.

Several of the players were centuries her senior, and they wrote it off to "beginner's luck", but the attitude changed as the same results came night after night. Any questions of cheating were squelched when she showed that she performed just as well in word games, where there was no equivalent to sleight-of-hand or marked decks.

"If it wasn't that ye've been here all yer life, Tiniki," one elder pointed out, "I'd be thinkin' that ye was a ringer and we was yer marks!"

Everyone laughed, but the willingness to play against her nonetheless continued to decline. Her expertise had quite rapidly grown to a point where it surpassed everyone else, and she was simply winning too large a share of the money at the table. She realized that she was going to have to travel to other villages if she wanted to be a gambler.

This brought on conflicting emotions. She was apprehensive about leaving the small community that had been her only home for fifty years. At the same time, she had a desire to put distance between her and the all-too-recent tragedy, accompanied by a gnawing curiosity to see how the rest of the world varied from this nook in the mountains.

She had amassed enough money to be able to repay Lesk's loan, but he told her to hold onto it for now. As she packed to depart, her small family joined her in her little room. She filled her small backpack with spare clothes and a waterskin, plus two decks of cards.

"Remember that we'll keep this room for you, whether it's for when you're just passing through or if you decide to move back in," her brother said.

"Thank you, Lesk. You know how much that offering means to me!"

"We also each have a parting gift for you," he said, motioning for Grandma Pali to go first, being the family elder.

"I know that the stone that Gatan gave you will always offer you light," she said, watching Tiniki reflexively grasp it within the fold of her clothing. "Even so, there may be times when you need a flame, if for nothing else than warmth on a cold night."

She held forth an old but well cared for tinderbox.

"This had belonged to your grandfather. I want you to have it, that a part of the family may be with you wherever your feet may take you."

"Oh... Thank you, Grandma!"

"Here is my gift, little sister," Soki said, opening her fist.

Tiniki stared at two new, square-cut, bone dice. The dots were painted in blue, the same color as her moonstone. She knew that that was no accident.

"I hope that you may maintain the luck at the games tables that you have shown thus far in your new profession!"

"They will travel close to my heart, keeping your caring, helpful face in my thoughts," Tiniki said.

Rather than placing them in her belt pouch, which had a little traveling money, she reached within the bodice of her dress and pulled out a second pouch that she wore about her neck. She deposited the dice in the pouch and then repositioned it, concealing it from sight.

When she was done, Lesk turned her to face him and stared deeply into her eyes. His look made it clear that he wanted to be serious. Taking a deep breath, she settled her thoughts and complied as best as she was able. She actually surprised herself by becoming calm and attentive.

"I had a hard time in deciding what to get you. I hope that it serves you well, but only in such uses as cutting meat or severing rope."

He held forth a sheathed, hilted dagger.

"I hope you are right, brother. If I come to needing it to defend myself, I will most truly be in trouble!"

As she started to withdraw it from its sheath, she froze in motion and tears welled up. She recognized it as the dagger that had belonged to Gatan's father. Gatan had told her how it had been in the family for many generations, passed down as a traditional wedding gift.

"I could think of nothing more meaningful to get you," he said softly, "and Gatan's family agreed."

Tiniki found that her vision was blurred as they each exchanged long, warm embraces with her. Taking a firm hold of her walking stick, she headed westward on the only road out that passed through their village.

As the well wishes of her family and the other village folk were left behind her, Tiniki made a serious request of Firsh.

"Please favor me by letting only harmless jokes befall me and my family. We have already suffered more than our share of the other type."

Wiping her eyes clear once more, she began to hum as she picked up a more forceful stride.

***

As Tiniki traveled, she found that she developed a true wanderlust. It grew more powerful as time went by. Over the course of the next twenty-two years, she visited every village and town in the Gnomish Kingdom, plus the two centers large enough to be called cities.

She also made rather regular calls upon her family's bar, taking deep pleasure in the brief stays in her old room. Her mobility gave her a role that was not normally played by members of her race. She got to know more distant relatives and relayed messages back and forth from one end of the kingdom to the other.

The culminating point came when she accepted a challenge from Gref. A friend of the queen, he was six centuries older than her and was renowned as the best gamemaster and gambler in the land. This venerable gnome rarely participated in games any more, so his mere interest in facing her was an honor. It awakened her awareness of just how great her reputation had become!

The competition was held in the courtroom of Queen Ideri's castle, and she offered a pouch containing one hundred gold pieces to the winner. Gref had selected a word game that Tiniki knew quite well: Consonants. It was a game of skill, depending in large part upon one's vocabulary, but reading an opponent's face might give a slight edge.

The scoring for Consonants varied, but the general rules of the game were uniform. A player selected a word containing three, and only three, consonants. These three consonants are stated in the order in which they appear. The other player or players then try to come up with the correct word, adding as many vowels as they chose, inserting them to make words, with the exception of proper nouns. If the correct word is found, the player scores points and selects the next word. If other words are stated, a lesser number of points is scored and the round goes on. If the word is not found, the poser scores points and selects the next word. The play continues until a set score is achieved. It is also critically important that one only chooses words that are in the opponents' vocabularies.

The queen selected the winning score to be two hundred. Gref and Tiniki agreed that naming the correct word would earn five points and selection of the next word. Stating alternate words would each earn one point. If the word was not named, the player who had chosen it would score ten points. If an unacceptable word had been selected, the player would lose five points and the opponent would gain selection, plus keeping any single points earned that round. Finally, if a player guessed a word that was not accepted as being valid, there would be a one-point penalty.

The final factor was deciding who would go first. Tiniki was willing to defer to her elder, but Gref would have none of that. He opted for a random means, such as simply cutting a deck.

"Would the role of dice satisfy you, Sir?" Tiniki asked, presenting her own pair.

"I accept that they are honest."

"But of course! You may select whether high or low will go first."

"May I try them first?"

Without any hesitation, she offered them to him. Gref

took them from her palm with his aged, wrinkled fingers. He cast them three times as she stood at his side. The audience in the courtroom was silent.

"They appear to be fine. High roll will go first."

Saying that, he shook the dice and let them free. His roll was eight.

Tiniki picked up the dice and rolled six.

"Gref shall go first!" the herald announced. "The beginning score is zero to zero!"

The game progressed slowly, as neither wished to lose points by being careless. Tiniki found that a movement of Gref's eyebrows let her know if her guess was close to the correct word, thereby helping her find the proper selection. However, his experience played to his favor. Though his aged body clearly displayed the wear of centuries of use, his mind was sharply honed and his vocabulary was extensive. As the afternoon advanced, he edged slightly ahead of her.

"Otter. Gref: 177; Tiniki: 161," the herald announced.

The gamemaster had just scored six points.

Writing his selection on a piece of parchment, he folded it and set it aside. As had been the case throughout the game, it would only be opened and read aloud by the herald after the round had ended.

"S-L-L," he said, which was repeated by the herald for the benefit of the audience.

"Sell . . . sill . . silly," Tiniki said quickly, watching Gref. He responded with a twitch of his eyebrows on the third word.

"Three points," he said.

Tiniki had become accustomed to ignoring the herald's repetition of their statements. She concentrated on her opponent while her mind mulled over the possibilities.

"Sally . . . and sully."

"Two more points."

Staring at his face, a spark flashed in her mind.

"What about slyly?" she asked.

"That is the word. The selection passes to you."

The herald unfolded the parchment and stated clearly the word therein.

"Slyly. Gref: 177; Tiniki: 171," the herald declared.

The game continued as the gap decreased. Tiniki finally stumped Gref on a rather simple word.

"So, what is this word you know that I can't think of?" he asked.

"Eggs."

"How did that elude me?"

"Perhaps it was just too plain," she offered, "or because no vowels go between the consonants?"

"Eggs. Gref: 191; Tiniki: 191. We have a tie!" the herald called out.

The first to score nine more points would win. If she could come up with another word that he missed, the game and prize would be hers. Now was the time to play the 'ace' she had saved and just hope that he didn't come across it in his thoughts.

She wrote the word, paused, and then folded the paper.

"B-L-L."

"Ball . . . bell . . . bill . . . boil . . . bull."

"That's five points, but you don't have the correct word yet."

"Hmm... What about belly or bully?"

"Two more points."

More time was spent in silent thought. The audience was hushed, limiting themselves to inaudible whispers.

"Belle. The one with a silent 'e' at the end, meaning a beauty, like yourself."

"Well, that earns you a point, though it raises questions regarding your vision," Tiniki said.

"Don't degrade yourself. Your face is nearly as becoming as your mind! Now I need but one more word.

Even if it is not the word you have chosen, the game will be mine. If I can think of no more, and your word is valid, the game goes to you."

He thought for several more minutes. The crowd in the courtroom began to grow restless. It almost looked as if Gref had fallen asleep, but he then raised his head, shaking it slowly from side to side.

"I can think of no other words. My only hope is that you have erred in your choice."

"No, I am confident that the word is acceptable and that it is one that you know quite well."

"Enough, then. Out with it!"

"Eyeball!"

"Ah...a triple vowel sequence. Quite good! I concede."

"Eyeball. Gref: 199; Tiniki: 201. The game goes to Tiniki."

The cheer of the people and the congratulations from the national celebrity meant more to her than the hundred gold pieces that Queen Ideri gave her.

***

"Good cannot be severed from bad" is an ancient gnomish motto. It recognizes that nothing is only good, just as nothing can be purely bad. Tiniki found that this applied all too well to her victory over Gref.

Tales of Gref's loss, the first in a non-chance game in nearly two centuries, spread rapidly throughout the kingdom. She found that she was now too well known, making it difficult to find anyone willing to gamble for meaningful sums. If something didn't change soon, she might be forced to once again take up a new profession!

Girding her courage, she decided to journey beyond the comforting protection of the Gnomish Mountains. No other races had been allowed to breach the sanctity of their homeland for over a century, as there had been too many cases of gross misconduct. A relatively small number of gnomes took the only road that led from their kingdom into Indrose, but usually only far enough to trade goods. Those who were willing to travel greater distances were the rare exceptions.

Trade occurred predominantly at Sonesetten, a walled city on the critical junction of three main roads. One led south to the Gnomish Kingdom, another led northwest into Glawynia and the third led east into the open grasslands of southern Indrose. In retaliation to the gnomish isolationist decree, gnomes were not allowed within Sonesetten after the gates closed for the night. A small community of gnomes had therefore developed in the shadows of the city's southern walls.

Four Feet Inn was a successful establishment a stone's throw from the city gate. Tiniki had heard that the owner was a distant relative of hers. When she arrived, it was easy to see how it had gotten its name; the ceiling of the bar and dining hall was only four feet above the floor, thus keeping out most non-gnomish clients other than occasional dwarves who preferred to avoid the taller races. She also learned that the tale of her triumph had preceded her, but only among the gnomes.

The city's ruling and the structure of Four Feet Inn each hampered Tiniki from practicing her profession in her preferred style. This was resolved quickly, however, when she learned of the Open Door Tavern, only a half-hour's walk to the west of the city. It welcomed anyone who had a pouch that jingled with coin, and it remained open all night.

The tavern master welcomed Tiniki, as he astutely noted through observation that activity at her table drew additional spectators and encouraged drinking. The flow of strangers on this major thoroughfare meant that she was almost always able to find new marks. She purchased a pony and paid for a permanent room at the Four Feet Inn and settled into a rather regular lifestyle, though it was generally nocturnal in nature.

This, however, did not quench her wanderlust. The elves, dwarves and humans were more fascinating than the tales she had heard, as was the walled city, but this only whetted her appetite. Nonetheless, she was always a bit uncomfortable in such a world of seeming giants and was uneasy about going too far from the mountains. On a sunny day, they were reassuringly visible on the horizon from her room in the inn.

The thoughts of her mother's motivational phrase frequently used in her youth came to mind. Whenever she was hesitant, her mother would query, "Be there something worth the knowing of?" A positive response, even if only mental, would suffice and she would take a risk. That probably accounted for her even being here outside of her race's realm.

Therefore, as a compromise to these conflicting forces, she made occasional visits to a few other cities. Her most common excursions were to Grenegrasen, Watarton and Estwatarton, all to the east. Two outings went even farther. One was to Cotounfeld, more than a full day's expedition to the east. The other was to Sundtimmer, the closest actual city in Glawynia.

She also tried to make it back to celebrate the two most important days of the year with her family, succeeding during most years. Things in the village hardly changed. They marveled at her newfound ability to stack a deck, but both her personal pride and the fear of the possible reprisals if caught using it at the game table kept her from applying it when she gambled. It was merely used in performing parlor activities with familiar acquaintances. She considered it a way to please the Trickster.

Lesk was surprised that his sister actually became competent at using the hilted dagger he had given her, again influenced by her mother's phrase. She also learned to use throwing daggers, as the other races were less trustworthy and often had a more violent nature. It turned out that this skill saved her life.

***

This happened a year after her nephew, Tink was born, named in her honor. She was eighty-six at the time of the not fully unexpected incident, which occurred in Grenegrasen.

The warmth of spring had just begun in earnest, and the rich odor of the manure tilled into the fields surrounding the city was pervasive. The game at the Red Cock Bar ended shortly before dawn, and a thick fog swirled around the building, creating an eerie setting.

The torches on either side of the pub's doorway were unable to penetrate far into this murkiness. The thick air further muffled the limited sounds of this early hour. Tiniki wished that she had someone with her as she exited to make her way down the street to the room she had rented the day before.

A figure suddenly lurched out of the alley she was passing. It was a dwarf, not much taller than her, but far stockier. He was drunk, made obvious by the way his body swayed as he moved. She recognized him to be the young fellow who had lost quite a sizable sum a few hours earlier.

Was his name Pantargor? If not, it was something close to that. She hastened her pace to get past him.

"Jush shtop fer a shecon'," he muttered. His arm shot out and firmly grasped her shoulder, forcing her to turn and face him.

His slurred speech was accompanied by bleary eyes and the stench of sour beer on his breath that heightened her uneasiness. His hair and beard were dirty and matted, and his tunic and jerkin showed that he had at least lain on the ground. Perhaps he had even rolled in the dirt.

"Pardon me," she said, trying to pull free. "I'm tired and I want to go to my room and sleep."

"Thass what I'm talkin' 'bout," he said, followed by a loud belch. The street was dark, and he was pulling her toward the darker alley.

"As I's figger'n it, you gots s'fiscien' money thass I'm owed sumpen, an' I wants to take it!"

With his dwarven strength, he tore open the top of her dress, making his intentions unquestionable. This was something she had often heard of since exploring this foreign world, but she had never envisioned experiencing it herself.

Tiniki was physically frozen in fear, unable to run, but she opened her mouth to call for help.

A dirty hand quickly gagged her.

"No noiss!" he demanded.

The chocking, rancid odor that entered her nostrils freed her from the state of paralysis. Reflexively grabbing her hilted dagger, she thrust it into his gut and then twisted it.

He pulled away, a look of utter astonishment on his face as his hands automatically moved to his stomach. Red blood surged around his grimy fingers. Dropping her dagger, she screamed as he teetered against the wall and then collapsed to the ground.

The baronial court easily decided in her favor, declaring it an action of self-defense. Nonetheless, it was made clear to Tiniki that she was no longer welcome in Grenegrasen. She could pass through, or even spend a night at an inn, but she was not to gamble anywhere in this barony. This decision was not debatable, and she would take up residence in a dungeon cell if she did not comply.

***

This had been a traumatic experience for Tiniki, and

she withdrew into the homeland for several months. During this time, her family helped her heal the mental wounds and ease her anguish by offering soothing, nurturing support. Tink played an important role, and she developed a strong bond with this little infant.

The death of the would-be rapist was difficult to accept, but she finally did so. The image of his intent was harder to erase, and it continued to reoccur in her dreams. Gnomes are not without fault, but their actions rarely include violence, and rape is unknown in their records or memories. It is not even a word in their vocabulary!

Against Lesk's advice, Tiniki decided that she had to once more face the other races. She was uncertain whether she would be able to stay there, but she had to at least attempt it. Otherwise, it would be a weakness that would continuously nibble away at her self-confidence. Grandma Pali said that she understood, and her support bolstered Tiniki's courage.

When she reached Four Feet Inn, she found a message waiting for her. A distant relative, "Uncle" Patov, wanted to see her.

Patov was a bit over four centuries old. He operated a trading shop in this gnomish community and seemed to do fairly well, though he kept pretty much to himself. He actually often spent much of each day within Sonesetten.

Finding that his shop was closed, Tiniki decided to wait for his return. She sat on an old wooden bench in front of the inn. The seat had been worn smooth over a very long period of time, and she found it comfortable to wait until the sun started to descend. As expected, she saw him shuffling out of the city, walking past the city guards. She got up and followed him to his shop. He remained silent until they were inside.

"Grant me a few more moments, if you please, Tiniki," he said as he carried a package through a curtain into a region beyond the rear of the room. He returned shortly afterwards and lit an oil lantern.

Slowly walking across the room, he shut and latched the door. He then returned to the small table and gestured that she should take one seat. He eased himself into another.

"I have some information that should be of great importance to you," he said in hushed tones. "Actually, I have several things I wish to discuss with you."

He looked straight at her, staring calmly into her eyes by the yellowish light. While his motions had implied the wear and tear of age, his eyes were clear and alert. Tiniki rested her arms upon the table and nodded.

"First, I must warn you that the brother of the dwarf you killed has sworn vengeance. He is quietly searching for you."

A surge of panic passed through her body, causing her to suddenly become very tense. She felt the nails of her right hand pressing into the heel of her left hand. At the same time, her teeth were biting into her lower lip.

Forcing her muscles to relax, she took a deep breath.

"How do you know this?" she asked as a cold shiver ran through her body. She tried to ignore it, intently awaiting his response.

"I am willing to take a risk and answer that question if you will do two things."

"What?" She noted that she was talking through gritted teeth.

"You must swear by Firsh that what I confide in you will not leave this room, and you must be willing to hear a proposition that I have to offer. Can you agree to that?"

"Yes." She felt another shiver go down her spine. What great secret was she about to learn? She struggled with the implications of what might result from this secrecy, feeling she had to pay total attention to everything he was about to say.

Patov held up his right hand with his knuckles facing

her. A silver-gray ring was on his index finger. The symbol of Firsh was clearly engraved on its face. With his other hand, he lifted her right hand and placed her palm against the ring.

"This ring is a conduit of the Trickster. Do you swear by him that what you now hear will be shared with no others unless he or I release you from this pledge?"

Tiniki's hand felt ice cold. She stifled the turmoil of the questions wanting to be answered and cleared her mind. Shaking her head once, she began to regain control of her thoughts. In a solemn tone, she said, "I so swear."

The cold sensation instantly ended. The room, which had grown dim, returned to the full brightness that the lamp could offer. She had no question that the god had been witness to this oath.

Releasing her hand, Patov got up and went behind the shop counter. He brought back a bottle and two glasses. Pouring a little brownish liquid in each, he lifted one glass and swallowed its contents in one fast gulp. Tiniki followed his example. It was a sweet wine, and she found that it took the edge off the tenseness that seemed to have been draped over her body.

Patov cleared his throat.

"I have learned of the threat against you through a very effective underground grapevine. You see, I am a member of the Thieves' Guild, at a rather high echelon."

Tiniki gasped involuntarily. She had heard of this guild, predominantly in her time outside of the Gnomish Mountains, but she had somehow not expected it to include gnomes, especially not as an officer!

"I understand your disbelief. I had a similar experience when I was approached to join the guild. However, the fact that I am a gnome has proved to be most advantageous, as few picture our kind as potential members.

"Sonesetten is well-situated, and I have been able to

serve the guild well in two manners. I have been a contact point for the transfer of information. As a trader, I also am in a knowledgeable position to be aware of who is leaving the city, what they carry and where they are headed. In addition, I have been able to serve as a very good fence."

"A fence?"

"Yes. I buy and sell stolen goods. Items that might be too easily recognized elsewhere can often be sold within our kingdom, as others thereafter never get a chance to see them. I make a good profit, and things are sold at prices that are attractive to members of our race. The thieves are also pleased. Only the victims lose out. I hope that it pleases Firsh, but that is most debatable.

"Anyway, I believe you can see why this must not be disclosed. You have no friendships outside of our kingdom. Acquaintances, yes, but not friends. I do not do you any harm, but there are those who would view my actions with displeasure."

"Undoubtedly!" A small snort accompanied the statement.

"Do not be too quick with your disdain. I wish to invite you to join our fold."

"What?! Why should I?"

Tiniki pushed back from the table and stood up. There was anger in her eyes, and her shock was most evident in her facial expressions.

"Calm down, Tiniki," he said in a reassuring tone. "I have been observing you for quite a while now. You have been under my consideration, and you have also been under my protection to a certain degree."

A series of emotions flashed across her normally controlled face. Many questions sought to be asked, but she suppressed them. Regaining command of herself, she sat down. She decided to let her "uncle" reveal what he selected. She would then progress from that point.

"When you gamble with others, you draw them into

open chatter that has frequently proven to be very useful to the guild. Your winnings have made you a possible target, but I have had those cutthroats and rogues who are in our organization refrain from plucking your pouch. On two separate occasions, we succeeded in stopping independent individuals from robbing you. In all honesty, however, that was done mainly because we dislike competition.

"Anyway, I have been seeking something that might make you become interested in enlisting. I believe that the venomous attitude of the dwarf in question should suffice."

He stopped talking and poured himself some more wine. He then sat back. After a moment of silence, Tiniki recognized that the issue had been turned over to her.

"How do you feel that this threat against my life will make me want to become a thief?"

"Well, first let me point out that you won't have to be a thief, just a member of the guild. I know that you have limited fighting ability. You therefore either have to hire bodyguards, which are expensive, or retreat into our mountains, which I am willing to wager is not your preference. On the other hand, the guild can supply a guard to unobtrusively shadow you. We will also train you to be able to better defend yourself. And I will, in a bit, add something else that I'm willing to offer to sweeten the pot: a last line of defense."

"You said I wouldn't have to be a thief. What would I then be expected to do as a member of your guild?"

"The most important thing would be to keep playing against others and getting them to tell you all sorts of trivial facts about themselves. As in the past, guild members would be present to collect the gems that are dropped so carelessly. However, we will sometimes let you know of specific topics that should be mentioned, depending upon whom you are playing.

"At times we may ask you to go to a certain hall, as a ripe plum may be ready for the picking. There may be cases where we are unable to have someone observe your gambling table. In such cases, we may arrange an inconspicuous meeting to learn what had been disclosed.

"I also want to assure you that we will only very rarely hit these targets. In most cases, the information will be collected and stored. We have no desire of creating a pattern that might be recognizable."

"Hmm... What if I say that I want to be a thief?" Tiniki was curious to see how Patov would respond.

He showed no change.

"I plan to have you trained in the necessary skills. I hope that you will not apply them against your marks, but they may be of use to you if you become as well known among the other races as you are among our own. I just wish to point out that if you go beyond Indrose, as I believe you have done once before, report to the local guild before doing anything."

"Why?"

"Well, if you don't, they will view you as an independent operator. What they choose to do will be at their discretion."

"And if I register with their guild?"

"They will allow you to practice your trade, as long as they get a cut of the action."

"And what will it cost me here?"

"Here? We will only ask one gold piece a month, plus ten percent of anything you steal. That will not include your winnings, as I trust they are earned honestly."

"You've really thought this all out, haven't you?"

"I've invested a few years of careful observation and contemplation leading up to this point."

"And you had nothing to do with the incident that appears to place me within your grasp?"

"I swear by Firsh that that is so!"

"Well... One gold piece a month is clearly far less than a paid competent bodyguard would cost. Once the impending threat is over, what would it cost to exit?"

"I'm sorry, but that option isn't in the hand that you hold. You join for life, unless the guild decides that you are not needed any more, which unfortunately is about the same thing."

"How appealing!"

"I believe that I should be totally honest with you. Remember, if you don't accept what I'm offering, that end may be in the very near future."

For several minutes, she mulled over the different alternatives.

Each had its down side, another example of the old motto. Comparing the negative aspect of each option, she considered the net worth. She didn't want to be forced to return to the homeland, shutting the door to the rest of the world she had only barely seen. Bodyguards were expensive, and there was always the risk that an enemy might make a better offer. In the third choice, there was a lifetime commitment and, while thieving sounded distasteful, she never had to do it.

"You said that I would gain training that I might be able to defend myself? Would that mean learning to use weapons?"

"Certainly."

"What weapons?"

"To start, we'd try to make you an expert with the dagger, both held and thrown. A short sword might be a good addition, extending your reach. A garrote could be a nice finishing touch, as it is silent and can easily be hidden."

Another tremor went through Tiniki's body as she thought of possibly killing another person, but she then remembered that a dwarf was planning on killing her.

"I think that I may take you up on your offer. However, tell me of the final factor, the one you said could 'sweeten the pot'."

"I could get the Trickster to be on your side."

"What?"

"I am willing to give my ring to you."

He held up his hand so she could again see the symbol of Firsh.

"It has a few charges, but it is becoming ever harder for me to recharge it. I've just had it too long."

"Please explain." This interesting offering had captured her total attention.

"This ring lets the wearer call upon the Trickster for assistance. All I need to do is point my finger at a foe and state his name. However, I am never certain in what manner he will offer his aid. It usually reflects his twisted sense of humor.

"To replace the charges, the wearer must make offerings in the usual manner. Whenever a new prank is successfully played upon a different friend, an additional charge is added to the ring. The limitation, though, is that it must be a different prank, and it must be upon a different friend.

"Strangers do not count, nor do mere acquaintances. The one compensating aspect is that he ignores what you have done prior to putting on the ring."

Patov removed the ring and held it out to Tiniki.

"Do you accept the offer?"

"Yes, I do."

She was actually surprised that she felt no hesitation in taking this innovative step in a new direction. Reaching forward, she took the ring and slipped it onto her right index finger. She found that it adjusted to fit her perfectly.

***

Patov started her training the very next day. It adjusted into a pattern of perhaps an hour or two each day, fitting in unobtrusively with her normal activities. He also had operatives keep an eye out for the dwarf who had sworn to slay her, and one guild member often followed her, though she found she was usually unaware of when one was present.

However, he only had a limited number of guild members whom he could call upon, and the dwarf entered Sonesetten unobserved.

The end of the day was approaching, and Tiniki was making her way toward the southern gate when a strange voice confidently called out behind her.

"Turn and face me, that you see who is avenging Pantragor!"

It had only been six days since the meeting with Patov, and there had been no noticeable improvement yet in her use of the dagger. Her mind was spinning through various options as she turned around, but they were all desperate and none seemed to stand out as a clear solution to her imminent calamity.

The dwarf who faced her wore chain mail and brandished a battle-axe with a very sharp blade. She recognized the similarity, but he was older than the dwarf she had faced in Grenegrassen, and he was sober. He stood less than twenty paces from her, and no one else was visible on this portion of the street.

She then noticed an elf step forward from the shadows, carrying a thin, drawn sword. He was clad in a dark gray tunic and breeches and she didn't hear any sounds as he crept up behind the dwarf. Tiniki avoided changing her facial expression, maintaining the image of the fear that was actually beginning to subside. Things no longer seemed hopeless.

Unfortunately, the dwarf was somehow aware of the elf behind him. Just as the elf was close enough, he swung around. The blade of the axe made a clean, horizontal slash, cutting through the elf's tunic and rib cage.

Completing the circle, he once again faced Tiniki, not

even looking back as the body of the elf quietly crumpled to the ground.

"Now it's your turn!" he leered, resuming his forward motion.

The disruption had, however, allowed the gnome to remember the ring Patov had given her. Having seen how the dwarf handled the axe, she knew her dagger was of little worth. Depending on her small weapon would be the same as surrendering her future to the merest span of time. She pointed at him with her index finger as he steadily sauntered closer.

"Firsh!"

This entire section of the street turned into a muddy swamp. She and her foe were both over waist deep in a thick, noxious muck. It clearly slowed her foe down, but it was just as limiting to her.

"Please, Trickster, offer me more meaningful help! I promise to repay it in kind! If I die, I will be unable to further serve you."

The dwarf continued to draw nearer, raising the axe above him, preparing for a downward swing. She pointed at him once more. This time there was desperation in her voice.

"Firsh!"

The axe vanished! The sudden shift in weight caused the dwarf to fall forward into the mud, swallowing a mouthful of the mire.

Not waiting to see what would happen next, Tiniki pulled out her dagger and drove it into the back of his neck as he struggled to get up, entering the exposed region just above his chain mail and below his thick leather helmet. A violent jerk went through his body, and he then sank beneath the surface.

With difficulty, Tiniki fought her way to the edge of the swamp. As she pulled her second foot out, the street returned to dirt and the mud caking her body became dry and began to flake off.

Looking back, she found the street to be bare. Both bodies were buried somewhere beneath it.

"Thank you, Trickster. I promise to be a loyal servant to you for the rest of my life!"

There was just enough time left to reach the gates before they closed.

***

Over the next four years, Tiniki proved to be a good student. She learned the skills of the trade and even did a little pick pocketing, although she was very selective in her targets. Rather than steal belt pouches, she just lifted coin pouches that were within them. This made it more difficult to notice and harder to place when it had actually occurred, even if it limited her take. Being overly cautious, she also only stole from people who were drunk.

This solely took place on evenings when there was no game, due to an absence of decent marks. She was aware that she now had an innate, strong dislike of male dwarves, but she may not have been conscious of the fact that her victims were always from that subset of society.

She was uncertain whether another thief ever observed her actions, but she didn't feel it was worth the risk to hide it from the guild. The amount she garnered was a pittance, anyway, as she did it for sport, not as a livelihood. Thus, she always turned the proper cut over to Patov.

The other thing she was careful to do was to try to please Firsh. She found that she could tell when an acceptable prank had been pulled on an appropriate person, as the ring became very warm for an instant. This happened on only five occasions: when she played jokes on Lesk, Soki, Grandma Pali, Tink and Patov. She thought the best was when she took the time to remove all the buttons on her brother's set of clothes and then reattached each button with a single strand of thread. Once the first gave, the rest followed in rapid succession. As his breeches fell to his ankles, he tripped over them, falling on his face right in front of the house! He even wound up joining the spectators in their loud round of laughter.

***

The crowd at the Open Door Tavern was lean. And their pouches were even leaner. No game this evening! Being Moonday, the day of thieves, it seemed to Tiniki to be appropriate to follow that path rather than honoring Firsh. She therefore would 'assist' someone by lessening his burden, unless a more appealing prank made itself evident.

She calmly took inventory of who was present, other than the tavern master and his two daughters, who served as barmaids. She counted six regular customers. They were in two groups, talking and sipping at their drinks. There were also five strangers.

One tall human sat at a table by the door. He seemed to be almost asleep. Another pair of humans, one male and one female, were at the bar, conversing and laughing loudly. Tiniki would willingly give high odds on what his goal for the evening was!

A dwarf sat at a table by the wall. He was keeping to himself, drinking heavily. A woman who seemed to be a human and elf crossbreed sat at the bar, sipping at her wine as she talked with one of the girls. Tiniki's glance returned to the dwarf.

As she casually walked past him, she noted that he was fighting to keep his eyes open. His speech was slurred and he was drinking sloppily. His belt pouch was resting on his seat, meaning that it wasn't pulling at his belt.

Loosening the laces of the bodice of her dress, she

reached into her pouch and removed the cloth that protected her lucky dice. She then waited a bit before walking past her target.

Just as she passed her victim, she dropped the piece of linen. She carefully positioned herself so that he got an eyeful while she was bending down to retrieve the cloth. She knew that her moonstone would be supplying enough light to catch his total attention, or as much as he was able to muster in his present state.

As she slowly rose, her left hand deftly removed the coin pouch that was begging to be taken. It was easily palmed and simply slipped behind her dress before she was upright.

Acting as if she was unaware of his presence, she moved smoothly toward the bar. Once his gaze ended, Tiniki strode to the doorway and stepped out. She dropped the pouch within her own and tightened the dress laces. Finding out what she had actually gained would wait until she was in her own room. For now, she walked smoothly toward the stable to get her pony.

"Pardon me, ma'am."

She spun around to see that the single human she had noted as being seated by the door was following her. She whipped out a thin dagger, ready to throw it.

"I'm not meaning to threaten you!" he said quietly but with emphasis, holding both empty palms up to her. "I would like to talk a bit, though, if there's a place where it can be done in confidence."

Keeping her dagger ready to throw if the need arose, she motioned for him to go around the end of the stall. In passing, she heard the stall-hand inside. If necessary, she could call for him.

Once they were off the street, Tiniki signaled for him to stop.

"My name is Stalif," he said in a hushed tone. "I am seeking a band of adventurers to carry out a specific task. A variety of skills will be needed, including perhaps picking locks.

"I noticed your adept action inside. Are you able to do as well with locks?"

"Perhaps."

While her response was cautious, she was very careful to talk in a calm and confident tone. Tiniki wasn't about to disclose more than was necessary, but she was interested in learning more.

"What do you want to have done, and what are you paying?" she ventured, as he had said naught.

"I can't reveal the task at this time, and it's my brother-in-law who would actually do the paying, but I know he would make it worthwhile. Could you be at Castle Vork four days from now?"

"I don't know. Where is it?"

"It's in the center of Glawynia, perhaps an unrushed three-day ride from here."

"I've never been there. It might be worth going just to see the land. No promise that I'll do what you want until I know more. I'll have to see who shows and learn more details."

If she wasn't interested in the offer, she felt the odds were good that she could find some worthwhile games. All she might lose was a little time, and this served as a good excuse to see more of the world. Why not?

"I'll consider it," she continued. "Can you give me clearer directions?"

"Most certainly. Let me first give you a small disk. It will serve as your pass so that the castle guards will let you in. May I remove it from my pouch for you?"

Tiniki nodded. As he took out the disk, she lowered her dagger. After having watched his face in the light of the nearly full moon, she felt that she could trust him.

This might prove to be interesting.

6 – DWARF MATES

Ginderbar had had the misfortune of being an orphan right from his entry into the world. His mother died while giving birth to him and his father had been killed almost two months earlier in an attack against their village by orcs. Shelsinbar, his father's older brother, had raised him, but living with a wizened, old bachelor had been a cold childhood.

As an infant, Ginderbar had daily been left with other supportive families in the mountain village while Shelsinbar went to work in his mine. Once Ginderbar could walk, he was taken to the mine in a sling across his uncle's back. He played with the gemstones that were carefully extracted from the igneous rock in the depths of the ground. As far back as he could recall, he had handled both the hand ax and the pickax. He never learned to read or write, having had no formal education, but his uncle taught him to speak well and he learned everything his uncle knew of the trade.

He gained a well-tuned perception of how to judge the strata of the rock and figure which direction to dig. The pick and shovel were extensions of his limbs, and he unerringly sensed when structural supports were needed before signs were visible to anyone else. His guardian claimed he had gained this uncanny ability by growing up in the mines, breathing in the dust. He also was able to easily judge the quality of the stones they pried out of the rock.

Lacking any social graces, he was shunned by the village girls. He watched the other youths interact, but he didn't know where to start, and none of them ventured to help him. It was surprising, then, that a spark succeeded in landing on dry tinder with Anndimfoss.

He was eighteen and she was sixteen when their paths first crossed. Ginderbar had taken a sizeable collection of gemstones, predominantly jade, down to sell to the jeweler in the central town in the valley. She was an apprentice at that time and was handling the shop he had happened to choose to enter.

However, it wasn't his parcel that attracted her. As soon as their eyes met, they stood staring at one another in star-struck silence. After introducing themselves with faltering tones, their confidence improved and they wound up talking comfortably of trivial matters. As their conversation continued, they learned much about one another, not noting the passage of time. It was only the intentional coughing that followed the entry of Anndimfoss's aunt that got them around to taking care of business.

As Ginderbar made the two-day trek back to his village, her face remained clear in his mind. He compared her stable childhood to what he had experienced. She had grown up in a solid family. Her father was a smith and her mother was an armorer. They worked together below their home, sharing the same anvil and fire. Her older brother had learned both trades and now worked with them. They very likely made some of the tools he and his uncle used.

He had to find reasons to make more visits to the town!

***

Once he was back at work in his uncle's mine, Ginderbar's mind continued to spin in loops, seeking an excuse to be able to see her again, but that seemed to lead nowhere. The only time he normally went to the town was to sell their gemstones, but it required a few months of work to gather a sufficient quantity that justified his absence from the mine. All the supplies that they needed were obtained from the small general store that was right here in the village.

Shelsinbar would never approve a four-day excursion simply because he wanted to see a girl. There was no way in which his uncle could comprehend what he desired, so it wasn't worth angering him by even venturing this 'frivolous' topic. What else could he do?

He swung the pick down with all his force, venting his anger on the stone. As he inspected the rubble and newly exposed surface, his eyes fell upon the tip of the pick. It was showing wear. He heard the sound of his uncle's blow softly echoing over the distance through the mineshaft. When they stopped for lunch, they would have to discuss buying a new one.

Lifting his pick over his shoulder, he prepared for another blow. The action stopped in frozen motion when an alternate thought flashed through his mind.

Repairing a tool would be cheaper than buying a new one if it wasn't for the time lost in journeying to a smith. This wouldn't be the case if several tools were being repaired at once, but they couldn't afford to wait until all the tools were in poor shape.

What if he collected worn shovels, picks, and so forth from around the village and made one trip for everyone? The savings would justify the time spent on this. He could probably use Gidsiftor's mule if he gave him a cut of the profit. And giving this business to Anndimfoss's father might even score a few points with her!

***

Ginderbar found that the idea bore fruit. Most of the families had one or more tools that needed mending. Each agreed to give him part of the money that would be saved by not having to purchase replacements, and Gidsiftor accepted the proposed deal for using his mule. The only objection, understandably, came from the owner of the general store, who recognized that this effort would cut into his profits.

When the mule was loaded, Ginderbar was surprised at just how much he was transporting. He took the money forwarded by the other dwarves to cover repair expenses and hid the pouch within his tunic. He then made the tedious trip down to the town. Only this time, it was not anywhere near as bad as in the past, since he knew he would be seeing Anndimfoss.

He reached the town in an early hour in the afternoon and easily found the smithy, as there was only one. Anndimfoss's family was pleased with the business he had brought them, especially as work was at a lull. They estimated it would take two or three days to complete it all and proposed that he stay with them; room and board would be a bonus for the large work order. He willingly accepted.

As he walked to the jeweler's shop, he found that he was actually elated with this good fortune. Anndimfoss wound up being quite happy to see him, and this increased when she learned he would be staying at her house. She had mentioned him to her family, but she hadn't described his features or given his name, so his invitation to stay under her roof was clearly a case of serendipity.

He waited until she finished work for the day and they walked home together. He enjoyed the warmth of her soft hand in his. He decided he would accept any task, no matter how menial, if it could let him be with her!

"Mother! Father!" she called out as they walked into the workshop. "Do you remember the young gem miner I had told you about?"

Her brother, Borkiften, looked up and the bellows were suddenly dropped from his hands.

"Oh, no!" he moaned. "We've welcomed the enemy and invited him into our home!"

"Come, dear," his mother said. "He's not our enemy. Does Iltsidtok's family talk of you that way?"

The look on his face changed from shock to a broad, sheepish smile.

"Only her brother, so I figured I should play that role," he chuckled.

"Enough," his father said. "Back to work. The oven needs more air to stay hot!"

"I'm going to prepare dinner," Anndimfoss told Ginderbar. "You can come with me or you can lend a hand here in the shop."

"I better stay here and prove to your brother that I'm not his enemy."

"Fine. We're having lamb today," she called out to everyone as she headed into the house.

Since the men were in the middle of a task, he turned to Oondimkif, Anndimfoss's mother.

"What can I do to help?"

"Well, you could straighten out the pile of tools you brought to us and then you could sweep the floor. We want to have everything ready when Anndimfoss calls us in."

"Is there something special about lamb?"

"Have you ever tried it?"

"Not that I recall. Does it require developing a taste?"

"No. I'm sure you'll appreciate the soft, tasty meat. However, it is best to eat it while it's hot. Otherwise, the fat congeals and it just tastes greasy instead of very good."

"Oh."

There was a brief moment of silence while Ginderbar tried to think of another topic.

"Does Anndimfoss do all the cooking?"

"Most of it," Borkiften called out. "She's actually halfway decent."

"Don't mind her brother's jabs," their mother

commented. "You'll find that she is a very good cook. And most of the time she isn't as picky about us being on time. While the stews, soups and ham dishes are better hot, they're still quite good when they've cooled down."

***

Ginderbar found the meals Anndimfoss prepared to be far better than anything he had had in the past. He felt that her mother hadn't even come close to doing her cooking justice. The repair work on the damaged tools took a bit over three days, but he wished it had been far longer.

They were together for all the time she could spare. Their relation grew stronger, and the parting was difficult. When he was able to visit her again after two months, they agreed the separation had been painful.

Before he left that time, they pledged themselves to one another. The blessing of Anndimfoss's family was unexpected, due to their youth, but it was most welcome. They had been impressed by Ginderbar's drive and energy. They agreed to a wedding when she was older, after she had completed her training and developed a business. The only complaint came from Borkiften, who felt his sister was slighting him by getting engaged before he did. However, Iltsidtok wasn't ready to make a life-long commitment yet, so he had to give in and accept that his little sister had finally beaten him to something!

***

During the last three years of her apprenticeship, having already gained the ability to shape precious metals, Anndimfoss learned the art of cutting gems. This opened up the true profession for her, as it enabled her to multiply the value of gemstones by converting them to exquisite gems. She gained the knowledge of how to select the correct angle to split crystals along their cleavage to produce the gem of maximum value. She also was taught to carve amber and jade, which she found let her express herself as she creatively liberated the figures she imagined to be locked in the uncut stone.

Meanwhile, Ginderbar worked hard in the mine, trying to amass some wealth. He had previously led a very simple life. Having seen her family's home, he wanted to be able to offer her an equivalent life style. He envisioned a shop for her and some nice furniture. These material goods, however, would not come freely, so he toiled longer hours and took on additional chores.

His uncle was actually disturbed by this display of energy, which he believed was counterproductive. He muttered how one should only work hard enough to meet his immediate needs.

"You can't know how long you'll live," he pointed out, "so what's the use of slaving away now. You may never get a chance to enjoy these things you envision in the future. A misjudgment in the mines, and a cave-in could end it all tomorrow. I'm not saying you shouldn't save some for the future, but don't live in misery now!"

Ginderbar understood that logic, but he had willingly accepted the responsibility to think beyond only serving his own needs. Anndimfoss would be living here in a few years, and there would most likely be a child or two after that. It changed his perspective; he didn't expect his uncle to see the world as he did, and it certainly was not worth getting into endless debates. He therefore listened to Shelsinbar and ignored this unsolicited advice, allowing the words to harmlessly wash past him as he nodded absentmindedly.

Even though he was making do with less, he found that he was feeling happier than ever before.

***

The years sped by. Anndimfoss completed her contract and was accepted as a partner in the jewelry shop. She and Ginderbar decided that they could wait a few more years before uniting, though the decision was painful for both of them. After all, he was only twenty-one and she was but nineteen. Most dwarves didn't marry until twice their age!

This period of time, in contrast, crept along. While they saw one another as frequently as was possible, there was no clear delineation point they could see approaching. After three years, the pressure was too great, and they succeeded in convincing her parents that they were mature enough to take on the responsibilities of married life. Their wedding day was heightened when Iltsidtok accepted Borkiften's proposal, capping the festive occasion. This meant that a similar event would be occurring somewhere in the future.

Ginderbar had kept the shop a secret from her. He had promised that one would be built, but she thought that would be in a year or two. Tears of joy welled forth when she saw the gift he had made for her, and he found that the emotions were infectious. In addition to working with the output of the family's mine, she planned on buying gemstones from other villagers to similarly convert them into works of beauty.

To operate properly, the jewelry shop would have to have a fair amount of money, as she had to be able to buy stones and gems when they were available. She frequently sold her products to people of their village and neighboring communities who were going to travel out of the mountains, as it was easier and far safer to transport a few good gems than an equal value in coin. The gems took up less space, thereby being easier to conceal, and they did not make the distinctive sound of a pouch of coins, which served as a magnet for thieves and ne'er-do-wells. The shop was therefore an important business in the small mining village, perhaps of more importance in some ways than even the general store.

The day after they arrived, a new streak of jade had been discovered in the mine. Anndimfoss took this to be an omen of good fortune. Jade is most commonly green in color, but other colors, such as white, yellow or red-brown, though infrequent, are sometimes found. This jade was mauve, a bit richer than the pastel blue-purple color of her own eyes. She took special care in cutting this stone, creating intricate animal figurines, and their wealth thereby increased.

The results were very visible. They became unquestionably the wealthiest family in the village, and Shelsinbar began to merit his nephew's decisions. However, the wealth did not buy friendship, and Anndimfoss was hurt by the way others shunned their social advances. They were a part of the community, but they were apart from it.

Miners no longer had to make the long treks to convert their gemstones to money, but they became more aware of the difference in value between the original stones and the final gems. They had to toil underground for long hours, investing much time and energy to extract the stones. While they were not aware that Anndimfoss put in equal hours to cut the stones, there was no question that she did not exert the same level of sweat and raw energy. This perceived difference in effort was actually the stumbling block that kept her away from being accepted, and it pained her deeply.

***

Such was their life style for nine years. Ginderbar and his uncle worked in the mine while she worked in the shop. They were together for dinner and the evening, but there was almost no contact with anyone else outside of business associations. Anndimfoss's feelings toward the neighbors unfortunately hardened, which lessened her personal anguish of loneliness, and she took great pleasure in the works of art she created. The visits to the town and her family were highlights that were unable to come often enough.

They made a vacation of Borkiften's wedding to Iltsidtok, even convincing Shelsinbar to join them, something he had not done for their own day of union. They were pleased to find that he hit it off exceedingly well with Anndimfoss's father, Purfossten. After an extended full eightday of celebration, they made the return trip to their mountain home.

A state of pandemonium greeted them. An orc attack had occurred two days earlier, while most were at work in the mines. Eight citizens had been slain, including the storekeeper and four children. The ravaged bodies of the seamstress and the storekeeper's wife had been found outside of the village. Several buildings had been raided, among them the general store and Anndimfoss's shop, and three others had been burned to the ground.

Some had wanted to make a retaliatory raid into the mountains, but cooler heads had convinced them that that would be suicidal. Ginderbar, Anndimfoss and Shelsinbar joined in the mourning and rebuilding. A decision was also made to permanently post a lookout at the single pass that led toward the orc stronghold. Several pointed out that this was an example of the clarity of hindsight, but all nonetheless agreed to participate on a rotating basis.

After this shared suffering, Anndimfoss found that the village was more willing to accept her, but she was unable to erase the stigma that had previously been implanted. Persevering, she and Ginderbar rebuilt their assets and her business. He also set aside time to teach her to use the hand ax, the village's preferred weapon. She immediately adopted the habit of carrying one with her at all times.

It took two years to get the shop back on its feet, which was fortunate. During the following year, the mine began to peter out. Ginderbar and his uncle found that their work was revealing fewer gemstones, and those they did unearth were both smaller and poorer in quality.

Over the ensuing years, they became more and more dependent upon the shop. The men considered seeking a new career but instead started excavating a new mine further away from the village where some evidence of copper was discerned. A bit was found, but barely enough to justify the effort.

After two years, the yield improved at a deeper depth, but not by much. Shelsinbar was thankful, as he was over two and a half centuries old, having predated the Great Earthquake, and was unable to picture himself doing anything else. The younger couple found it to be a quiet but stressful period of their lives, with an ever-present, negative undercurrent. It stretched on for another dozen years.

***

The mood then changed dramatically during a visit to the town. Anndimfoss had visited her sister-in-law's workplace. Iltsidtok was a healer, and Ginderbar found his wife's face had an aura of ecstasy when she returned to the smithy, where he was lending a hand.

"Guess what?" she asked as she strode in.

"Whatever it is, I can tell its good news," her mother replied.

"Uh-huh!" she beamed at everyone.

"Well," her husband asked, "are you going to tell us, or is it private?"

"I was pretty sure last month, but I wanted to wait until I was certain before I opened my mouth." She turned to face her brother. "Your wife just confirmed it!"

Rotating around, she gazed into Ginderbar's curious

face.

"We're going to be parents!"

"Really?" he asked, a blank look on his face.

"Would I kid you about this?"

A broad smile spread across his face as he welcomed her with a big hug.

Congratulations were offered from the other three as Ginderbar crushed her in his arms.

"We'll celebrate tonight!" Oondimkif said, removing her work apron and setting it aside. "This job can wait until tomorrow. I'll be in the kitchen."

She exited from the shop, happy thoughts of becoming a grandmother whirling through her mind.

The miner released his wife and looked down into her lavender eyes. His green orbs glowed just as brightly.

"Come. We have to go for a walk. We must consider our child's name."

Draping his arm over her shoulder, he steered her out into the street.

At the celebratory dinner, two names were presented and approved by the family. If the child wound up being a daughter, her name would be Elmdimder. If it proved to be a son, he would be called Kenfossbar. Everyone agreed that they were good, proper names. They then sat down and feasted into the night.

***

Things were joyful for the ensuing months, especially after active motion could be felt in Anndimfoss's womb. Then, about a month before the due date, the movement lessened. They became worried and returned to the town. Iltsidtok had promised to be the midwife, but they wanted her expertise and advice now.

She was uncomfortable about this symptom, warning that the infant's lethargy did not bode well. It stopped altogether the next day, and Elmdimder was stillborn late that night.

Three days were spent in sorrowful mourning. When they packed to return to the village, Iltsidtok pointed out that Anndimfoss was only fifty. This was an early age for giving birth. She should be confident that her body was still adjusting to the final stages of maturing, and the next pregnancy should be fine. Somehow, this information was not especially consoling. The pain was here and now. Thinking about possibilities for the future did not lessen the heart-wrenching anguish.

Things only got worse when they reached the village shop two days later. The door was unlocked, but Shelsinbar did not respond when they called out his name.

Behind the counter, they found the body with his skull caved in and his hair matted in a reddish-brown mess. A blackjack lay on the floor, one side caked with dried blood. All of the gems, jewelry and coins were gone. Their uncle had been seen the previous evening, so the heinous murder and robbery must have occurred during the night or early morning.

Tallying up the factors, they decided that there was no reason to stay in this village any longer. They had no wealth to revive the business, no family and no true friends. The mine wasn't really worth mining and the house was no longer a home. Two deaths within the span of six days necessitated a need for change.

They moved down to the valley, joining the comfort of her family in the town, but they were still enshrouded in a deep depression. Ginderbar decided that he needed a change in environment and that now was the time to select a new career. Anndimfoss agreed. She lacked the funds to start a new shop, and the threats imposed by potential repetition of either robbery or murder made her feel that she would become a prisoner if she set up a new shop, having to always defend it.

Contemplating the recent occurrences, they decided to face these fears and threats head-on. They would get the necessary training and then seek employment as soldiers or men-at-arms. At least they knew that they would be together and would be able to trust and depend upon one another.

Her family willingly loaned them the money they needed for now. Ginderbar approached the barracks of the royal guards stationed in the town. They were bored, rarely having anything to do beyond patrol duty. They enthusiastically agreed to earn some extra money on the side by training him and his wife.

They both quickly learned to wield the short sword, bearing fine weapons forged by Oondimkif. They also honed their skills in handling hand axes, particularly paying attention to the details of throwing them as missile weapons. Anndimfoss displayed a natural knack at precision in this aspect, extending her reach as she envisioned the target as the unknown enemy that had slain their uncle.

On the advice of one guard, Ginderbar learned to crank and fire bolts from a crossbow. He was impressed that accuracy could be maintained over quite a distance, thereby enlarging his region of influence. Anndimfoss added the use of the morning star to her repertoire. She liked the way it lengthened her reach and had the ability to bite into an opponent, even if wearing armor that would deflect a blade.

As before, her mother supplied the weapons. She then made hardened leather armor for each of them, studded with metal rings. She completed her gifts by supplying two small shields. She pointed out that these were investments to ensure that her children would return and make her a grandmother.

When they were ready to depart, Purfossten and Borkiften gave them two ponies and a mule. Iltsidtok gave them a large vial of salve that would help heal wounds and prevent infection. They loaded their gear on the mule and headed out of town toward the kingdom highway, promising to return to visit within a year.

They had heard very recent rumors of the possibility of civil war, so they decided to seek their fortune by journeying to the capital. If there was any truth to those tails, they should be able to gain employment in King Linoan's troops.

***

As they made their way northward, they found that there was minimal traffic leaving or entering the valley. They encountered more once they were on a main thoroughfare, but most were not too talkative, which was contagious. They stopped even trying to initiate discussions, which extended to stays in inns as they progressed.

However, there was one exception. A human who called himself Stalif rode up in the same direction and stopped once he overtook them, attracted by the armaments they bore. After a brief discussion, he made an offer that merited at least a side trip for investigation. They accepted a stamped iron disk he gave them, plus directions to the castle of one Lord Pitar.

He rode off on his long-legged horse, leaving a small cloud of dust behind himself on the dry road.

"Well," Anndimfoss said, "let's get going. We have two days to get there if we want to be considered for this job."

Looking forward, she got her pony to resume its trot in the same direction. Ginderbar followed, tugging the resistant mule behind him, struggling to keep it moving at a pace faster than it desired.

7 – THE COTERIE

As the door closed behind Tobba, the eight people Stalif had gathered in three separate kingdoms found themselves alone. For a moment or two, they merely glanced around the room, sizing each other up.

Fitessa was the first to speak.

"I don't know who will take on the mantle of leadership in this venture. However, the first step will be to decide who is going. While some of us have met informally during the course of this day, I figure that we should each introduce ourselves, tell what skills we have to offer, and then state what our intent is at this time. We'll then be in a better position to make some real decisions."

"Sounds good to me," the gnome responded.

"Sure," Reph added, nodding vigorously. "I says it soun's good too!"

"Why don't you go first," Jienna asked of the half-elf.

"O.K. My name is Fitessa, as I had said earlier. I'm a Trademaster, dealing in wines and other alcoholic beverages. I've sold to Castle Tiufrann in the past and thus am a recognized face there, which means I can get the group in – or at least part of it, depending on how many go. I'm considering taking part in this, though it may mean that I can never do business there again."

As she stopped, she scanned around at the others.

"Who's next?"

"I'm Jienna, a servant of Sylvan. Before becoming a druid, I was a forester. The berserker is my brother, Reph. He's a follower of Kreva, and his previous experience was as a hunter. We're both planning on trying to rescue the girl."

"An' so's Star, Ji. Don' fergit 'im!"

"I guess that means you're next," the druid said, deferring to her friend.

"Seems so," he said, rising to his full height. "I go by the name of Starspire and serve Lamanna as a member of the Order of Enchantment. As Reph has already declared, I plan to be a participant in this noble effort."

"We's 'The Trio'," Reph added proudly.

"Fine, little brother," Jienna said quietly. "Now it's our turn to be silent and listen."

There was a pause before the wood elf decided to contribute his part.

"My name is Uhu," he ventured in a soft voice. "I think that I'll be joining you on this excursion. It sounds interesting. I grew up as a fisherman, but now I'm earning a living through a combination of my brawn and my proficiency with my weapons. I'm pretty decent with the dagger, staff and sword, but my specialty is the bow."

"I was taught that your race can speak to animals," Jienna commented. "Is that fact or fable?"

"It's a fact. Which animals a wood elf can converse with varies, but I am able to communicate with owls, eagles, bears, boars, deer, lynx and pegasi, and they've often become my friends."

"Gee," Reph said, his eyes wide open.

"My husband and I have also recently converted to the occupation of warrior," the dwarf offered. "My name is Anndimfoss and he's Ginderbar. I previously earned my living as a jeweler and he was a miner. This sounds like a job that will let us know if it's the right choice for us."

"I fight wi' th' halber', th' sword an' th' big ax," the berserker added.

"What about you, Gnome?" Fitessa asked.

"My name is Tiniki. Ages ago I was a barmaid. Since then, I've made ends meet as a gambler and gamester. I've also developed an ability to read faces very well. I believe that we should lay all of our cards on the table, as it were, but this will require you to come clean – was it Fitessa? I have the impression that you were holding back a bit.

"Anyway, part of the reason that Stalif asked me to join this outing is that he feels there may be the need to pick a lock or two. I'm also a thief, but that fact is not to be told to any others, as I don't desire to rot in a dungeon. Understood?"

"Will we have to guard our pouches?" Starspire asked.

"No. If you will not disclose that aspect of me, your possessions are safe. I pledge this by Firsh!"

"However," Uhu noted, "if she follows The Trickster, we all better keep an open eye on her!"

"What do you mean?" the spellcaster asked.

"Gnomes in general, and particularly those under oath to their god, are notorious practical jokers. Our myths are intertwined, and I heard tales of the gnomes in my childhood. Perhaps I'll share them with you at a later date, if you're interested."

Starspire smiled at the elf and nodded.

"What about you, Fitessa," Jienna asked. "Do you have a card up your sleeve, as Tiniki implied?"

"My compliments to you, Thief. Remind me of your knack to read faces should I forgetfully start to sit down to play cards with you. I, too, am a member of the same guild, though I have never yet tried to apply those skills. Perhaps I will change that fact this time. I guess I'll toss my lot in with the rest of you."

"Then we will number eight in all," Starspire said, half to himself.

"Actually," Uhu responded, "the number will be nine. I have an owl, bonded in friendship, who I know will offer his assistance. His name is Swoop."

"I see two things that should be taken care of right

Saving Lady Noan

away," Fitessa said. "We will need to choose a leader, to speak in our behalf, when appropriate, and to make decisions when there isn't time for discussion. I remove myself from such consideration.

"The other thing is that we need to discuss Tiufrann. Have any of you ever been there before?"

She glanced at each of the others, watching as they shook their heads in turn.

"Well, I've been there several times. Let me share some points with you."

The half-elf fell silent as the door on the far side opened. Everyone shifted to watch a servant hold it ajar as Tobba came in, followed by Stalif.

***

As the servant exited, closing the door behind him, Stalif stepped forward.

"Welcome to Castle Vork. I am most pleased that you have come to our aide. It is a just cause, and it is most imperative." His eyes glanced around the room as he talked, looking at each member of the room, skillfully giving the conversation a personal tone as he also tallied who was present. "It is good that so many of you responded."

"Were there others you asked?" Jienna queried.

"Three others. But having eight out of eleven come on such short notice and with so little information is appreciated. Thank you!"

"Now," Tobba said, "we have the more critical question. How many of you are willing to help in saving Lord Pitar's daughter? Or do you need more time to resolve the issue?"

"No, we have had sufficient time," Jienna said. "We will all be going to Tiufrann to rescue his daughter."

"That is the news we hoped to hear," Stalif sighed.

"My brother-in-law will be most pleased to learn of this!"

"And are you willing to pledge an oath of fealty to Lord Pitar, pledging to do all you are able to rescue Lady Noan and return her unharmed?" Tobba asked.

After they had agreed and each had, in turn, taken the oath, he resumed talking to them as a group.

"I will see that facilities are made ready for you for the night. The promised advanced payment will be given in the morning. I will go to take care of those matters. Lord Stalif has a bit more to discuss with you."

He turned and went to the door, but his step seemed to be a little lighter than before.

"I have only two things that I wish to offer, but I am also willing to attempt to answer any questions you might have," Stalif began. "First, I cannot stress enough the importance of trying to keep this endeavor a secret. We hope that there are no spies here, but we cannot be certain. We likewise hope that the three who did not come are not spreading word of this venture. If word leaks out, you will have failed before you begin.

"The other thing is the pair of promised maps. I have never been to Tiufrann, but you have, Fitessa, so I trust that you will be able to interpret them." He placed two rolled parchments on the table.

As he withdrew his hand, he queried, "Do you have any questions?"

"Would it be possible to have any forces behind us, to help escort Lady Noan back here?" Jienna asked.

"If you can think of a way to do it without tipping our hand, we will willingly have it for you."

"It is a nice idea," Fitessa commented, "but it won't work with a stealth project such as we are undertaking. Perhaps an attachment can leave after the equinox, planning to meet us on our return trip."

"I will discuss that with Lord Pitar. It may not be exactly what you want, but it might be an acceptable compromise. Other questions?"

"We have to pool our thoughts," Starspire said. "That may lead to other questions. May we continue to use this room?"

"Most assuredly. I will see that fresh food is supplied, too."

"See that a better wine is brought to us," Fitessa added.

"I will."

With that, he bowed and exited.

***

"You had some points you wished to share with us," Ginderbar said, addressing Fitessa.

"Yes. As I said earlier, I have been to Tiufrann quite a few times, though not during the celebration of the equinox. I have regularly sold supplies to the castle and to the One Claw Inn, plus sometimes to two bars within the walled city.

"I therefore will be recognized, and my presence won't raise any suspicion. The same will not be true for the rest of you. You dwarves will probably be most easily accepted. You might also easily be admitted if you accompany them, Tiniki, though I have never before seen a gnome in that region. Come to think of it, I've never seen any of your race outside of South Indrose."

"My race," she replied, "does not often travel far from our mountain homeland; but there are exceptions."

"Obviously, as you're here with us. Anyway, you will need to be careful in your actions, as you will be a wild card, to once more play upon your profession."

"I understand," Tiniki responded with a nod.

"You will be the most difficult factor, Uhu. It was difficult for me to become accepted, and that was in better times. I doubt that you would even be allowed within the walled city, but I have an idea how we can handle that.

"The other point that stands out regards you, Starspire, and I am not referring to your height, though that will not be missed. You must hide your profession, as that would only draw further attention, and most likely attention that would be quite unfavorable. That means that you need a drabber cloak and a different name."

"Anudder diff'ren name?"

"Silent, Reph!" Starspire's tone got the berserker to clamp his lips shut.

"You said you had a suggestion for Uhu." Jienna mentioned, steering the discussion back to Fitessa.

"Yes. I always have two guards travel with me to protect both me and my wares. They are used to that and expect it at Tiufrann, where I always stay at the One Claw Inn. Uhu could pose as one of the guards and could serve on the outside, managing such things as communications and steeds. You might pose as the other guard, spellcaster."

"Perhaps, though I don't know how to use anything other than a staff. I could wear another weapon for show."

"Just don't try to fight with it," Jienna said with a giggle. "I picture you doing more harm to us and yourself than to any foe in a fighting situation!"

"Isn't that the truth," he agreed, glancing briefly at his friend.

"Now, when it comes to selecting a leader," Fitessa suggested, "I think it would be a more natural role for a spellcaster or druid."

"If it comes to that," Starspire countered, "I would defer to Jienna. She is more comfortable in dealing with a group, and it wouldn't fit in well with my role as a guard for others to turn to me."

"Good point," Jienna noted. "But I will depend upon you for advice...and everyone else, if I am to take this position."

After a short exchange of opinions, it was found that

the others were willing to accept her as the leader of the party. The conversation then stopped when servants entered, bearing platters of food and, at the same time, clearing away what remained from earlier in the day. Fitessa tasted the wine and rated it as adequate, though not to her level of preference. None of the others were unhappy with the noticeably improved quality, so they accepted the offering and sat down to dine.

***

While they ate, Jienna asked the dwarves to describe the festival of the equinox. They explained that the balance of day and night was taken to reflect the balance and duality of the world. Each equinox, in both the spring and fall, was given over to celebration.

Hard toil was avoided as much as was possible on this day. At sunset, everyone celebrates with food, drink and dance. All people – high or low, rich or poor – are viewed as equals. Ill feelings are forgiven and efforts are made to form new friendships or to strengthen old ones.

"Tobba and Stalif are clearly correct," Ginderbar concluded, "in judging this to be the best time to rescue Lady Noan. The castle banquet hall and ballroom should be open, and the defenses, at least that of the dwarves, will be down.

"You've been there, Fitessa. Are the guards dwarves or humans?"

"As I remember, it's about evenly split."

"Then we must hope that the humans have learned to participate in the holiday spirit!" Anndimfoss stated emphatically.

Everyone agreed.

***

Once the servants had cleared away the platters and

the remnants of the dinner, the members of the group had the room to themselves and Jienna placed the two maps on the table.

"We must once again call upon your experience, Fitessa," she said.

The half-elf spread out one parchment that showed the region while the others took positions that enabled them to see it clearly.

"This rectangle in the center, labeled 'Castle Tiufrann' is really the walled city. The castle is actually the eastern portion. The Tiufrann River runs diagonally across the map, flowing in a southwesterly direction. The walled city is actually on an island. The line running more or less across the middle of the parchment is the highlands cliff. It is perhaps forty or fifty feet in height.

"I take it that the thick lines running across the bottom and the top right corner mark the edges of the forests. The thinner lines are the roads passing through the region. We will be coming up from the south, along this route."

She pointed this out with an extended finger.

"A rather steep ramp runs from the bottom to the top of the cliff, marking the disjoint part of the roadway."

Her finger took a shift to the right.

"The small squares are probably farmhouses, with the exception of the two larger ones where the southern road meets the road that parallels the northern forest. The one on the left is the One Claw Inn, while the other is the stable.

"The drawbridge shown here on the eastern side of the castle crosses the deep, narrow chasm eaten away by the river. I've never seen it down and I presume that it has a portcullis behind it. On the northern side, a guard tower arches over the drawbridge. There then is a portcullis in the city wall, leading into the walled city and market. That is where I have always entered to do business.

"I figure that we should try to get there at least a full day before the equinox, that we can get rooms at the inn and get a chance to look around. I can do some business then, too, which will help cover our presence."

"What are these other markings on the map?" Starspire asked.

"Those are hills. They aren't too high, but the rest of the land, above and below the cliff, is very flat."

"Let's look at the other parchment," Jienna said as she unrolled it.

Fitessa rotated it 90 degrees to the left.

"Now it has the same orientation as the map," she explained. "It is a sketch of the walled city. The arched entryway is in the north wall. As you enter, guard barracks are to the left and their stables are to the right. The marketplace is this open area in the center of the city, with the two bars I sometimes service being here," she paused to point with one finger, "and here. At the northeast corner of the marketplace is the entrance to the castle itself, with both gates and portcullis.

"Inside the castle, the courtroom is to the right and the large room to the left is the banquet hall. I believe that stairs ascend from there to the ballroom, but I'm not certain on that, having never been in the banquet hall itself. I have heard that the pantry and kitchen are behind the banquet hall and the guard mess hall and castle barracks are in the northeast corner of the castle.

"The two high towers are in the middle of the eastern wall, on either side of the drawbridge. The one next to the mess hall and barracks has the control for the drawbridge. I know this because the wine cellar is at the bottom of this tower, as is the entrance to the dungeon. I've made deliveries directly to the wine cellar on two occasions.

"Unfortunately, I don't know what is in the other towers or the other portions of the castle. I wish that this parchment was labeled, but I guess we should be glad that we have this. However, if this parchment was found to be upon us there, our future would very likely be most dismal.

With your permission, Jienna, I suggest that we store it and the other parchment in a hollow rod in my cart."

"A hollow rod?" Jienna whispered to Starspire. "How interesting."

Looking up at Fitessa, she said, "By all means! I take it that it has been used for similar reasons in the past, but that is your own business."

"I have one other suggestion to offer at this time," Fitessa said. "In journeying to Tiufrann, we should move as three separate groups, though we can stay in close proximity to one another. That would be less likely to raise questions.

"I suggest that I and my 'guards', one on horseback and the other on the cart with me, would be one group. The dwarves and gnome would be a second group. The last would be the druid and berserker. We would request rooms separately at taverns along the way and would only interact together when in uninhabited regions or after we reach the One Claw Inn."

"That seems reasonable," Jienna responded. "I think that we should each take care of whatever preparations are necessary in the morning, once Tobba has given us the advance money. We will aim to depart by midday, if that is alright with each of you. Is there anything else that we need to take care of before retiring for the night?"

"We needs a new name, Ji," Reph stated. "We's not th' Trio no more."

"My brother has always identified with having a group name," Jienna explained. "Does anyone have a suggestion? Just to use among ourselves?"

Working to please the berserker, several ideas, including 'the group', 'the pack' and 'the menagerie', were suggested and discarded. The one that was finally accepted was to go by the name of the Coterie, which Tiniki explained meant a closely associated group of people. As she pointed out, they better become closely associated, as their lives might very likely depend upon one another.

As they exited the meeting room and reclaimed their weapons, Uhu had everyone accompany him to the castle's parapet. In the darkness of the cloudy night, he hooted and a similar sound echoed from the distance. A moment later, Swoop appeared silently and alighted on the elf's shoulder. He was introduced to everyone else. They then descended and were shown to their rooms.

***

In the morning, after breakfast, Tobba escorted the members of the Coterie to the courtroom. They took time to carefully study the portrait of Lady Noan. He then gave them the promised advance on the reward, and Jienna told him to inform Stalif that they would be starting northward in a few hours.

She, Reph and Tiniki decided to stay at the castle, as they had nothing they felt they needed to do. Starspire left to get simpler clothes to hide his profession. He assigned his friends to come up with a new name that he could use for this venture while he was out.

When he returned, he was wearing a worn, brown cloak that hung very loosely over his gray clothes. He had a leather belt and a rather worn backpack. The fine blue garments he had previously worn were packed away and carried under his arm.

"Nothing else was available in my size," he explained, shrugging his shoulders. As he moved it aside, he revealed a long sword in a scabbard attached to his belt.

"Ginderbar suggested that I could ride in the cart with Fitessa and keep his crossbow by me. Combined with this piece of metal, I should give the image of a guard. I only hope I never have to try to use either."

"Well," Jienna chuckled, "you will look the part. Reph suggested calling you Gork. How does that sound?"

"Gork? Why not? For the next eightday or so, I will be Gork!"

***

Uhu attempted to obtain some armor. With the time limitations, he visited a few different venders. On short notice, however, the best he could get was a shirt of chain mail that was a bit loose, even with an acton worn beneath it. He bought it anyway, figuring that he could always improve on it if he survived, and survival was of great importance! He just hoped it would not in any way impair his use of his sword.

***

Fitessa made her way to a seedier bar on the outskirts of the town. Ordering ale, she sat down at an end of the room near the door where she could see the other customers and likewise be seen

Scanning her audience, shifting her head from side to side, she slowly used the index finger of her right hand to clean out her ear. She then rubbed her chin, followed by pulling on her ear lobe. Hearing a loud cough, she focused her attention on an old man to her left.

He stood up and ran his hand through his thinning hair. With both hands, he adjusted his belt and tightened it one notch. As he glanced obliquely at her, she started to reach into her pouch and then changed her mind, removing her empty hand, tightly shutting the laces. She then rubbed her cheek.

The short man began to walk out of the bar. He coughed while passing and then waited at the doorway until she got up. He was standing outside and led her to a quiet alley.

"Yer've need of the guild?" he asked softly, keeping an attentive eye on the minimal traffic on the road.

"No. I'll be on private matters for the next eightday and will supply my own guards. Simply pass that on. I'll get back into the normal pattern after that."

With no other discussion, they parted. Fitessa made some purchases from a usual supplier before returning to the castle, telling the dealer she would pick them up shortly with her cart. She then headed back to Castle Vork.

***

"Where are we going?" Ginderbar asked his wife. "Considering the local attitude, I'm not sure this is a good idea."

He glanced at the stares directed at them. However, the manner was not as vehement as when they had ridden in the previous evening. Perhaps the fact that they had been guests at the castle had tempered the townsfolk's disposition.

"A servant told me of a seeress, and I have some questions I wish to have answered."

"But think of it, dear wife. If she has psychic powers and were truly able to foresee the future, don't you think that Stalif would have visited her, that we might be acting on fact rather than on conjecture?"

"Who knows? As I understand it, the accuracy of the prophecies of a seeress depends on the strength of the emotions of the one posing the questions. Perhaps Noan's family has seen this seeress, but chooses to keep the issue cloaked in uncertainty."

"Why would they do that?"

"Because one can never be sure of the interpretations of prophecies. They may prefer a margin of safety."

"Well...remember to recognize this uncertainty in regard to the answers to your questions. Do you plan to share them with me?"

"I don't know...yet."

They walked in silence until they reached the small house with the three red lines marking the presence of a fortuneteller. Anndimfoss reached up to knock, but the door opened before her knuckles reached the wood.

An old, white-haired man stood before them. While short by human standards, he was still a full head taller than either of them.

"Eh! So, my wife was almost right. She said to open the door as a dwarf was seeking answers. I thought she was assuredly wrong this time, but it seems only partially, as there be two of you."

"Only I come with questions," Anndimfoss said. She stepped in as the old man moved aside.

"I'll wait out here for you," Ginderbar said.

"As you wish, beloved."

"So, she was right, as usual," the man muttered as he shut the door.

The room was dark, as the curtains were drawn and there was but one candle.

"She awaits you in the side room," he said. "Leave your weapons out here, unless your questions be specifically about them. Her fee will be one gold piece, and you'll be able to ask no more than three questions, so be careful in selecting them."

He cleared some space on the table for her sword and hand ax; her morning star was back at the castle. He then pointed to one room as he shuffled into the kitchen.

Anndimfoss went into the indicated room.

"Shut the door behind you, lass."

The room was dim, being lit by a single, large red candle, giving eerie highlights to everything. An old woman with long, silver braids sat at the table. A white, finely brocaded cloth was beneath the candle and a bowl, probably used for scrying, was before her. Shadows danced on the walls as the candle's flame flickered, but she was unable to make out any specific details.

"Please, be seated, place your coin on the table and state your name."

The dwarf followed her directions.

"And what is your first question, Anndimfoss?"

"I will be leaving on a dangerous undertaking later today. Will we survive?"

The woman stared into the dwarf's eyes. There was a long pause before she responded.

"You shall survive, but I foresee much suffering. Your next question?"

Anndimfoss was not happy with this answer. She decided to spend another question to try for a clearer image.

"Will this suffering be too great?"

The time before an answer was even longer. Anndimfoss watched the candle as the seeress stared blankly at her. It was not clear if she was actually awake, but is seemed totally inappropriate to make any sound. She thought of coughing quietly, but before she came to a decision, the woman spoke with a hollow voice, showing no emotion.

"I am unable to clearly measure what is too great. I see that you shall lose something dear to you, but you shall gain many-fold in return. What is your final question?"

"I have so many other things that I wish to ask, but I must ask the one that caused me to come to you."

Taking a deep breath, she continued. "Recently, I lost my daughter. I do not know what caused her to be stillborn. I must ask – will Ginderbar and I have a healthy child?"

The answer was almost instantaneous.

"You will have a healthy child by Ginderbar, and it will grow to adulthood. That is the limit to your questions. You now must depart to face your future."

The old lady sat back, closing her eyes and breathing deeply. Tears of happiness clouded Anndimfoss's vision as she rose, quietly thanking the seeress as she took her leave.

She smiled warmly at her husband as she stepped out into the sunlight. Hugging him affectionately, she found she was unable to talk with him at this time. The emotions surged too strongly through her body. She leaned her cheek against his shoulder as they headed back to the castle.

***

The dwarves left their mule in the castle stable, loading their gear onto Fitessa's cart. The trademaster explained that she had to pick up wares on the way out of town, but the three groups would meet on the northern road and each would travel just far enough apart to be within eyesight of the next party.

Stalif saw them off with wishes of good luck. He reminded them that rescuing Lady Noan was the purpose and priority of the venture. As they mounted their steeds and headed out, Lord Pitar and Lady Nimina came to the lower parapet, worry showing distinctly on their faces.

"May the gods be with you in this venture! Bring back our daughter!"

8 – NORTH

At the time of their adventurous departure, the weather was pleasant. It was sunny and warm, and the road was dry and firm. The light rain before dawn had wetted the road enough to keep down the dust without producing any mud. All in all, it was excellent conditions for traveling. If one was looking for an optimistic message, this might easily be interpreted as a good omen.

Jienna and Reph rode ahead at a steady but leisurely pace. Fitessa had Starspire keep the cart as far back as possible without losing sight of the pair that preceded them. Swoop had settled on the cart's rim. He at first complained about the motion, but it fairly quickly had rocked him to sleep, his hooked claws imbedded firmly in the wood. Uhu rode just behind them. The three ponies traveled as far behind the cart as the first two were ahead of it.

The road rolled through farmland, meadow and woods. The sky was blue with a few puffs of white clouds floating by serenely overhead. The fields were gold and amber, with farmers taking advantage of the fine weather to harvest their crops. Hay was spread in the sun to dry before being stored away to feed the livestock through the winter months.

The woods also reflected the coming seasonal change by showing the first signs of fall. The willows by the Tiufrann River had begun to turn yellow and early bright red coloring appeared in the sumacs and wood bane. The vines of wood bane climbing up the trees looked like flames leaping up the trunks.

To some, especially Uhu and Tiniki, the approach of autumn was even audible. The calls of the birds were clearly different from what was heard in spring or the height of summer and the chorus of insects had likewise been distinctly altered. When they rode over stream-spanning bridges, the water seemed to be moving faster, and there was a distinct tinkle as it passed over the pebbles. A sense of change was in the air.

Tiniki also noted a rather mellow warmth between the dwarves that had been absent the previous night. They rode close to one another, talking quietly, frequently accented by chuckles. Ginderbar and Anndimfoss were using terms of endearment in their conversations, and she was certain that some chill was melting away. Whatever it was, she felt that it most likely would be beneficial to the party as a whole, so she planned to do whatever she could to help it along. Perhaps, lacking love on a personal level, this was a vicarious enactment. She didn't know, but, if that was the case, so be it!

For her own part, Anndimfoss had been motivated by the answer the soothsayer had given to her third question. Elmdimder had been stillborn and she had placed the blame upon herself. She had feared she was unable to bear a healthy, happy child for her husband and herself. The mood of the self-doubt had inadvertently eroded her relation with Ginderbar. It had begun to cause an unintentional separation between them. When he chose his new career, she imagined how he might die and never return. This had subconsciously caused her to decide to join him, but the resulting awkwardness had led to relations that were stilted and uncomfortable. Knowing that she was able to have children – and that such would come to pass – suddenly removed all the negative forces, and things had returned to an earlier time, before all the difficulties had begun to accumulate. The change was not consciously planned, but the effects were very much appreciated by both of them.

***

Jienna's thoughts were of a different sort. Since the days of The Pack, she had thought of going adventuring, doing good deeds and saving the world. Now that they were actually on their way, she found that there were much more immediate aspects, things that even superseded saving Noan, though not at the expense of stopping that goal.

Part of her responsibility as a druid was to go out across the land as a missionary. She was to serve her god and proselytize his faith. She also was empowered to protect nature and to strive for a balance in the world. It should not deter her from the Coterie's quest, so she must try to find a way to achieve it at the same time.

This influenced her actions when they reached the town of Poldoff in the late afternoon. Thus, as the others went toward the lone tavern – the Green Rooster by the image on the signboard – and Swoop perched on a pine branch far above them and well out of sight of the town's humans, she directed her steed into the marketplace. Reph followed his sister.

The presence of the berserker hushed the crowd, who had been haggling over prices, as customers knew the farmers had no desire to haul their produce back to their farms. Jienna took advantage of this opportune momentary silence.

"In the morning, I will hold service that Sylvan might bless your crops and the harvest and the haying. It will be here, an hour after dawn, before I resume my journey. You are welcome to come. If you do, bring some of your farming implements with you.

"Also, while I have your attention, is there anyone who needs special aid at their field or orchard? I cannot make any promises, but I will hope that I will be able to entreat Sylvan to offer you assistance."

One woman came forward, explaining that they had an infestation on their fruit trees. Jienna and Reph dismounted and followed her to the town's outskirts.

After inspecting the trees, she knelt and prayed to her god, seeking his assistance. She buried a holly leaf in the middle of the orchard, asking him to first and foremost stop the spread of the borers. She also appealed upon him to drive off the infestation, removing these villainous insects or at least depleting their numbers.

When she was done, the family asked her if she would please them by being their guest for the night. Accepting their kind offer, she and her brother followed them to the farmhouse. Noting rodents scampering about in the midden, she turned to the farmer.

"Get a cat," she said, "but be selective. Find a young one that still lives with its mother. You want one whose mother is a mouser but leaves birds alone. You will then have an ally to remove unwanted vermin while allowing the birds to still help protect your trees." She wondered to herself whether a mouser would turn to killing birds once the furry prey were depleted. Such was probably the case, a part of the balance of nature.

"Yer d'rections shall be followed, Druid!"

"Thank you, and thank you again for your hospitality. I will not intercede any further with unrequested advice."

"Nay. If ye've advice, it's most welcome!"

The evening proved to be both friendly and pleasurable for everyone.

***

Back at the Green Rooster, Tiniki's quiet and solitary actions had caught the dwarves' attention. They watched as she played cards by herself in the common room. Finally, curiosity overcame Anndimfoss and she asked the gnome what she was doing, seemingly playing cards with no one but herself.

"When you play by yourself, it is called solitaire."

"But why play by yourself? Who are you trying to beat?" Ginderbar asked.

"Actually, it is a way to pass time and the challenge is to see whether you can succeed at winning the game. However, this version, called Dragon Solitaire, is said to have a side benefit. You can only play 13 games in an eightday, but, if you win, it is said that no nonmetallic dragons, nor certain other evil creatures, will be able to attack you for a year. I just lost my last game for this eightday and my protective period will end if I don't succeed in the next round, starting after the equinox."

"Is that protection true?" Anndimfoss asked.

"I'm uncertain. It may be fantasy, but just in case there is any truth to the rumor, I figure it can't hurt to have extra protection, especially with this new profession I am now undertaking."

"Could you teach us this game?" the dwarf queried.

"I'll just watch," her husband interjected.

"Sure, but while I am teaching Anndimfoss how to play, you can also learn and you can watch that she doesn't miss any moves," Tiniki responded.

She spread the deck out so that they could see the faces. There were four sets of dragons – red, green, gold and silver. Each set had different numbers of dragons on the card, varying from one to thirteen.

"Thirteen seems to reoccur in this game," Anndimfoss noted.

"Yes," Tiniki replied. "Thirteen is supposedly the lucky number of dragons." She collected the cards and handed them to Anndimfoss.

"First, you shuffle the deck. Do you know how to do that?"

Her new student nodded, so Tiniki waited until the dwarf had done that a few times.

"Now, count out three cards face down in a pile and place the fourth card face up on top of it. Then repeat this step three more times, making a row of four piles. Sixteen cards will be in the piles and thirty-six cards will remain in your hand."

Once this had been done, she continued explaining the game.

"Of the face-up cards, cards may be played upon one another with the following restrictions. The cards must descend in order and they must alternate between metallic and nonmetallic dragons. For example, you can move the card with ten red dragons onto the card with eleven silver dragons, but the card with nine green dragons cannot be moved to the card with ten red dragons."

She paused while this direction was followed.

"Good. Having moved that card, the facedown card beneath it is uncovered, so it must be turned over. Let's see what this one is."

A single red dragon appeared.

"That's good! Cards with a single dragon are always moved above the four piles, thus potentially creating four new piles."

The dwarf followed her tutor's direction.

"These piles are built upward by number, only playing cards of the same color dragon on each pile. This pile will collect the red dragons. As other single dragons appear, you can create the three other piles. You actually win if you can succeed in getting all of the cards on these piles."

Tiniki paused so that the dwarves could internalize these rules.

"There are a few more rules. Cards in your hand are turned over three at a time. If the visible card can be played to either an ascending, common-color pile I just described, which will hopefully continue to form as you play, or a descending alternating pile, you may do so, but the move is not mandatory. This is why it is a game, as some choice comes into play. Any questions so far?"

As they both shook their heads, she continued.

"Once you go though the cards in your hand, the pile will be lifted, turned over and the play resumes, three cards at a time. If the last set is less than three, it is played as is."

Anndimfoss began to count out a set of three cards, but the gnome shook her head while placing a hand on the dwarf's.

"Hold off playing until I finish the rules, OK?"

She again paused briefly.

"If any of the original piles disappear, you have a void. It must be filled. That is not an option. However, you will have a choice. Select one of the other piles and move the face-up cards from that pile into that space, exposing another card to be turned over. If there are no longer any facedown cards on the table, the uppermost exposed card from the hand immediately moves into the void. Since such is the case, you should sometimes consider when you create the void, because that can have a critical effect.

"That is Dragon Solitaire. Much of the game is luck, but you do have choices of which pile to move into a void and when or whether you move cards, either from the hand or onto the common-color piles.

"I will watch as you play, but I cannot give advice, as I have already played my thirteen games for this eightday. Are there any questions?"

The dwarves decided they could best learn by actually playing. Tiniki was happy to see that the game increased the interaction between Anndimfoss and Ginderbar. Even more surprising was the fact that the dwarf won her fourth game. Her face glowed with the positive potentiality as they went to the dining hall.

***

Tiniki took a separate tavern room. She had no special

desire to be by herself, though neither did it particularly bother her. She knew, however, that Anndimfoss wanted to be alone with her mate. The sounds she heard late into the night from the neighboring room reassured her that she had made the right decision.

The tavern dinner had been fair, but nothing more. The only one who feasted that night was Swoop. It was a warm, clear night and he found rodents everywhere. While Jienna's recommendation might change things in the future, he gorged himself this night. He had not eaten so well in years!

***

As was now her natural habit, Jienna automatically arose for her pre-dawn prayers. She tried to be quiet, but Reph opened his eyes and rolled over to view her.

"Rest," she whispered. "I'll be back shortly."

He nodded and snuggled back under the wool blanket. She wished that the problems of the world were as easy to please.

Stepping outside, she found the air to be a bit nippy, but not yet the cool crispness that really marked fall mornings. Clouds had moved in and completely hid the stars, but it did not feel like rain, at least not until much later in the day. The thought crossed her mind of how she had become more attuned to nature, a natural aspect of being a druid.

Adjusting her cloak, she maneuvered in the dim light, heading for the orchard as she walked through the edge of the vegetable garden. Going from tree to tree, she found many shriveled insects. Looking upward, she offered her thanks to Sylvan and asked that he continue to offer his assistance in this battle.

When she reentered the farmhouse, she found that everyone was up. The fire in the hearth was radiating heat throughout the kitchen, and breakfast was being prepared. It was simple but wholesome: boiled, ground meal with fresh cow's milk, sweetened with berries.

Before departing, she told the farmer that a small offering should be burnt every Sylvanday in the midst of the orchard. This would gain the god's attention so that he would continue his positive support. He promised to faithfully see that it was done. She and Reph then headed for the marketplace.

***

It was Beltetaday, the day of rest, but the farmers gathered in the marketplace, bringing tools that they soon would be using, such as scythes, flails, pitchforks, pruning blades, wheelbarrows and baskets. Jienna blessed these simple folk and all of their implements, asking Sylvan that each might have an easy and bountiful harvest. She then reminded them that the morrow was his day and that each should individually beseech his help in the morning.

As she went to Reph, who was holding both of their steeds, she saw that the other members of the Coterie were leaving the Green Rooster. They had timed themselves to allow a smooth exit from Poldoff and it seemed to be working very well. To any observer, they were three independent groups who happened to be going in the same direction.

"D'ya wanna go, Ji?"

"Yes, Reph. It's time to be on our way."

After mounting, she once again reminded the people of their duty to Sylvan. They waved her off and then began to disperse back to their homes.

As the crowd thinned, Fitessa got onto the cart beside Starspire.

"All right, Gork. Let's be off. I've business to tend to in Tiufrann. Ride a bit ahead, Uhu, and keep an open eye.

We'll be entering thicker forest before the day is over."

Once they passed the last farmhouse, the owl silently enacted his name and landed on the cart. Without any conversation, he settled into a comfortable grip and went to sleep.

Back at the Green Rooster, a girl brought the three ponies from the stall. She curtsied when Tiniki gave her a copper piece for holding the reins while they mounted. They thanked her for the fine service and commented that they might stop again in the future. They then nudged the ponies into a trot.

After they left the town, they slowed down once they were able to see the cart. Looking at Anndimfoss, Tiniki easily read happiness in the glow on her face.

"I take it that you two had a most enjoyable night. Did you get any sleep?"

They both blushed.

"Enough, I hope," Ginderbar answered with a chuckle. His face then reddened further when a yawn escaped.

Tiniki clucked her tongue as she shook her head.

"I guess I'll have to keep an eye on you two youngsters to be sure you don't fall from your saddles."

All three laughed as they settled into an easy-going pace.

***

The day proved to be rather uneventful. Jienna stopped to bless two farming villages during the morning. In each case, the others kept moving, but they slowed down further along the road until she and her brother had passed them. In the early afternoon, they stopped just after entering the thick forest to eat a meal together from supplies that were stored in the cart.

Tiniki commented how the clouds had been

thickening, wondering whether rain would come before they reached an inn for the night. A few of them were startled when Fitessa informed them that there was only one small village left between here and their goal. It had no tavern and they would not, in any case, reach it before nightfall.

"Well, we's jus' gonna hafta sleep outside," Reph said, grinning as he shrugged his shoulders.

The others recognized that that was what they would have to accept. None of them had raised this question and the half-elf had not thought of mentioning it. It was not like any of them had never camped out, but they had somehow just assumed that it would not be necessary. Making assumptions is not a good habit.

***

The rain still waited as they set up camp, but it was imminent, and the clouds were very thick and dark. They made sure that the horses and ponies were all hobbled and Swoop agreed to Uhu's request to keep an eye on them. Even if there was no rain, he wasn't going to be hunting this night. A tarp was firmly fastened over the cart and two others were set up so that each could serve as a lean-to. It would be crowded quarters, but it would hopefully keep them drier.

A large stock of wood was gathered for the campfire and they then had a light supper. As they ate, Tiniki and Anndimfoss talked quietly with one another. They found that they were beginning to develop a friendship and confided a bit about the emotional stresses each had undergone. Tiniki learned of the loss of the dwarves' daughter, and she told of the loss of her loved one. While it had been ages ago, it still hurt like a fresh wound.

Jienna then gained everyone's attention by calling upon Tiniki and Uhu. She was curious to learn about the common myths of gnomes and wood elves that had been alluded to two days before.

"How well versed are you on this lore?" Uhu asked Tiniki.

"Decently. Why do you ask?"

"Because I only know bits and pieces. I'll let you be the taleteller."

"Only if you intervene when I seem to be in error."

"Fine by me!"

Moving to a position where she could see all of the others around the fire, Tiniki took a deep breath and began.

"This is the tale of origins. It is told in village gatherings to gnomish children, and it is told with pride for the role the Trickster played in creating this world.

"There once was a time when this realm did not exist. The gods were, of course, present in their realm. As far as we know, those immortal beings have always existed. What they did in the distant past is not our concern.

"Anyway, eons ago, a few of the gods got together and created a new plane, the one in which we live. As I said, it was only a few gods: the Trickster, Oak Leaf and one or two others. I do not know their names."

"Nor do I," added Uhu.

"Somehow," Tiniki went on, "they had decided that they wanted to have beings that would worship them and show them respect, making themselves more important than other gods.

"That's why they created this world, with water, land, sky, plants, the sun and the stars. They created three beings. Firsh bound the gnomes to the earth, making it their domain. Oak Leaf formed the wood elves and made their domain the plants. The other beings were given the domains of the air, fire and water. They were all dragons. Does this agree with what you have been told, Uhu?"

"Yes, except I was told the gnomes were given their mountains and we were given the live oak."

Saving Lady Noan

"Where was we?" Reph asked.

"Humans didn't yet exist," Tiniki answered. "Actually, there were no other sentient beings—beings that can think and talk. Neither were there any birds or mammals or reptiles. I don't know if bugs and fish were there, so don't ask.

"Other gods got interested in this experiment. They wanted to also be worshiped. The gods of the dragons told them to go away, but Oak Leaf was willing to share this world. The Trickster decided to side with him, but in his own style.

"Together, they placed a spell upon the fresh water of the world. As each being drank, he or she gained the ability to take on a new form. Oak Leaf and the Trickster were very creative, thinking of everything that inhabits the world. The other gods selected forms that appealed to them and made them sentient. When they were in their alternate form, they became aware of their patrons and thus shared their worship.

"But, as was to be expected, Firsh made a twist in the spell. If a being stayed too long in its other form, it was unable to change back. The new animals had to discover ways to live and survive in these forms, which amused the Trickster.

"Eventually, he and Oak Leaf ran out of ideas for new forms. They removed the spell on the water, and the Trickster pulled a new prank. Everything had to replenish their numbers by reproducing! It is said that this is the greatest prank he ever conceived.

"Thereafter, life migrated outward and populated the world."

Tiniki had been leaning forward. She now sat back and took a few deep breaths.

"Most interesting," Jienna said. "Is that what you heard, Uhu?"

"Almost. The final prank that Tiniki said was not in

our tale, but our version never tells why we reproduce, which is certainly different from the actions of the gods. Also, I was told that they kept the spell on the water on one spring. If one drinks from it, he gains the ability to change into some other form, with the risk that he might not be able to change back."

"Where is this spring?" Fitessa questioned.

"No one knows. The story says that it is either forgotten or hidden. But the tale is used to teach children to not drink from a strange spring or stream. First observe other animals and see if it affects them in any manner. This way, you can better judge if the water is safe."

"My parents said that most myths are meant to teach us something," Starspire noted, "but the reason has been forgotten for most of them. Also, in my training as a spellcaster, I was told that all dragons have the ability to polymorph. That would be compatible with this story."

Ginderbar yawned loudly, and several others found it to be contagious. They decided that they should turn in to get some sleep so that they might be ready to travel in the morning. Starspire and Fitessa agreed to take the first shift on guard duty, as they had ridden on the cart. Tiniki, Anndimfoss and Ginderbar volunteered to take the middle time. The last three would finish the night.

***

Shortly after the others had fallen asleep, the patter of rain against the leaves formed a backdrop to their snores. It grew in volume until it was all that Fitessa and Starspire heard. The rain became very heavy, and they had a difficult time keeping the fire from going out.

They were wet and miserable when their shift ended. The rain stopped just as they were wrapping themselves in their cloaks to try to go to sleep. By the time the last shift began, the clouds were departing and stars began to peer through small openings in the forest canopy.

Reph tended to the horses while his sister carried out her morning rituals. Uhu watched her, talking quietly with Swoop. It was very different from the stiff, formal ceremonies that he had observed at Panasi. The ceremonies were carried out with smooth motions, and he sensed references to nature, though he was unable to understand the druidic tongue. The prayers were all recited in mellow, soothing tones.

When she was finished, he approached her.

"May I ask questions about your religion?"

"Most assuredly. Our faith is non-secretive and open to all, despite the use of our own language."

"What are the concerns of your god, Sylvan?"

"He protects the forest, farm and field."

"That is much the same domain as Oak Leaf. Is he also strict and vengeful?"

"Only if one willfully does unjustified or evil harm to nature."

"Are restrictions imposed upon those who worship him?"

"Not really. His followers are expected to protect nature when such action is not threatening to themselves, and they should not make vain or boastful claims of what he will do for them."

"And what else is expected of those who follow him?"

"Only that they attempt to protect the fauna and flora, within the web of life, and at least set aside some time to thank him once each eightday, on his day, which is today."

"The web of life?"

"That is the recognition that a predator is allowed to feed upon its prey if it does so in the proper place. No animals or plants are wantonly destroyed. Whether a plant is a weed depends upon where it grows. Moving a plant or predator is better than removing it, if such is possible."

"I was pushed away from my tribe. At that time, I

turned my back on Oak Leaf. Your god seems to be far more caring and benign. I think I would like to be a follower of Sylvan. Is that all right with you?"

"Unquestionably. I feel certain that he will welcome you."

Jienna knew that her god would be pleased. She hugged the elf and spent some time instructing him on how to properly address Sylvan. She was happy with the sincere interest he displayed and believed that it was a positive step that would help heal this wound he seemed to bear.

The sun was rising as the others got up. It appeared that it was going to be a fine, warm day.

**

After a couple of hours, they came upon the village of foresters Fitessa had mentioned. These people drew their livelihood from the woods, cutting lumber and hunting game. Jienna spent a short time amongst them, offering blessings and advice on how to avoid stressing the resources. As before, the others slowed down until she and Reph again passed them.

Swoop was more energetic this day and he silently glided between the great trees, scouting ahead of them. At midday, he came back with a warning, which he shared with Uhu. The wood elf then called a meeting of the Coterie.

"My friend has seen a band of men camped by the road, before a bridge, perhaps two miles ahead of us. They are armed with both swords and bows and arrows. Some are on each side of the road. I would guess that they are bandits."

"What are our options?" Jienna queried as she took on her leadership responsibility.

"Well," Fitessa answered, "we could ride forward as we were and hope that they simply let us pass or at least don't slay us first and then take what they want. We could try to outflank and ambush them. We could have two or three go ahead to discover their intentions. I figure they will demand a payment for us to go by, which we could pay, or we could fight them. Anybody have other ideas?"

"If we wish to fight them," Jienna mused, "I could appeal to Sylvan to enmesh our foes with the branches of the trees and bushes in which they are hiding. That would make our task easier."

"Unquestionably!" Fitessa exclaimed.

"What spells might you be able to cast to aid us, magician?" Ginderbar asked.

"The only true offensive spell in my repertoire is Pyrra's Flame," Starspire said, "but..."

"Not openly, in the forest!" Jienna retorted.

"I understand," he said in a soothing tone, "plus, we're trying to hide my ability. I'm now Gork, remember?"

"Ah, yes," muttered the dwarf.

"Does anyone have anything else to offer?" asked the druid, looking around.

"I have a blue moonstone," Tiniki ventured.

"You do?" the dwarves said in unison.

"What's a moonstone?" Uhu inquired.

"The important point here is that it could help us move more silently, that some of us could more easily sneak up behind them," she replied.

"Wait, everyone," Anndimfoss stated. "We're looking at this the wrong way. We don't want to tip our hand before we even reach Tiufrann. We need to go ahead as simple travelers. If they attack us, then we can react, but not before. However, if your god could grant your prayer, Jienna, it could be saved as a surprise, should it be needed."

"You know, you're right. I will pray to Sylvan before we move on to be prepared, and Reph and I will shift to last position. I just hope they talk first."

"We's not gonna fight?" the berserker moaned. He'd

been touching up his bright body paints in preparation.

"Hopefully not, little brother, but if they start something, we're depending on you to be able to finish it!"

A broad smile returned to his face.

"We'll go first," Ginderbar offered, "but we should all stay closer together. Can Swoop discretely inform you of any changes in the conditions?"

"If they see him, then owl hoots shouldn't seem out of the ordinary. However, once we're near them, I won't be able to share the information with the rest of you."

"Just remember to not let them know we are aware of their presence," Fitessa advised. "That could initiate unfavorable reactions."

"Take care, an' be ready, Gin," Reph suggested.

He smiled back at the youth.

"Right. Let's ride."

***

Before they reached the bridge, they had been informed that there were eleven men in the ambush. One, armed with only a sword and wearing metal, was in the shrub by the bridge. The others, dressed in leather, were evenly distributed on each side of the road this side of the bridge. They had bows, and arrows were notched but not drawn, at least not when Swoop had passed over them. He was unable to be any more specific.

As the dwarves and gnome approached the wooden bridge, the swordsman stepped forward. His armor was chain mail, a bit rusty and a few rings seemed to be missing. He had unkempt, brown hair and a scraggly, ruddy-brown beard. Yet his eyes were clear and steady, with a visible glint, and a slight smile came to his mouth as he inspected them.

Spreading his feet, he hooked his thumbs into his belt, one on each side. His sword was sheathed, hanging untouched from his belt. The scabbard, like the rest of his clothes, was nondescript.

"Ho! Ye wish ta cross me bridge?"

"That seems to be the way this road is leading us," Ginderbar responded.

"Then ye'll have ta pay tha toll!"

"And what would happen if we can't afford it, or if we decide not to pay?"

"I don' think ye're too poorly. An' should ye na pay tha toll, then ye'll be quite sorry."

"How will you make us sorry?"

"Well, na just meself, ye see. I does ha some friends what's about ye, but ye'll do betta ta trust me."

He motioned to their sides, and arrowheads became barely perceptible through the brush.

"And what is your toll?" Anndimfoss asked.

"Ten pieces of gold."

"Ten? Do we have that much, dear," she asked, turning to her husband.

"Na, na. na... Ten pieces from each o' ye, an' don' play games. Ye keep us waitin' too long an' tha rate'll go up."

Each paid, with some hesitancy, as did those behind them. Reph growled at the swordsman, who withdrew a step, but the money was given.

They weren't happy with the expense, which they agreed was very stiff, but Jienna reminded them that their true purpose was to find and rescue a maiden, and it assuaged their feelings. Uhu muttered about reclaiming their gold on the way back, but the others reminded him that their role then should be escorting and guarding Lady Noan.

***

The afternoon continued to be sunny and warm,

though this was only sporadically apparent when the foliage above the road opened enough to allow a view of the blueness that existed above it. Uhu and Reph were most vocal in making evident their pleasure in the radiant warmth, but the others were also glad that the road sliced the forest open, allowing in the sun's rays. To either side, gaps in the roadside brush permitted them to see into the inky realm of the great trees, where the infrequent openings in the canopy created an image akin to the few stars scattered across the sky on a partially cloudy night.

The forest seemed to roll on endlessly, but, as the sky began to turn a darker shade of blue with the approach of dusk, an opening in the trees before them revealed Castle Tiufrann, perched on the lip of a cliff, its towers reaching upward from the castle's stone walls. They had stopped as a single group to gaze at their goal when a scream reached out from the forest to their left. It was high-pitched and there was a distinctly feminine tone to it.

Reph and Uhu kneed their horses, charging through the brush. They entered the darkness, responding to the wail that had reached their ears. Only a heartbeat later, Jienna followed, chasing her impetuous brother. Starspire leaped from the cart and ran after them, taking advantage of the breech in the brush created by the horses. Shouting over his shoulder, he told the others to wait unless they were called.

As they entered this ebon realm, a bright point stood out perhaps six hundred feet before them. The piteous call came from there. As they neared, details became clearer to their straining eyes while a nauseous, unpleasant odor simultaneously filtered into their nostrils.

The light emanated from the wings of a slender, apparently nude, feminine figure, at most maybe eighteen inches from head to toe. One wing was bent in a distorted angle and her scream appeared to be a combination of pain, anger and anguish. She was in the grasp of an ill-formed humanoid, towering well over eight feet in height. Its body consisted of olive-green ooze, with a mop of matted brown hair running from its head down onto its back. Some of its slime was smeared on the sprite-like female, sticking to her breasts, shoulders and legs. Her captor was shielding its eyes with its other hand as it slowly moved its prey toward its open maw.

"A forest troll!" Uhu called out, drawing and notching an arrow as he rode.

The first arrow went wide, but the second hit its target, sinking into the troll's body all the way to the feathers. An agonizing howl issued from the monster as it released its catch. She started to fall and then began to flutter upward in an erratic flight pattern until she reached a limb beyond the troll's reach. The brightness of her light dimmed a bit as her attention was diverted to her damaged wing.

Uhu imbedded the troll with another arrow, but the fourth missed as his horse shied back. The odor was becoming too strong, and his steed refused to advance. Reph's and Jienna's horses were reacting in like manner. All three dismounted, almost absent-mindedly wrapping the reins around convenient branches as they focused on the troll. Reph started to run forward, ignoring the rich aroma, while Uhu drew yet another arrow.

"Be careful, Reph!" Jienna called out.

The troll turned in the direction of her voice. Its eyes were nearly completely shut as it squinted to identify its enemy. A renewed bellow followed the entry of an arrow deep into its chest.

The wood elf was unable to fire another feathered shaft at it, however, as the berserker was between them. Starspire caught up to the others just as Reph thrust his halberd into the wounded beast, adding the force of his momentum.

"For Kreva!" he shouted.

As he pulled his weapon back, a sickly green liquid flowed out of the wound. Reph had drawn blood, of sorts, and the drugs in his body took charge, pumping adrenalin into his system. The blood lust clouded his rational thought, and he entered a state of mind frenzy where, unless his sister intervened, he would continue fighting until he or his foe was dead.

The troll flailed out with both clawed arms as Reph swung the halberd around in a full circle. Both sets of long nails raked into the berserker's painted body, creating deep gouges. Blood seeped forth from each line. Even so, the halberd completed its path and sank into the troll's head, cleaving it open. There was a loud, slurping sound, more akin to dropping a large rock into a swampy mire than the expected crack of a split skull. The troll collapsed to the ground as Reph glared around for other adversaries.

"Thank goodness that's over," the spellcaster said. "Let's tend to your brother."

"First we must finish the troll," she responded. "Strike it again, Reph!"

They watched as Reph swung his weapon down once again into the troll's inert body.

"But it's already dead!" Starspire protested.

"It's down, but that won't kill it," she called back as she ran forward. "Its body is reforming even now. It is like a simple slime mold, on a large and terrible scale. All the cells must be destroyed to defeat it."

"How can we do that?" he moaned.

"With fire, acid or direct sunlight," Uhu told him.

Turning quickly, Starspire cupped his hands around his mouth. "Ginderbar! Bring oil! Now!!"

He and Uhu ignored the message their minds were receiving from their noses and went to join the others. They and Jienna watched as Reph continued cutting into the greenish-brown mass. They also watched as previous cuts slowly but relentlessly closed as the tissue reorganized.

While it was actually quite revolting, it somehow mesmerized the three of them. Nonetheless, their stomachs tightened and their throats gagged. They were glad that they had not eaten recently.

A noise behind them broke the awkward trance. Looking up, they watched as Ginderbar approached. He glanced up at the source of light and then at the shifting blob that Reph continued to periodically and methodically deform.

"What is that?" he managed to ask between coughs as he handed two vials of oil to the young magician.

"It was a forest troll, and will be once more if the task isn't completed," Uhu said with a tone of disgust.

Starspire poured the oil over the monstrosity and then had Jienna disengage her brother. She instructed him in druidic, and he complied with her request. Everyone then retreated a bit as the spellcaster began to chant phrases that they heard but neither comprehended nor remembered.

Fire surged forth from his fingers, igniting the oil. The flames continued to flow into the conflagration, and a new noxious odor even worse than its predecessor accompanied the thick smoke that spread out. Their eyes were tearing and Jienna found that she did disgorge the contents of her stomach. But the spellcaster persevered, making sure that all parts of the troll were consumed while keeping the fire from expanding to the surrounding forest.

As the flame died down, Jienna tended to her brother's wounds, cleaning them and stopping the bleeding with strips of her blouse.

Gasping for breath, Starspire staggered over to where they stood.

"I hope that the fire wasn't visible from the castle. I tried to control and contain it, as it will be far harder to rescue Lady Noan if our cover has been blown," he said.

"I think you did an adequate job on all counts," the druid commented. "It isn't quite full darkness yet, which also helped. We'll just have to go ahead and adjust as is necessary."

"Ji, Star – I mean Gork, Uhu an' Gin...c'mere!"

The other four turned to face Reph.

The winged female they had rescued was alighting on a branch before the berserker's face. Her wing had somehow been mended and her nubile body, a lilac shade close to that of Anndimfoss's eyes, was totally clean. As they approached, their full attention was drawn to her diaphanous blue wings, her short, pink tresses and her diminutive but properly-proportioned, bare female form.

A smile was on her small face, and her blue eyes sparkled as she looked at her benefactors. She then spoke in a melodious tune:

"To you all,
I owe my life –
Let me help
you in your strife.
Give your hands
and, with a spell,
Your future
I will foretell."

Reph held his palm before her. She stepped onto his hardened, calloused hand, which he held steady. Starspire, Jienna and Uhu placed their hands around her, and she rubbed her fingers against their skin, barely touching them. The sensation was as slight as the brush of a cat's whiskers. Her lips were moving, and a barely audible buzz reached their ears, as she seemed to sing to them. Reph's hand was too high for the dwarf to reach, so he silently stepped back, not wishing to interfere with her spell.

Her eyelids closed as the chanting sound stopped. There was a moment of silence, and the others withdrew their hands. Without opening her eyes, she began to speak in a hushed monotone:

> "She is there,
> pretty Noan...
> She's not dressed...
> up in stone...
> Up, then down...
> Underground...
> There beware...
> king uncrowned."

Her eyes reopened and the lilting melody they had first heard returned to her voice:

> "Two days hence,
> pursue your deed.
> Best of luck...
> and with great speed...
> In my name
> and by my will
> Floralee
> Sassasaspill!"

There was suddenly a blinding flash of white light. As their vision returned, they discovered that the winged sprite had vanished. A thin silver ring was on the middle finger of Reph's right hand, where she had been standing. The makeshift bandages on his chest had also disappeared and the long scars from the troll's claws had sealed, looking like the wounds had been inflicted at least a full eightday before, rather than less than an hour ago.

"What happened?" Jienna asked.

"I think we exchanged aid with an ooph," Uhu answered.

"An ooph?" queried Starspire.

"Yes. The oophs are a powerful sect of the fairy-folk that were in some of the tales my mother told me. She said they have great magical powers and can both read one's mind and see into the future. She also said that they are able to only speak the truth. How the troll was able to capture her is beyond me."

"Well, what should we do now?" Ginderbar posed in a querulous voice.

A lone wolf howl sounded far to the south. Several other wolves then rapidly echoed in response, all in the same general direction.

"I think that decides matters for us," the elf said. "Let's immediately get our steeds, return to the others and make our way to that inn!"

Their actions revealed their agreement.

***

As they rejoined the rest of the party, they noticed that clouds had moved in, totally masking the heavens. Swoop flew in, informing Uhu that the wolf pack was headed in this direction, but fortunately not yet at a fast pace, so they pushed northward and ascended the ramp to reach the top of the cliff. As they went, they filled the others in on what had happened, pondering on how to correctly interpret the ooph's message.

Welcome light and noise issued from the One Claw Inn. They stopped at the stable to see that their steeds would be cared for properly. Fitessa paid one hand she recognized a bonus to make certain that the goods in her cart would not be disturbed, making it clear in definite terms that he would personally be held responsible if anything happened. They then went into the inn. The stable hands did not notice as an owl silently swooped into the open hayloft.

***

"Welcome, Fitessa!" the innkeeper called out. "You

have come at a good time. That is, if your cart is full."

"It is, Bultoo."

They firmly shook hands as they smiled with an air of comfortable familiarity.

"Are all these people with you?"

"No. Only Gork and Uhu, my two guards. I just met the other two parties as we reached the edge of the forest. As always, I want two rooms, one for me and one for my staff. Usual rate?"

"We want two rooms, too," Tiniki called out.

"And one for us," Jienna said, placing her hand on Reph's shoulder.

"I wish I could give you the business you desire, but only three rooms are available," Bultoo said, shaking his head. His full beard, streaked with white, shook back and forth over his copious stomach.

Tiniki aimed a questioning glance at Anndimfoss. The dwarf nodded and then smiled at her husband.

"We'll make do with one room," the gnome said.

"I guess my men can stay in the stable," Fitessa grumbled. "One should be there with the cart, anyway."

The room seemed to shake with the boom of thunder that rumbled on for more than just a few seconds. They hadn't seen the lightning, but it must have been close. Heavy rain began to pelt against the tavern, and the conversations in the barroom were stilled for a brief moment.

"If they don't snore, I won't object to sharing my room with whoever is not on duty," Jienna suggested.

"That is most generous of you, Druid," the innkeeper commented.

"Gork doesn't usually snore," Fitessa said. "Let me know if he gives you any trouble, Druid."

She sternly eyed the tall youth and then turned to the wood elf.

"Uhu, you'll be up tonight. Wait until this kind lady

awakens before switching with Gork."

Fitessa turned back to the innkeeper and the friendly smile returned to her face.

"And, Bultoo, let me pay you for three days, through the Equinox. If we stay longer, I'll settle with you then."

Jienna and Tiniki each paid for their room for four days. They were able to see that this pleased the innkeeper. He urged everyone to go into the dining hall while enough food was still available to feed each well.

They all ate in the crowed and noisy room and then retired for the night, except for Uhu, who made his way quickly through the rain to the stable. He had been very aware of the spiteful attitude that had generally been directed at him by the others present during dinner in the large room. Many were dwarves, but the humans expressed the same animosity. When everyone else in the stable was asleep, he eased his tension by talking with Swoop, who had been able to find a passable meal of mice in the stalls.

"The gnome was also an oddity there, but none of the spite was directed at her – only at me!"

Swoop reassured him that he had been judged solely by the way he looked and that things would change once they got to know him as an individual. The talk continued into the night, as each found points to compliment in the other. Thus passed the night as the heavy rain beat on the sturdy roof overhead.

9 – TIUFRANN

Starspire awoke to the murmur of Jienna's morning prayers. Looking at the window, he saw that the sky was clear. While raindrops sitting on the glass reflected the light from the druid's candle, he could also see sparkling stars.

Moving as quietly as he was able, he sat cross-legged on his pallet and stretched his arms, working out the kinks that had developed during the night. He had slept well and felt that his manna was fully recharged.

As Jienna completed her daily rites, the first reds and oranges of dawn began to streak the sky, spreading from the horizon. Reph began to uncurl, so the spellcaster rose and went to the pitcher and basin on the side table. He splashed some water on his face and rinsed his mouth to remove the normal morning's sour taste. Turning around, he looked at his friends.

"Let me inspect your ring, Reph. I should be able to identify whatever magical powers it has, if there is any."

"D'ya think its magic, Star?"

"Hey, little brother, remember! That's not what we're to call him, even if alone."

"Oh, right, Ji. D'ya, Gork?"

"I won't know until I look."

Accepting the ring, he sat down at the plain desk in the room's corner and set the silver circlet before him. He removed his birthmanna from within his tunic and held the ring against it. He then started to recite the now-familiar spell, making finger motions as he reached certain points.

Jienna noticed that her brother was staring intently at what was going on, his full attention directed at what was occurring. His breath was shallow and there was a glare to his eyes. She hoped that the gift from the ooph did have a power of some sort. How would Reph react if this turned out to merely be a plain ring without any magical traits? Were his sudden expectations too high, a habit he too often experienced? Would he be upset?

The casting of the spell finally came to an end. The spellcaster returned the amulet within his clothes and placed the ring on the desk. With his fingers, he rubbed his eyes while taking a deep breath.

Curiosity overcame Reph's patience.

"Well? Watcha find? Anythin' good?"

"You might say that, Reph. The ooph has given you a protective ring that is quite impressive."

"What's it do?"

"Several things...and it works whenever you're wearing it. It doesn't need to be invoked, and there's no limit to its use."

He paused as the berzerker carefully picked it up and studied it with a degree of reverence.

"Put it back on, and I recommend keeping it on the finger where she placed it."

As Reph returned it to its original position, the spellcaster stood up and stretched.

"Well, what *does* it do?" Jienna asked, her impatience evident in the tone of her voice.

"First. It makes it harder for him to be harmed, as if his skin was thicker. In addition, most harmful spells are more likely to fail when cast against you, Reph. Finally, it will assist the hand wearing it, increasing the likelihood that you will succeed at harming your foe.

"Just don't let it get to your head. It doesn't guarantee that you will always win in battle, nor are you invulnerable. Remember to use common sense before entering into battle, right?"

"Uh-huh, Gork." Reph was staring at the ring,

entranced by how much such a little piece of metal could do.

"It's still too early for breakfast," Jienna noted. "Before you replace Uhu, I'd like to go over what the ooph told us, while it's still fairly clear in our minds and before we make the plans for today and tomorrow."

Starspire sat down next to her. "Sounds fine by me," he agreed.

"First," she said, "the ooph said that Noan is there. According to Uhu, an ooph can't lie. That means that Stalif was right and we're not on a wild goose chase."

The druid stopped for a moment as she shifted in her seat to a slightly more pleasant position.

"The ooph then said that 'she's not dressed up in stone', right?"

"Yes. Perhaps that means that she's not being kept in a stone cell, such as the dungeon Fitessa told us about."

"Makes sense. I couldn't see her uncle mistreating her, just in case his brother becomes king."

"Well, Ji, the last line warned us to beware the 'king uncrowned', didn't it? Might that mean that her uncle will be the new king of Glawynia? If so, we don't want to be on his bad side, either."

They both thought for a while.

Starspire broke the silence.

"Look... The ooph said to beware him underground. If we meet him there, we'll decide what to do. If Noan isn't in the dungeon, I don't see why we'll be going underground at all. I figured that the part about up and down meant that Noan is in a room in the upper floor, so we have to go up and down to get her out.

"What I can't figure out is what was meant by underground. Could it be two separate words...under and ground? In that case, what might it mean?"

"I'm as stumped as you. Maybe Tiniki or one of the dwarves will have an idea. They have a heritage of digging into the earth. We'll have to see if we can get a chance to talk to them in an unobtrusive way."

"Hey, Ji an' Gork, when we gonna eat?"

Jienna looked at the window. A cloudless sky was visible and sunlight was pouring in. They recognized that Reph was right and further talking could wait. It was time to break the evening's fast. Then Uhu could be replaced so he would be able to eat and get some sleep. The spellcaster went down first, with the others following a few minutes later.

***

Fitessa slept late, enjoying being lazy. When she finally got up, she made her way downstairs, resuming her normal pattern. She usually visited Tiufrann about twice a year, so it was a very familiar setting, though noticeably busier at the time of this special holiday. Eating a full meal, she joked with Bultoo's daughter, Sheelta, who managed the One Claw Inn in the morning.

Only twenty-two, Sheelta had taken over this responsibility two years ago when her mother died. Fitessa had known her for seven years or so, since she had started working in the family business as a barmaid. She had a solid build, but nowhere near as large as her father. Her red hair and freckles stood out against her pale skin. Like her mother, she was sensitive to sunlight and stayed inside most of the time when it was not overcast. Friendly and open, she certainly was far from being able to be called shy, and she found it easy to share ribald exchanges with the inn's customers, both human and dwarf.

While a few boisterous voices were constantly heard in the background, no one else was in the dining hall at this hour. Talking together, Fitessa learned that most people were still abed, as they had been drinking heavily the night before, preparing for tomorrow's festivities. Sheelta and

Bultoo expected as least as much business tonight. Since Lord Blavin would be supplying free food and drink tomorrow, however, they expected the inn to be empty until people staggered back to their beds.

Fitessa was informed that her guards had each eaten and had changed shifts. Sheelta made several comments about how easy they were to recognize – a human beanpole and an elf – and hinted how Fitessa might have selected these males for qualities other than simply guarding her wares. On hearing the expected denials, Sheelta volunteered to personally test their abilities. This had become a common exchange over the years, and Fitessa was willing to bet that Bultoo's daughter had gone beyond verbal innuendos on at least two occasions.

The half-elf also learned that the druid had eaten and had left the edifice with her berserker. She had asked the locations of the farms in the area. The only others who had come in to eat seemed to have business to tend to in the city and they had wanted to get there when the gates were to open.

After the meal was done, Fitessa and Sheelta talked business. Bultoo had drawn up a list of what he wanted and now left it to his daughter to haggle over prices. With years of previous experience, they quickly came to an agreement that each found satisfactory. Sheelta then had the cook's aide go to the stable with Fitessa. He helped Gork unload what was being bought and the two of them brought it into the rear room. Fitessa carefully put the money in her pouch.

The stable hands harnessed the horse to the cart, and Fitessa and Gork rode to the castle. As expected, the northern drawbridge was down, the city gate was open and both portcullises – the one in the guard wall and the one in the city wall – were up. Five guards were on duty at the entrance: two at the guard wall archway, one atop the guard wall and two at the city gate. The first three were humans and Fitessa knew two on sight. The two at the city gate happened to be dwarves. One recognized Fitessa, though she couldn't recall his name.

"Ya' goin' to the castle or the bars?"

"To the castle first. If anything's left, I'll check out the bars."

"Good 'nuff. Ya' knows where to takes it."

"Iffen I might ask," the other ventured, "does yer also have a full elf with yer, like we's heard rumor?"

"Yes. My other guard is an elf. Why?"

"Jus' wond'rin is all," the first said. "No accountin' fer taste, but I guess what with elf blood in ya'self..."

"Anyways," the other added, "it'd be best iffen yer would have that one stay outta the city, if yer knows whats I mean."

"I understand," Fitessa answered. She nodded and then turned back to her supposed guard. "Let's get back to work, Gork. Through the gate and turn left."

Other than that short bandying with the two dwarf guards, Fitessa and Starspire found the mood of the city and castle to be quite jovial. Everyone was looking forward to the festival, and everyone who was up was busy with one task or another.

The castle majordomo was pleased to see Fitessa, and Starspire wound up driving an empty cart back to the inn later in the day. He had helped carry supplies both down to the wine cellar and up to the ballroom and stood beside his 'employer' as she was asked to sample some of the food being prepared in the kitchen.

He was tired, but they had seen part of the castle, including going to the second floor. They didn't know if it would help, but it certainly could not hurt. To maintain the cover of her normal pattern of business, Fitessa had also stopped in at the two bars, even though she had nothing to sell to them. She discussed what they might want her to bring on her next visit, as the castle normally did not purchase anywhere near such large quantities.

***

Jienna made a point of spending the day visiting many of the farmers and foresters in the region. Reph, of course, accompanied her. She offered the blessing of Sylvan, whether or not they worshipped him. The day was sunny and quite warm, so most of the workers she visited did not mind taking a break from their toil, especially as tomorrow was to be spent in celebration. The mood pervaded everywhere, and everyone was caught up in it, whether dwarf or human.

Frequently, people questioned their nationality. She was able to unearth that this was due to the ever-present fear of civil war. Once it was learned that she and her brother were Indrosian, they were viewed to be impartial and non-threatening. Even so, the local folk tended to keep away from Reph, eying his brightly painted body and the diagonal scars running across each side of his chest. He had modified the pattern of the body paint to draw attention to them, as he was proud of his first wounds earned while serving his god.

By being attentive to the chatter, Jienna picked up quite a bit of information that might be of value to the Coterie. She got a chance to share this with Fitessa when they returned to the One Claw Inn. Purely by coincidence, they returned at the same time and were alone at the stable entrance while the stable hands were working with Starspire, removing the horse's harness and putting away the empty cart. Reph waited near the entrance to the inn.

"Since dwarven-human crossbreeds are rarely fertile, there is much doubt whether Blavin will ever have any offspring. If such proves to be the case, many feel that his ascension to the throne would only be a temporary matter, and the question of his succession would return the nation to the same state of uncertainty. Even so, without exception, the citizens seem to be totally loyal to him and seem to be willing to lay down their lives for him."

"Then we must rescue Noan by stealth," Fitessa murmured, "and we will have to avoid returning here after our task is done."

"That is certainly true! I also found that a large portion of the people worship Pyrra."

"Pyrra? The god of fire?"

"His domain also includes change and the unknown, which are critical issues to farmers. While change is expected, as reflected in the seasons and the rotation of crops, many were very nervous and requested prayers to protect them from the unknown. They see the future as being very foggy.

"The important thing is that they will be taking tomorrow's holiday very seriously. I have the impression that everyone – and I truly mean everyone – will be drinking heavily. If we keep our minds clear, it should give us an edge. But we need to be as careful and as observant as we are able, so that we don't give Pyrra a chance to foil our plans."

"Have you considered how we will make our exit once we have gotten Noan out of the castle?"

Jienna quickly glanced around.

"Stop using her name!" she hissed. "Just one person accidentally hearing it could be our undoing!"

She again checked that no one was within earshot before continuing.

"And, yes, I have been thinking about it. We need to have one person outside, ready with the horses. Some signal will have to be worked out that can't be mistaken, but I haven't come up with it yet. Do you have an answer?"

"I believe so. Since Uhu won't be going into the walled city, he is our outside man. And as he was on night duty yesterday, I'll maintain that. He can have Swoop fly around the castle and let him know when we're exiting. Tonight, I'll draw up some letters of sale for everybody's horses and gear. Uhu will be able to show them if anyone questions why he is taking all of the steeds."

"That sounds perfect, Fitessa! Your expertise as a trademaster is proving most valuable."

"Well, thank you, Druid. I think that the price sounds most agreeable."

Hearing Fitessa speaking in her normal voice, Jienna then became aware that someone was approaching the stable. Thank goodness for the acute hearing of elves! Though only a half-elf, she had clearly picked up the sounds in a timely manner.

"I'm glad we were able to do business together," Jienna responded, shaking hands to close the deal. They then parted, she to the inn and Fitessa to instruct Starspire to stay on duty here in the stables.

***

Upon reaching the inn, Fitessa found Uhu sitting on the porch, lazing in the late afternoon's sun. His eyes were closed, but she was able to discern that he was clearly not asleep. She watched as his ears continuously shifted to catch the various sounds.

"Up and on your feet, you lazy fool," she said, laughter rippling after the final syllable. "It's time to eat, before the dining hall is crowded. You then have to take a dinner to your partner when you go to replace him."

"My shift already approaches?"

"Look at how low the sun is! Gork has worked while you rested. You'll now be earning your keep."

Inside, they took a corner seat and the half-elf ordered three large meals, one to be delayed until they were leaving. Bultoo stopped by to approve the morning deal with Sheelta and to find out how Fitessa had fared within the city's walls. He congratulated her on her success and then questioned why Uhu would be going to the stables.

"You know that your cart and horses are safe enough."

"First, friend, you have to remember your shortage of rooms. One way or the other, he'll be staying in the stable. And if I pay him for doing nothing, it might go to his head. What would he do when I have actual work for him? Would he demand a bonus?"

Both Bultoo and Uhu joined her as she chuckled. The innkeeper's deep voice momentarily drew the attention of all the others in the room, both staff and patrons.

"A point well worth remembering," he said, nodding in agreement with the trademaster as he returned to his own responsibilities.

As they ate, Fitessa watched for safe periods when no one was close to their table and unobtrusively explained to Uhu in an almost inaudible whisper what she and Jienna had decided. When they finished, Uhu took the food to the stable and shared this information with Starspire. The tall youth returned the tray to the dining hall before retiring to the room upstairs.

***

Two minstrels had entertained the crowd in the barroom after dinner. The holiday spirit was growing, and Reph was whistling as he and his sister finally went to their room.

Opening the door, he saw Starspire at the desk, bent over a parchment lit by a tallow candle. As Jienna shut the door, he walked over to his friend.

"What's ya' doin', Gork?"

"Reading," he mumbled. His eyes stayed fixed on the open scroll and his lips resumed their silent motions. His fingers made some quick, complex movements.

His attention was broken when he became aware that his childhood allies from Kilgali were standing to the side, silently watching his actions.

"What <u>are</u> you doing?" Jienna echoed.

"I'm studying a spell I'm trying to master."

"Oh..." The sound was uttered by Reph as he nodded. To him, that explained everything. He was fascinated with the scroll. The more intently he stared at it, the faster the squiggles of ink seemed to change and move, as if more than a hundred small worms were gyrating before him.

"Can you say any more?" Jienna queried.

Removing the crystal monocle from his eye, Starspire carefully rolled up the scroll and placed it within a narrow leather cylinder. He then inserted that into a prepared, hidden fold within his tunic, below his left arm.

Taking a deep breath, he stretched his arms and rubbed his eyes. He then stretched the fingers of each hand a few times. Turning, he looked at the others, appreciative of their patience.

"It is called Petit's Spell of Enhancement. If used properly, it can enhance any spell I am able to cast. For example, remember how I used Pyrra's Flame to destroy the troll?"

Jienna nodded while her brother absent-mindedly ran his fingers over two of the scars.

"By directing some of my manna to cast this spell, I could modify the flame. If I want, it would enable me to make it hotter, or it could last longer, or I could project it a farther distance. Do you both follow that?"

"Yes."

"Uh-huh."

"The problem is that I must memorize the words and motions perfectly. This is a very tricky conjuration. If I make any mistake, it won't work. Even worse, there is a chance that it could sour the other spell. That is, it would change and do the unexpected. It might, for example, cancel the flame, or it could cause it to flash back, consuming me.

"Therefore, once I do have it down cold, I will only use it in extreme cases."

"A wise choice," the druid noted. "You look tired. Why don't we all turn in and rest for tomorrow. We need to be ready for whatever comes our way. Let's hope that we can learn just where she is and that things all run smoothly."

***

The dwarves and gnome had spent the day inside the city, going from shop to shop. Anndimfoss and Tiniki inspected the wares, carefully comparing quality and prices, and chatting as if they were life-long companions. They talked with everyone in a friendly manner, making promises to some to be back tomorrow. While they were busy, Ginderbar got into separate discussions with the people he met.

He had an especially congenial conversation with a local miner who was visiting his brother's family. They debated the merits of the various materials each had extracted from the earth and the differences in the methods they had used under certain conditions. While he had dug for gemstones, he learned that the mines in this region mainly yielded metals. When they parted, Ginderbar felt that he had made a friend that extended beyond the professional experiences they had shared.

Anndimfoss likewise became friends with a dwarf who was a jeweler. His sister served as a castle servant, and Anndimfoss was able to get invited to have lunch with his family for the next day. She viewed that as a good investment of her efforts.

In similar manner, Tiniki depended upon her experience as a gamester to open relations at one of the bars. She learned that a group was looking forward to a high-stakes poker game in the following afternoon, and she managed to get included. While it did not relate to the group's goal, it seemed to give an explanation for her being here in the city. If nothing else, it made her feel more comfortable.

As they made their way back to the inn, they compared notes. Each had a strong contact that could be tapped for details on the morrow, but they all agreed that Anndimfoss's was the most promising.

They conversed socially with Jienna while listening to the minstrels after dinner. They agreed to walk to the city together after breakfast, hoping that they would then get a chance to talk confidentially.

When Anndimfoss mentioned that she was tired, Tiniki could read from her face that this was far from the actual reason she wished to go to bed. The gnome told the dwarves to go upstairs without her, as she hoped to find some evening activity at the tables in the bar. She assured them that she would not be up for a few hours, and she was pleased with the grateful smiles on their faces. The thoughts in her mind flashed back to when she was younger. If only that landslide hadn't taken Gatan.

A lively group of gamblers attracted her attention when she walked into the other room. She started studying their faces as she got into the random chatter of spectator conversation. Eventually, an opening formed and she took the seat. She had already developed a good interpretation of the other players' expressions, but she intentionally lost a few hands to be more certain of herself.

She then began to play in earnest, aiming more at the pleasure of winning than at the amount she was able to pull to her edge of the table. Nonetheless, she became aware of negative undertones that began to be exchanged by the on-lookers. This was especially true of the humans, who didn't seem to be aware of how well she could hear. The influence of the alcohol also had a role and the undertone began to grow hostile.

Some raised questions as to whether she served Vegar, and not merely as a gambler. They felt that she was winning too often and that this was not possible if one was being honest. Another person responded by pointing out that today was Moonday, the day for thieves. Tiniki decided that she had to clear the air.

She lost the next four hands, giving up almost all of the evening's profits. That actually did not really matter to her. She had proved to herself that she was able to beat them, and that was very satisfying. Under what wound up being a more amicable atmosphere, she called it a night.

Rainfall began to be heard as she made her way up the stairs. It was gentle but steady. Turning the key quietly in the lock, she went in and shut the door. She then closed the open window, as the rain was beginning to become heavier. The room was close to silent, with only their calm but steady breathing being audible. She gazed in the direction of the two young dwarves.

As her eyes naturally adjusted to the dim conditions, her infravision took over. They were snuggled together, Ginderbar's chest against his wife's bare back. The blanket only covered the lower half of their bodies, and she saw that one breast was cupped in his firm hand, his arm cradled over her side. They slept with smiles on their faces.

Feeling that she was invading their privacy, she turned away. Removing her dress, she crawled under the blanket on her pallet. Anndimfoss had something she had missed and a mixture of envy and wishful thoughts washed through her mind.

Though she was with friends – and she was certain that these two dwarves were friends – she was still so much alone. But she was young, having only experienced ninety years. And she also knew her body was attractive. She was able to use it to turn an interested male's head when she so desired. The problem was finding someone she was interested in attracting.

Should she just return to the mountains and find a mate? She knew that her wanderlust was too strong to allow her to merely settle down. Was the Trickster toying with her emotions? Perhaps she could find another gnome who was willing to leave the mountains and see the rest of the world with her. If not, could she find a male of another race whom she could trust with her true, open feelings?

Might she be able to find someone she could love, as she had felt so passionately for Gatan? The legends about Atiri, the great gnome illusionist who lived many centuries ago, told how she had gone abroad and had married a human archdruid. If the story was true, might not a similar future be possible for her? She just wished she could find the pleasure her friends had.

Thinking of them, she decided to carry out the prank that she had concocted earlier in the day. She exposed her moonstone, that first gift of love she had received, and used its quieting effect to move about silently. She removed the stone that she had earlier placed in her pouch and went to Ginderbar's boots.

He had the habit of jamming his feet into his boots in the morning, first the left and then the right. She had never seen him check to see if there was anything inside, even when they had camped out. That had been the kernel of the prank. Carefully, she inserted the stone into the tip of his right boot. She then returned to her pallet and went to sleep, dreaming of erotic love with a faceless person.

***

Ginderbar's scream of pain awakened her in the morning. That was followed by a sudden sensation in her hand. The ring grew warm for a brief moment.

"You're welcome, Firsh," she whispered as she began to sit up.

10 – EQUINOX

Everyone staying in the inn, other than the staff, seemed to sleep even later this morning. It was cloudy and cool, which did not encourage anyone to get out of bed. In addition, though this was court day, it was also the equinox, which superseded all else in regions heavily populated by dwarves.

The noise from the crowd in the barroom downstairs finally overpowered the urge to sleep late. Knowing there would be almost no business in the evening, the One Claw Inn was capitalizing on the morning throng as people began to pour into town for the evening celebrations.

As they prepared for the day, Tiniki confided in Anndimfoss that she was responsible for the stone that had appeared in her husband's boot. This brought a giggle from her friend. The gnome explained how this pleased her god and how he then charged her ring. She noted that the warmth of the ring had signified that Firsh accepted Ginderbar to be her friend, which pleased Anndimfoss. The point was then added that, while she may pull additional pranks on him just for the pleasure of his reactions, it couldn't be done again to charge the ring.

Over breakfast, all members of the Coterie heard several of the locals complaining about the poor weather. The wet nights were hampering haying, and the cloudy sky, today of all days, boded ill. A few made signs to Gwynterg, fearing that he was unhappy. If that was true, then a major storm was brewing. A few asked Jienna if she could answer that question, but she had to be honest. She responded that she was new to the order and could only foretell the weather for a few hours into the future.

One clear effect was that it increased the level of drinking. It had started early and was heavier than the inn had expected. Silently, the members of the Coterie considered this to be fortuitous from their perspective. Heavy drinking should make it easier for the rescue of Noan to be a success.

***

The hallway was quiet when Uhu went to the upstairs room. Jienna had gotten the others to sign the sales papers, which were left with him. Each member had agreed to leave most of their gear in the rooms, and Uhu also got the keys. Each member had been instructed to carry limited, concealed weapons and not to draw them unless no other option was possible. One risk accompanying the flow of liquor was that brawls would be more likely to occur, and bared weapons could be a catalyst. They definitely had no desire to draw attention to themselves!

With reluctance, Reph left behind his halberd and battle-axe. Jienna fastened her scimitar to her belt. The dwarves each opted to take a hand ax, while Tiniki took her dagger. Starspire continued to wear Ginderbar's sword, though it still felt out of place. Fitessa had her broad sword. Unknown to the others, two throwing knives were also hidden up her sleeves. With the exception of the berserker, the weapons were kept out of sight beneath their cloaks.

While the others started for the city gate, Fitessa and her guard went to the stables. She checked the cart, carefully transferring her thieves' tools to the inside of her tunic. She then gave a few copper pieces to the hand on duty to keep an eye on the cart until Uhu came on duty in the evening. The boy was unquestionably pleased with the bonus, which he shook in his hand a few times.

***

As they entered the gateway, Fitessa turned to Starspire.

"You need not stay right on my heels, Gork. As long as you're within sight, it will suffice."

The others had had a chance to exchange notes on the walk over. Starspire now went to Reph and talked quietly with him. Whenever anyone else was close, they heard a simple discussion of the comparison of their 'professional experiences'. A few of the guards who were off duty occasionally added their perspectives. They also compared the merits of Hispere to those of Kreva, but they avoided getting into serious religious debate.

In the late morning, a large crowd gathered in the open market area to view the entertainment that went on to pass the time. It varied as different groups displayed their abilities as a way to build up to the evening festivities. There were those who played instruments and sang, offering a wide range of styles and levels of skill. The most popular was a family of five that performed athletic and acrobatic skills. The loudest cheers and hoots came when the younger son controlled a set of eight balls, bouncing them while keeping each and every one in total control. He ended the act by passing one ball at a time to his sister as the number decreased, switching to having four all aerially juggled, which extended for several more minutes before ending the act.

All in all, the morning was entertaining but uneventful. No new or interesting information came up in the townsfolk's chatter. They did find that no one appeared to pay any notice to their meetings with one another, but they made sure to interact with others, too. They did not want to be identified as a single group.

***

At midday, Jienna and Reph stopped before an eatery

with outside tables.

"Find a table and order some food for us, Reph. I'm just going to the apothecary across the way to get some healing items. If you get in a fight again, I'd prefer to be prepared."

"Good 'nuff. What's ya' buyin'?"

"Not much. Just some disinfectant balm, a package of clean cotton strips, and probably some willow bark. I'll be back shortly."

Gork saw Reph and came over with Fitessa. They had just visited the bar next door.

"Can we join you for lunch, Reph?" Starspire asked.

"Sure, Gork."

As a serving girl approached their table, Starspire played the role of introducing the others to one another.

"This is my boss, Trademaster Fitessa. This berserker is Reph. He's the one I'm sharing a room with at the One Claw Inn."

"Yes. I've seen him before." Fitessa sat down and looked at the girl.

"The seasoned meat pies smell good. Do you feel their taste matches their aroma?"

"Yes, m'lady."

"Fine. I'll have that. You, too, Gork?"

He nodded his approval.

"Do you serve wine?"

"I can get it from next door," she responded.

"Then get me a bottle of sweet red."

"Yes, m'lady."

"What tea do you recommend?" Starspire queried.

"Spicebush, sir."

"Then I'll have that, please."

She turned to Reph.

"And you, sir?"

"Same's him, an' fer m'sister, too."

He then turned to his friend. "I'll be back, Gork. Jus'

goin' t'use th' privy."

As he looked around, Starspire saw that an off-duty guard whom he and Reph had talked to earlier in the day was staring in their direction. He was large and solidly built, with a scraggly black beard, and it was easy to recall how uncouth he had been. Starspire watched as he advanced with an uneven gait, showing the effect of the quantity of liquor he had been drinking.

He came toward their table and stopped only a few feet away. Leering at Fitessa, his eyes scanned up and down her body.

"Can't think o' much good use fer elves, lessen poss'bly in bed. Never tried one m'self...yet! Int'rested in 'sperimentin'?" A deep, guttural laugh issued forth as he continued to ogle her.

The spellcaster stood up and stepped into a position between them. He revealed his sword and nervously placed his hand upon the hilt. This was one of the worst scenarios he had imagined.

"You didn' seem to look like much o' a fighter when I metcha earlier, an' even less so now. Let's see whatcha can do, awright? But jus' fists, so's those on duty won' hafta get in the act."

The drunk stepped back and started to get ready to fight. Others cleared a space around them. Starspire was glad that at least he would not have to draw the sword. He hoped that the effect of the alcohol would give him a chance to avoid being clobbered.

At that point, Reph forced his way into the open space. He placed his fists on his hips and stared at the instigator.

"Fer 'im, it's a job." He gestured at Starspire with one thumb. "Fer me, its fun! What says we play wi' one anudder?"

"Mebbe, but I don' like takin' 'vantage o' halfwits. I hear 'zerkers don' have much upstairs!" The same laughter rolled forward again, and some of the crowd joined in. Starspire noticed that Jienna had pushed forward, a bit to his right.

"By the by, 'zerker, how'd ya' get them scratches?"

Reph glanced at his chest and caught sight of his sister in his peripheral vision. She mouthed the word "druidic" to him. He nodded as he looked back at his adversary. Clear, fluent speech flowed forth, but the drunk just shook his head.

"What's ya' say?"

Jienna took a step forward.

"Let me translate. My brother just told you that the scars are his story. If you beat him, perhaps he'll tell it to you. However, he warned you that he expects to win, and he'll be making your blood an offering to Kreva. He also added that it isn't wise to judge him by how he speaks in one language."

Reph gave a big, toothy grin.

The guard backed into the crowd, retreating to a chorus of catcalls and laughter. As the people dispersed, the serving girl brought their meals, which they consumed with pleasure. They were glad the fight had been avoided, but they wished that the event had never occurred at all. They did not need the attention, as it might prove to be a difficulty later in their effort.

***

Anndimfoss and Ginderbar had their lunch in the home above the jeweler's shop, as had been scheduled the previous day. The host's sister was a bit late, and complained loudly about the delay as she entered the room.

"I was just about to get off duty, Fin, when I got stuck feeding the prisoner Lord Blavin has up in the tower, so I had to trudge all the way up and then back down again. Why she doesn't get a single meal like the prisoners in the dungeon is beyond me!"

"Hush, Ull," Finsimpen said in a soothing tone. "Enough with your complaints about your chores. Let me introduce you to the two friends from southern Glawynia I told you I'd met yesterday. Then I'll get to the kitchen and help Ean serve dinner."

The meal was plain, but the atmosphere was friendly and more than compensated. There was a strong rapport and the five dwarves found that they all got along very well. The topics of discussion varied greatly, but neither Anndimfoss nor Ginderbar was able to unobtrusively direct the conversation back to the tempting entry statement, so they failed to learn any more details about the prisoner before Finsimpen had to end the meal to reopen his shop.

They did learn, however, that the guards were on eight-hour shifts, with one rotation being at midnight. The only dwarves who were to be on the morning shift were two who would be on duty in the dungeon. Ulltommid explained how she looked forward to celebrating with her fiancé when he got off gate duty, as her shift was to end at the same time.

As they parted, she told their new friends that she would be serving food in the castle and hoped to see them later in the evening. Finsimpen and his wife also looked forward to seeing them again.

Once they were back on the street, Ginderbar whispered into his wife's ear, "I'm glad we won't be doing anything against this family, Ann. It's too bad that we'll probably never be able to return to Tiufrann and see them again."

"Well," she responded, "there's always the possibility of getting them to visit us, once we settle down and have a home again."

Ginderbar was unsure how to interpret the quirky grin or the glint in her eyes. He wished that there were classes in reading body language.

Saving Lady Noan

***

Tiniki had chosen a lunch of pastry delicacies. While she in no way received the outright disrespect that would have been directed at Uhu, she knew that she stood out like a sore thumb. She had learned that no other gnomes had ever been in this city. Her entry with two dwarves had eased the tension a bit, but it was still present, especially with the common knowledge of gnomes being pranksters.

She discovered that she was truly pleased to see Anndimfoss and hooked arms with her friend. They then sought out Jienna. The three had agreed to spend the early afternoon shopping together, including returning to some of the merchants they had visited the previous day.

"Remember," Jienna said, "we're not going back to the inn before the celebration, so we can't burden ourselves with too many purchases."

"True," Tiniki agreed. "What if we limit ourselves to one purchase each?"

"But we shop until each of us has one item!" Anndimfoss added. The other two concurred.

The dwarf easily selected a fine shawl she had favored on the previous round. The weaver complimented her on her choice, noting how it matched the shade of her eyes.

The two shorter women then showed Jienna a skirt that had caught their attention in the seamstress' shop. It was colorful, with lemon yellow and lime green predominating, and had a matching blouse. Jienna was interested and promised to seriously consider returning to purchase them.

Out on the street, a brief discussion led them to resolve that the skirt and blouse would qualify as a single purchase. Finding nothing more appealing, they eventually returned to the shop and the druid left happily carrying her parcel.

Tiniki considered a squat sandalwood-scented candle,

but it would be awkward to carry around all day. She also liked a pair of intricately designed leather boots at a cobbler's display. Her final decision, however, was to purchase a new deck of cards. Her old cards were slightly worn, which made them only useful for playing solitaire. For those who preferred to play card games with an uneven edge, unintentional scratches marked the cards more clearly than hidden ink marks and worked just as well. Even if not used in such a manner, they could all too easily be so interpreted by one who was losing in a game played for coin or gem.

Jienna and Anndimfoss escorted Tiniki to the poker game at the dwarf-owned bar. They then joined the circle of spectators. The bouncer, a brawny youth, was over two hundred pounds of solid muscle. He warned everyone that they could only make comments and side bets between hands. If they caused any disturbance during the play of cards, they should expect to find themselves bodily hurled out into the street!

The gamblers were told that they would be playing dealer's choice, with the deal rotating after each hand. The only limitation was that no cards could be wild. No one was opposed to that. The ante for each hand was set at one gold piece, with one coin from each pot going to the house.

Finsimpen then stepped forward and offered to convert gems to coin for the players. Anndimfoss watched him evaluate the stones and found that, in general, her judgment matched his. Tiniki withdrew an emerald from a pouch within the bodice of her dress. The dwarf gave her 130 gold coins, which she stacked before her. When he finished with the last gambler, he withdrew to the bar, smiling at Anndimfoss as he passed her.

During the first hour, the gnome depleted half of her coins, folding almost all of her hands as she carefully studied the methods and mannerisms of her opponents. She then began to play more seriously. She was partial to seven-card, high-low stud poker, but she also occasionally selected five-card draw when the deal came to her.

The crowd quickly responded to the fact that she was consistently drawing in big winnings and only lost a few coins when she folded. The money steadily shifted to her side of the table. Three other players had to call upon the jeweler to convert more gems to coin.

It began to drizzle outside, which matched the mood in the room. Derogatory comments about gnomes in general and Tiniki in particular became louder and more frequent among the spectators. There were speculations that nobody could win so often if the game was being played honestly.

Then the dwarf seated opposite Tiniki abruptly stood up, knocking over his chair as he rose. He had been losing more heavily than anyone else at the table, and his face was flush with anger. He stared at the gnome, who had just finished dealing five cards to each player.

"I knew we shouldn't have let a gnome into the game! She don't have it in her to not cheat! She just slipped two cards to herself from the deck's bottom!"

The crowd erupted, but the bouncer somehow succeeded at keeping them from physically harming her. Guards were called in and Tiniki was taken into their custody. One guard took her dagger and another collected the large pile of coins at her seat.

The captain strode into the bar and the shouts suddenly simmered down to mutters. He listened to the complaints and Tiniki's denials. He then questioned the barkeep and Finsimpen.

"Considerin' the day, Lord Blavin's not goin' to hold a court session this day. We'll take the gnome to the dungeon and the money in question to the castle. It'll get sorted out in court in a couple of days. Until then, everyone better just cool down. I declare this game over!"

Anndimfoss and Jienna stared blankly at one another

as Tiniki was led away.

***

Four guards and the captain led Tiniki across the market area toward the castle. The drizzle was chilling, but at least it was thus far only intermittent. The catcalls and laughter, plus slurring comments and "I-told-you-so" refrains accompanied her passage.

While she felt panic-stricken, she kept a calm exterior exposure, just disclosing a little bit of nervousness. She remembered the advice she had received from "Uncle" Patov: "If you are ever captured, plead innocent and then appear confident. It will support your statement, even if it isn't true."

As they approached the castle gate, she saw that the portcullis was up. Two guards were on duty, and they straightened up upon seeing the captain. The party then proceeded directly down the hallway, though two of the guards, including the one carrying all of her money, turned off to the right.

A lowered portcullis blocked their progress at the end of the hall, but they turned to the left. Tiniki remembered that this was the second exit from the walled city. They then turned to the right and took a spiral stairway that descended to a lower level.

At the bottom, they turned left and followed a short hallway to a metal door. The foremost guard knocked and then pushed the door open. An odor of musky, stagnant air reached her nose as she was turned over to the two guards who were within this room. Her dagger was given to one as the captain briefly explained what he believed had happened.

Cells lined the left, right and far sides of the room. Most of them appeared to be empty. There was one dark hallway to the left, and other hallways appeared to go to the left and right at the far corners of the room. A table and two chairs were to the right and a large, metal gong was behind the door. The room was lit by two large candles in sconces situated on either side of the room. A fetid smell combining both urine and defecation was also all too present.

As she was placed in a vacant cell on the right side of the room, the captain left with the two guards who had escorted her to the dungeon. She heard the large metal door clang shut as she turned to inspect her hopefully temporary abode.

The cell was perhaps six feet wide and ten feet long, with stone walls that she could tell had been cut into the bedrock. The metal grating was closed and locked behind her. The only things in the room were a rotting straw pallet and a chipped ceramic chamber pot.

"Yer'll get dinner ev'ry night. The tray'll be taken in the morn when yer pot's dumped. If'n yer lucky, yer case'll be heard afore the nex' court day. If'n not, yer'll be 'ere fer a full eightday. If'n yer found guilty, yer may be 'ere much longer!" The dwarf chuckled.

"If yer quiet and gives us no grief, time'll jus' pass. If'n yer gives us trouble, yer'll get it back wi' int'rest. An if'n yer so inclined, we might be able to trade favor fer favor." He and the other guard both laughed heartily this time.

Tiniki watched as they returned to playing dominoes on the table. She saw a cave cricket at the edge of the pallet and feared what other creatures might be hidden within it. She sat down on a clear spot on the cold stone floor and settled into a depressed mood.

What was to happen to her now? And, even more worrisome, what would be done to her when the others rescued Noan?

**

Anndimfoss wanted to get the others and save their friend. Jienna quietly reminded her of their sworn priority and repeated that message to the others as they became aware of what had occurred. She stressed how they first had to liberate Noan. Once that was done, they could return to save Tiniki. The point was raised by Ginderbar that this might be the ooph's line of "then underground". If so, that would be when they had to beware Blavin.

"Just remember to not base our actions on fulfilling a prophecy," she warned. "It can always be explained by modifying interpretations with the clarity of hindsight. We need to keep clear minds and base our actions upon what we actually encounter."

They again dispersed to await nightfall and the celebration. For each of them, this time went very slowly and their overall mood was quite dark. However, the cessation of rainfall had a positive effect on the city's residents. Even though the clouds remained, they willingly chose to view it as a good sign, and the drinking began in earnest a couple of hours ahead of time.

The clouds prevented seeing the sun set, but the marked darkening of the sky was almost as effective. At the blast of a herald's trumpet, the entire populace of the city quieted down and generally moved toward the market area in front of the castle.

A resounding cheer issued forth as Lord Blavin appeared before the loyal audience, standing on the parapet above the ballroom. While nobility normally wore brightly colored garb, he refrained from that custom. Nonetheless, the rich quality of his distinct black and white raiment, which stood out clearly in the torchlight, identified him to everyone below.

A tall, aged man with a long, gray beard stood to his right, dressed in a plain, gray robe. A young, female dwarf stood to Blavin's other side. She wore a low-cut gown in bright orange and yellow and also had a matching conical hat. The cheers of the crowd informed any who had been unaware that this was his mistress, Esthinpeem.

"Welcome, citizens of Tiufrann! Also, a big welcome to all other guests who have come to share in the celebration with us! While this marks the turning of the year to the cold season, the well-known soothsayer, Postif, my advisor and friend, has some pleasant, warming news to share with you. Let this precede the evening's activities."

Shouts of support grew in volume and echoed off the walls. When these energetic calls of encouragement finally died down, Postif stepped forward. He waited until there was almost pure silence and then cleared his throat to obtain their undivided attention.

"Lord Blavin had asked me to foresee the answer to three questions that he felt were of great importance to both Tiufrann and all of Glawynia. Thrice have I sought the true answers. An eightday before today and again yesterday, I tended to this task by scrying, first with pure rainwater and then with boiling oil. At first dawn this morning, an augury was performed with a virgin ewe.

"The answers were the same all three times. I then spent this day in prayer, conversing with Shlomit, the goddess of knowledge. She confirmed my readings. I therefore am confident that my results are correct."

As he paused to gather his breath, a few calls rang out. They wanted to know what the questions were, and, even more importantly, what the answers were. He again effectively waited for silence.

"The first question regarded good king Linoan. The prophetic answer is that he will not last out this moon."

Lamentations arose from the audience. It was honest and came from the people's hearts. It was a combination of bemoaning the loss of their king and a fear that the nation might be thrust into civil war. The emotions washed back and forth through the multitude, but it was eventually calmed by those who reminded the rest that there were still two more prophecies and how their lord had had such a positive attitude. Eventually, the throng quieted down, with nearly every face returning to the aged man who stood atop the castle.

"The second question was from whence our new ruler would come. The answer was unquestionable. Each source said that our new monarch would come from within Castle Tiufrann!"

Happiness welled up, stronger than the response to the first prophecy, and the positive emotion spread rapidly, reaching the people in the shops and even those that were yet outside the city's walls.

Jienna was standing by Starspire and Fitessa. "The king uncrowned," she murmured at a barely audible level.

Blavin was smiling proudly, which could easily be seen by those below him. Chants of "King Blavin" began at one point and were repeated again and again until it became a uniform call of the crowd. This took even longer to die down, and Postif had to spread his arms to still the few who did not wish to stop.

"The final question was whether our new ruler would have offspring, thereby guaranteeing a smooth succession. To this, the answer was that this monarch shall start a long and undisturbed dynasty!"

As the cheers resumed, Postif stepped back and Blavin moved forward. He was beaming as he drew Esthinpeem to his side. Together they waved to everyone, and the volume redoubled. This time it was allowed to go on for a much longer period. At last, it finally died down as voices became hoarse.

"We have more to celebrate than just the Equinox!" Blavin called out. "Before you, as my witnesses, I hereby announce my betrothal to Lady Esthinpeem! May the bonfires be lit, and may you all join us in drink, dinner and dancing!"

With that, he accepted a torch that was held forward

by someone behind him. Holding it up, he turned and, as the protective tarp was removed, he lit the stack of wood on the castle rooftop. At the same time, a similar bonfire, though much larger in size, was lit on the hillock outside the wall.

The gates to the castle were thrown open and kegs were tapped. As people surged forward, the cries somehow grew even louder than they had been before. The members of the Coterie were the only ones who remained silent, but no one noticed.

11 – UP

As the celebration progressed, the six members of the Coterie operated as pairs and investigated the accessible portions of the castle. People milled around inside the entrance hallway, where a tapped keg was available just beyond the guard posts. To the right was Blavin's courtroom, with the door closed and a guard on duty. At the end of the hall there were the bases of two large towers, one on either side of the lowered portcullis before a raised drawbridge.

A guard was on duty in each, and they smiled and nodded as curious people went down the short hallways and glanced in. The portcullis was controlled from the position on the right and a flight of stairs spiraled both upward and downward. Common discussion disclosed to the members of the party that they led up to Blavin's quarters and descended to the well. Fitessa had described the opposite tower on that evening that now seemed like ages ago. The drawbridge was also controlled at this point.

Most of the traffic in the hallway flowed into the banquet hall, which was to the immediate left of the gate guard posts. Inside, there was a broad stairway going upstairs. Distributed around the room were large tables bearing trays of various foods. Servants moved in and out of the kitchen, removing empty trays and replacing them with ones laden with new offerings, meeting the demand of the happy throng.

Anndimfoss saw Ulltommid and exchanges greetings.

"How are you holding up, Ull?"

"It's not too bad, Ann. We prepared the foods, and

most trays are ready in the guards' mess hall. The dancing will be starting upstairs, and most folk should soon direct their efforts to simply drinking. Within an hour, this room should be fairly quiet. The last two hours before I'm off will be easy!

"I look forward to seeing you and Gin then. For now, I better get back to my job."

A small group of musicians were situated in one corner of the ballroom. As they began to play, people danced to the lively, active music, building up a sweat while adding to the merriment. Blavin and Esthinpeem set the tempo. Two guards stood by the archway that led into a hallway that had to go to the various rooms on the castle's second floor. They scanned the multitude in motion, keeping a careful, protective eye on their lord and his lady.

***

As had been prearranged, the three pairs met outside in a shaded corner of the market area, keeping a careful eye that they were not being watched. They quickly exchanged their notes in terse statements. They then turned to Jienna to decide their course of action.

"Since your friend told of a female prisoner in the tower, Ann, that will be our first target. Too many witnesses would see us forcing our way past the pairs of guards in the ballroom or before the courtroom, so they are both out.

"I therefore suggest that we take out the dwarf guard in the left tower. If you look up, you can see that the top of the other tower is partially collapsed, so I don't think it is in use. Also, note that a guard is on duty at the top of the left tower."

Everyone quickly glanced upward and confirmed Jienna's comments.

"That means we'll have to be quiet. I wish we had

Tiniki's moonstone," Ginderbar murmured.

"So do I," she responded. "Anyway, to conceal our activity, I figure you'll slip on the guard's tunic and replace him, Gin."

"Where will the body go?" Fitessa asked.

"It could be hidden behind the crank that lowers and raises the drawbridge," Starspire suggested.

"Remember," Fitessa added, "servants may be going downstairs for food. The stock of drink will hold for a while before they have to go to the wine cellar. Don't get into any discussions, Gin."

"From what my friend said," Anndimfoss offered, "they shouldn't need to get food for several hours."

"Fine," Jienna said. "We'll try to move as rapidly as possible while staying quiet. What spells do you have that will assist us, Gork?"

"The only three that I think will be of any use are two cantrips – Lamanna's Light and Distract – and a Throw Voice spell. The last two can give an edge against the guard or anyone else we meet."

"Those are better than any I can offer for inside a stone structure. It is not my god's realm. You will help Gin and Ann displace the guard. You and Reph will then lead the ascension. Ann and I will follow, and you will come behind, Fitessa, as we may have to call upon your skills with locks.

"Any questions?" She looked around, making eye contact in turn with each of the others. "We want to be done before the guards rotate, so we have a bit over two hours. Let's sift back in and meet at the end of the hallway. When I make a downward hand motion like this, the three of you will go in and take out the guard." She gave a quick demonstration. "We'll give you one minute and then join you.

"Good luck, everyone, and may Sylvan aide us!"

The rest added quiet appeals to the gods they served,

and the party split up.

***

Within ten minutes, they all were in the hallway. No one was stationed at the gate guard post, but that was not surprising, as the castle – or at least a portion of it – was open to everyone. Fitessa got into a conversation with the bored guard at the door that led into the courtroom. Jienna and Reph stood by the empty keg. Enough drinks were available elsewhere so that this one had not been replaced.

The other three drifted to the far end of the hallway, where Ginderbar and Starspire chatted quietly. At this point, there was only one other couple in the hallway, and they were walking toward the gate. Jienna gave the signal and the three disappeared around the corner to the left. Reph began to walk slowly toward where they had been, and Jienna then followed.

At the entrance to the tower, Starspire stopped just before the archway. The two dwarves stepped in, acting as if they were slightly drunk. Ginderbar had a mug of ale, which he offered to the guard on duty as he staggered forward.

"Mights ya' like ta' share inna Equinox spirit?" he slurred.

"Thank you, friend, but I'm still on duty...but only a couple of hours to go now."

"Well, frien', my name's Ginderbar. Wha's yers?"

"Pastiffon. Again, thank you for your offer, but you'd best be heading back to the banquet hall."

At this point, Ginderbar dropped the mug. Taking the signal, Starspire glanced around the corner and quickly cast a distraction cantrip on the guard. Pastiffon had glanced at the broken mug and now found that he was studying it.

Anndimfoss was moving cautiously to the right. With the guard turning his head, she was fully behind him.

Rapidly drawing her hand ax from beneath her cloak, she hit Pastiffon squarely on the back of his head with the side of the blade. His body crumpled to the ground. A little blood seeped up into his hair, but he was breathing.

They quickly removed the tunic bearing the Tiufrann coat of arms. Ginderbar took off his cloak and tunic and redressed. Dragging the unconscious dwarf out of sight, the other two tied his hands and gagged him. Ginderbar placed his clothes and ax with the guard and transferred the short sword to his belt.

A colorful motion made them jump, with both dwarves going for their weapons. They relaxed when they saw Reph at the doorway. He had moved up silently, thereby startling the three of them. Jienna and Fitessa appeared behind him.

Moving the mug out of sight, Ginderbar assumed Pastiffon's place. He gave the others a signal of good luck as they began to silently ascend the stairs in the order previously set by the druid.

***

At the top of the stairs was another guard station, but it was presently unattended. There was an archway into a dim hall, with some light coming from a more distant source. Starspire cast a cantrip of Lamanna's Light. The pale blue light radiating from his palm was enough to tell that the rest of the small area was empty.

He and Reph continued up the next flight of stairs. However, when Fitessa reached the landing, she stopped and went to the archway. Peeking out, she saw that no one was there. Glancing back, she watched as Jienna followed Anndimfoss up the stairs. She then listened carefully and stepped into the hallway.

Their action was permanently shutting off a profitable market. It would probably have far-reaching repercussions.

Her desire to accumulate wealth superseded her other motivating forces. She rationalized that the others could rescue the girl without her assistance. Meanwhile, Blavin's wealth was unprotected. How could she pass it up when she was this close?

She eased her way slowly and silently down the short hallway. A doorway was on the left. This was probably an alternate entry into Blavin's quarters, aside from the other tower stairway. The half-elf decided to explore further, so she passed it and approached the end of the hall.

It ended at a moderately lit hallway running in a perpendicular direction. Carefully peering around the corner, she heard music to the right. She could make out the back of a man – perhaps a guard? – at an archway farther down the hall. That was probably the ballroom. She withdrew and returned to the door she had previously passed.

Placing one ear against the door, she held her breath and listened. The only sounds she perceived were the beating of her own heart and faint strains of music echoing down the hallway. The room beyond this door seemed to be silent. Placing her hand on the knob, she was not surprised to find that it was locked.

She glanced at the lock as she withdrew a strong, thin pick from the kit stored under the waistband of her skirt. Inserting it into the keyhole, she found that her mentors had been successful in their training. She slowly turned the knob and then slid into the darkened room, closing the door behind herself.

***

As Starspire reached the third floor, he motioned to those behind him to wait, cupping his left hand over the light emitting from his right palm. An archway opened onto the castle's roof, and voices could be heard outside.

Looking out, he saw three guards standing around the bonfire, feeding the flame and joking with one another. None were facing inward toward the tower.

He used his cupped hands to signal the others to follow and began ascending the next flight of stairs. If they were now discovered, they would certainly be in a difficult position. They were fortunate that no one was expecting them. He hoped that their luck would hold out.

At the next landing there was a door with a grated opening...obviously a cell. Letting a bit of the light project through the bars, he saw that it was empty. A few strands of straw were all that lay on an otherwise bare stone floor. A pair of chains hung from the wall, and a grated window was on the far side. Reph and Anndimfoss had joined him on the landing, and Jienna was already visible.

Holding a finger to his lips, he started to move toward the next level. The others followed.

As they ascended, they came upon another cell, but this one had a dark cloth hanging over the grating. Moving it aside with one finger, he peered inside.

The floor was covered with straw and a body, wrapped in a blanket, was beneath the chains. The prisoner appeared to be asleep, but Starspire somehow had a strong gut feeling that this was Noan. He carefully tried the door, but it was locked. He would have been astounded if it was otherwise.

Silently, each member of the group joined him. After Jienna was there, they waited for the thief, but she did not appear.

"Where is Fitessa, Ji?" Starspire whispered.

"How do I know?" she hissed back. "I thought she was behind me."

"With no thief, how do we open the door?" Anndimfoss queried.

"What if'n I breaks it?" Reph suggested.

"Someone down there?" a voice called from above.

They froze in place as the magician cancelled the light.

"You complainin' again, miss? If so, you'll just hafta wait 'til mornin', so go on back to sleep."

As they waited with stifled breath, their eyes adjusted to the limited light coming from the level above. Starspire tapped Reph and pointed at the berserker's sword. He silently slid it from his sheath and then followed the spellcaster, staying merely a single step behind him.

They moved in slow motion, avoiding making any sharp impact with their boots against the stone steps. The light increased as they spiraled upwards. Starspire finally reached a point where he could see a torch and a large metal gong. Another step enabled him to see a guard leaning against the parapet. His eyes were halfway closed.

Signaling Reph to charge, he cast a distraction cantrip, hoping surprise would give his friend the edge he needed.

Moving forward past the spellcaster, Reph shot at his target, sword held out as an extension of his arm. The guard looked up as the name of the berserker's goddess issued from Reph's lips. Eyes opening wide and mouth forming a broad "O", the guard's hand was just beginning the motion toward the hilt of his sword as Reph's long blade forced its way through his leather armor. It punctured a lung, and blood spouted forth as the metal was withdrawn. His arms swung outward as his body fell forward. First his knees hit the stone floor, and the rest of his body finished the motion. A red pool began to spread outward over the stone.

It had all occurred in an instant, and Starspire hoped that no one below had been looking upward. Reph looked around, seeking additional enemies. Taking a deep breath, he shook his head and stared at his friend, fortunately recognizing who he was. He shook his head once more and then wiped his blade clean on the guard's tunic before resheathing it.

Starspire noticed a ring of keys on the guard's belt and

unhooked it. He then motioned to Reph to follow him back to the others. The bloodlust and adrenalin were both draining from the berserker's system, and he would need to sleep before he could again perform at anywhere near this level.

***

The keys were held up as they joined the others. Reph and Starspire were smiling broadly.

"It looks like we solved two problems," Jienna noted. "How are you, Reph?"

"Jus' fine, Ji. Mebbe a bit tired, but I knows I pleased Kreva!"

"Mm-hmm. Well, keep it down, little brother. Now let's see which key works and if we can make it out without any more confrontations. I don't want to push our luck."

Starspire began to go through the ring, one key at a time. He succeeded on the fourth try and swung the door open. It squeaked slightly, but the body didn't appear to move.

"I'll keep an eye out here," Anndimfoss offered.

"Good. You stay with her, Reph, and you come with me, Gork."

It was hard to see, but Starspire noticed an unlit torch in a sconce just within the cell. He lit it with a Fingerflame cantrip. As it sputtered into life, light flooded the small room.

The chains from the wall led into the ball curled within the blanket. All that was visible was a bare leg that stuck out the other end. Jienna went over and slowly peeled the blanket back. A mop of dark hair came into sight, followed by Noan's face.

As her eyes popped open, the druid clamped a hand firmly over Noan's mouth.

"We're here to rescue you. Please, you must stay

silent!"

In a reflexive movement, Noan kicked outward, throwing the blanket aside.

"She's naked!" Starspire exclaimed as he spun around, blushing, until his back was to her. "The ooph's statement had been two separate lines, Ji, telling us about her being 'not dressed' and 'up in stone'!"

Meanwhile, Jienna had released Lady Noan's jaw. "Your father sent us to get you out, m'lady."

She saw that the chains were attached to the girl's wrists.

"Gork, give me the keys."

He reached out behind himself, dangling the ring from one finger. Jienna took it and fumbled until she found the right one.

"Thank you! Please, just call me Noan. How do you plan to sneak me out?"

"First, we have to dress you. Put on my cloak. On second thought, take this skirt and blouse. You're a bit larger than me, but they will have to do."

She offered the package that had previously slung over her shoulder and had been dropped absentmindedly by the doorway as she had entered the cell. Once Noan had donned the garments, Jienna gave her cloak to the girl.

"I only wish I had spare footwear for you."

"Don't worry. My feet aren't overly tender. Might you have a sword I can use, though? If need be, I want to be able to help in any fighting."

"Take this one," Starspire said, offering Ginderbar's. "It belongs to another member of our party, and I can't really use it, anyway."

She eyed him as she fastened the sheath to the waistband of the skirt. Noan then looked at the others, partially visible outside the cell.

"How many are you, in all?"

"Eight, or perhaps nine, if you count Uhu's owl," the

druid responded. "I am Jienna. This tall one is presently going by the name of Gork." She led Noan out of the cell. "Here's my brother, Reph. And this is Anndimfoss." Each bowed his or her head in turn.

"I'll introduce the others later, once you get a chance to meet them. For now, we need to get out of here.

"Before we go, though, we need to know how many people will recognize your face."

"Not many. Besides my uncle and the few soldiers who brought me here, only three serving women have seen me."

"We hadn't thought you would be mistreated like this...being chained and naked in the cell, even though your party was slain, with the other women raped," Starspire said.

"Actually, my uncle wasn't guilty of that. We had been attacked by an orc raiding party. They were going to hold me for ransom when my uncle came upon them. He rescued me, but then decided to take advantage of the opportunity."

"The carnage that was described matched my experience with orcs," Anndimfoss said in disgust, remembering the raids upon her village.

"You said your uncle was taking advantage of having rescued you," Starspire ventured. "Can you explain?"

"After he brought me here, he was trying to decide what to do. When his soothsayer said he was to be the future ruler of Glawynia, he chose to hold on to me as insurance. Once he became king, he said he figured my father would be unable to take any action against him.

"The cell conditions were to keep me from socializing with the guards and influencing them. The only people I've seen in over a full eightday have been three dwarven servants. I knew Father would send help, but I was starting to wonder when you would get here!"

"Enough!" Jienna declared. "We can talk more later.

Now our priority is to get out. Reph is drained, Ann, so you and Gork will take the lead. You'll guard our rear, Reph.

"Now, let's get going, quickly, quietly and carefully!"

12 – DOWN

U hu had gone to each of their rooms, and everyone's gear was packed in the cart, hidden under the tarps. It actually was not really that much, and the cart still appeared to be void of anything worth taking. He was pleased with that and hoped that any others passing by would perceive it the same way.

The one boy on duty in the stable was asleep, snoring soundly. Uhu had the signed letters within his tunic, but they would only be needed if he was questioned outside of here, and then they would only be useful if that party could read. He could probably take a few extra horses without being noticed, but he saw no reason to create problems.

He just wished that the waiting would end. Time seemed to be merely creeping along.

As if on cue, Swoop glided into the stable, alighting beside him on the edge of the stall.

"Have you seen them? Are they on their way here? Is it time for us to go?"

"Calm down, my friend," the owl responded. "I'll try to answer your questions, but I am only able to reply to one idea at a time.

"First, there is still time before they will be out of the castle, but it may be soon. I have seen some of them and just wished to inform you before I return to patrol. I figured you would be restless by now."

"You read my clearly, even when we are apart. Fine. What do you have to say?"

"I saw the ones you call Reph and Gork atop the stone spire, where Reph slew the human who was there. They then withdrew within the stone structure."

"Thank you! Unquestionably, they have begun the action that was the purpose of this trip. Return to your patrol, friend, and keep your keen eyes searching for their exit from the castle. I will gather the steeds and move out onto the road headed southward toward the descent from the cliff's edge. When you see them again, inform me. If you can, you will then direct them to where I will be."

As the owl flew off, Uhu saddled his horse. He then placed the rest of the saddles in the cart. Gearing the horses and ponies might raise questions that the letters would not answer. He harnessed another horse to the cart and tethered the other steeds in two lines at the rear of the cart. His horse was tied to the front corner.

Throughout these efforts, the boy fortunately slept on, oblivious to it all. Looking outside, the elf studied what he saw. A bonfire on the hillock to the northwest was lighting up the farmhouse in the region and a rather large crowd was gathered around it. None seemed to be facing in his direction. He also saw the tip of the other bonfire flickering above the castle's parapet, and he could make out some people at the castle's entrance.

No one was anywhere near the inn, and the two farmhouses along the road to the south were dark. The sky was totally clouded over, which meant he and the horses would be invisible to humans, and dwarves would only see them if they were away from any lights. The bonfire on the castle roof removed most risks, and Swoop had assured him that there was now no guard at the top of the tower.

Quietly and calmly, he had the horse pull the cart out into the street and turn to the selected road. The rest of the animals docilely followed along.

He would again be waiting, but it was with a more directed purpose and role. Nonetheless, it would also be riskier. That was why he had his bow and arrows on the cart seat by his side, with only his cloak shrouding their presence. He hoped he would not be placed in a position where he would need to test his ability.

***

Not many people passed Ginderbar at the tower guard post. Everyone seemed to be fully engaged in the celebrations, with drinking having almost fully replaced eating. He also heard the music and stomping from the ballroom above, with whoops and cheers occasionally reaching his ears.

A few curious souls just glanced in, and they accepted the smile and nod he offered, imitating what he had seen earlier. The deposed dwarf was still silent and motionless, which Ginderbar confidently felt would last until they had left the castle. His wife had given the fellow quite a sound blow!

Two humans, wearing tunics with the Tiuffran coat of arms, walked past, coming from the barracks or mess hall. They each had a large mug in hand and were joking with one another. Obviously, they were off-duty guards.

One glanced over at Ginderbar, holding up his drink in salute.

"Don't worry, Pastiffon. Drink'll be left fer you, too. It's less'n two hours 'til I'm to replace yer."

"If he ain't, start without 'im!" the other called out.

"Mm-hmm," Ginderbar answered, nodding and then looking aside.

They continued on their way.

Glancing upward, he made a quiet appeal to his wife and friends: "Find the girl and let us get out of here!"

***

Tiniki sat in her cell, bundled in her new shawl. The dinner had been plain, but at least it filled her. She had also watched one guard take a very large tray of food down one of the hallways and then a normal tray down another. Her curiosity was gnawing at her, but she forced her mind to put it aside, along with a couple of comments the guards had exchanged. Her personal concerns were more serious and far more immediate.

Working slowly when the guards' attention was elsewhere, she had carefully removed the garrote from her belt and her kit of tools from her boot. They were hidden beneath the straw, unobtrusive but right at hand.

She had resolved to make her escape tonight and was now working on the details. The lock was simple, and she was confident that she would be able to pick it fairly quickly. All she would need was a distraction.

That could be supplied in one of two ways. If the others succeeded at rescuing Noan, it should undoubtedly cause quite an uproar once it was discovered. That would be the optimal condition. The alternative would be the change of the guard, as these two dwarves were looking forward to getting drunk, and their replacements would hopefully be at least tipsy.

She planned to use the garrote to overpower one guard, taking his weapon from him. Acting quickly, she should be able to then at least disarm the other. If all else failed, she could turn to the Trickster and use her ring. The single guard at the top of the stairs would then be the only barrier between her and escape.

Of course, once she was out, there was the problem that she was the only gnome who had ever been in this region. Trying to maintain an optimistic attitude, she decided that she would have to face that when it came up. Cross one bridge at a time.

***

As the door closed behind her, Fitessa stood still for a few minutes, allowing her infravision to come into play.

She then cautiously advanced down the dark, narrow hallway until it opened into a room. She was glad that no animals were visible, but the heat in the room was so evenly distributed that nothing in particular could actually be perceived. The only exception was the fireplace at the opposite end. The dim warmth she was able to visually perceive meant that embers were buried beneath the ashes.

Feeling around, she found a candle on the mantle, and next to it were several long, wooden splints. She thrust one into the ashes so that it hit an ember and it was ablaze when she withdrew it. This momentarily blinded her, but her eyes quickly readjusted to normal vision. She then lit the candle and tossed the splint into the fireplace.

Looking back, she could see the short hallway leading to the door. Tapestries covered the wall to her left and the curved edge of the other tower. A doorway evidently led to the tower stairway. Another door was opposite it, on the same side of the room as the fireplace, but on the other side of a plush bed. Drawn curtains shut off the windows, though there would be nothing to see at this time on such a cloudy night.

A rapid visual survey of the room revealed that the other furniture consisted of a brightly painted wardrobe, a desk made of polished oak, a matching dressing table and two dressers. The floor was thickly carpeted. Some jewelry sat on the dressing table, and Fitessa went over to examine it. She was uncertain of its true value, but she nonetheless quickly transferred it to her pouch. An ornate jewelry box sat on the table, but it was locked, and the thief found that she was unable to pick the lock.

The box was too large to conceal and it would be difficult to carry. She also could not afford making the noise that would assuredly result from trying to break it open. Unhappily, she left it there. A cursory inspection of the wardrobe and dressers disclosed several expensive items of clothing, but nothing that she could easily conceal and take with her.

Swearing softly, she decided to check the other door before carrying out a more careful search of the room. Trying the latch, she was pleased to find that it was not locked. She slowly inched the door ajar, but she opened it fully once she ascertained that the next room was dark.

Holding the candle aloft, she saw that this room was windowless. The outwardly curved corner disclosed that this was the southeast corner of the castle, with the defensive crenelated parapet on the roof above. There was a bolted door on the right side of the room, and the walls were covered with tapestries. On second thought, she considered that there might be arrow-slit windows concealed behind the tapestries, but that was of no actual importance to her.

Three chests were arranged along one side of the room, and a ceremonial sword lay atop one, undoubtedly belonging to Blavin. Other paraphernalia, much of it ornamented with gems, was distributed on a pair of shelves. Fitessa assumed that this was the castle treasury, and she gloated over the wealth that was hers for the taking.

As was to be expected, the chests were locked. Setting down the candle, she withdrew a pick and finagled with the chest closest to her. With a bit of finesse, she got it to open. Removing the lock, she raised the top of the chest.

Before her was a multitude of coins. Most were silver and copper, but a reasonable quantity was gold, glistening before her eyes thanks to the candle's light. She ran her hands through the pieces of shining metal, enjoying both the feel and the sound. Unfortunately, she would be unable to take this with her. Perhaps one of the other chests contained gems? If not, she would have to select from among the jeweled items on the shelves.

A noise caught Fitessa's attention. Freezing, she gave her total attention to what was perceived by her ears.

A key was being used to unlock the entrance to the

other room! Moving quickly, she closed the door to the treasury. She then stood very still. Hopefully, she would not be discovered. Breathing slowly, she tried to calm her racing heart.

***

Anndimfoss and Starspire led the way down the spiraling tower stairs, proceeding slowly but steadily, valuing stealth over speed. They went step by step, regularly pausing to listen to the sounds. They could hear noises from the reveling crowds, but everything was distant, which was what they desired.

There was no trouble on the deserted fourth level, as they had expected. The next landing was different, though. It would be necessary to pass the archway leading out onto the castle roof. Guards should still be there, standing near the bonfire to keep it burning actively. It was hoped that the liquor would be clouding their attention and vision, but care was of the utmost importance.

Starspire discretely looked out at the blazing pile of wood. It was smaller than when they had ascended, but it still burned brightly. A voice rang out, completing a ribald tale, and was followed by a chorus of laughter. The guards were off to one side. Only one was visible, and he was facing away.

With a hand gesture, the spellcaster had the dwarf cross the opening, staying back in the shadowed region. As Noan and Jienna reached the bottom of the stairs, he traversed the flat stones. He waited for the remaining three to make it across and then took off to follow Anndimfoss.

***

As the players had stopped the music for a rest, Blavin and Esthinpeem had excused themselves from the ballroom and went past the two guards, taking a torch with them.

Blavin had been in a most high-spirited mood and had been exerting himself more than was his norm. On his lover's advice, he had agreed with her suggestion of freshening up and changing their clothes, as there were still many hours of partying ahead of them.

Unlocking the door, he pushed it open. Holding up the torch, he swept out his other arm, bowing to his dwarven mistress.

"After you, m'lady!"

"Why, thank you, kind sir!"

As he followed her into the room, they both came to a sudden stop. The wardrobe and several drawers were open, which was not how they had left the room earlier in the evening.

Esthinpeem was about to speak when Blavin placed a finger upon her lips. He then pointed to the door on the far side of the room.

The torchlight lit the door dimly, but a thin line of light ran the length of one edge of the doorframe. There was no question about it. Someone was in the treasury!

Blavin stepped backward, motioning her to follow. At the doorway, he whispered into her ear, "Get the ballroom guards, quickly!"

In but a moment, they were by his side, swords drawn. "M'lord?"

"A thief is within the treasury. Remove him by whatever means is easiest!"

As the guards strode across the room, Blavin placed the torch in a wall sconce. He then went to the tower door and opened it, calling for the guard below to sound the alarm and come upstairs at once.

The two guards in the room were already at the other door. The first stood to the side as the second pushed it open. He was greeted by one of Fitessa's throwing knives, but it just grazed his cheek. The cut burned as blood began to dribble into his beard.

The second knife missed him completely, digging into the wood of the door as he entered the room, his partner now behind him. She drew her broadsword as he stepped forward and met him so that he would be actively engaged. This would hopefully mean that the other would be unable to pass him and then move behind her.

He held back, allowing her to swing first. Yet, once her motion had begun, he quickly responded, parrying her blow. Fitessa felt the clash of metal against metal, stinging her hand. She felt trapped. Panicking, she made a wild, wide arc before her.

The guard, experienced and calm, waited for the blade to pass. He then took a half step forward and thrust his blade before him below her left collarbone.

Fitessa screamed out in pain. The sharp intensity caused her to reflexively release her sword, which fell to the ground. She blankly stared upward and her mouth opened wide, desperately drawing in air. As the guard withdrew his broadsword, she felt the warm flow of blood between her flesh and the clothing that covered it. The fluid seemed to surge down her body in slow motion as other sensations lapsed. Her eyes glazed over as she fainted and her still body then collapsed to the floor.

***

The scream rang out a moment after a loud horn had sounded. None of them knew what either meant, but they sensed that neither could be good. Anndimfoss had just reached the second floor and Reph had just left the roof landing.

Hand ax in her right hand, she waved Starspire on past her. She was certain she heard footsteps approaching, so she stood her ground as Noan passed by.

A guard appeared in the archway, facing the descending stairs.

"Pastiffon! Get up here! A thief is in our Lord's room! There may be others!"

Not wishing to lose the advantage of surprise, Anndimfoss swung the ax down, hitting him soundly in the back of the head. The blow dented in his helm and he fell forward. His forehead hit the stone floor with a resounding thump, and his body lay inert.

Jienna had stopped a few steps back, her scimitar out of its sheath. She now glanced behind her.

"Where's your brother?" the dwarf queried.

Jienna just shrugged her shoulders, an anxious look on her face.

***

Reph had stopped his descent when he heard boots stomping down the stairs. He knew he was in a weakened state, but he had enough sense to know he should not leave his back exposed to a foe.

His deadly instrument ready, Reph watched a half-soused guard stumble down the stairs. His sword was sheathed and he lacked a helm. He came to a stop as he discerned the berserker before him, uncertain of what he should do.

As he groped for the hilt of his sword, Reph responded.

"For Kreva!" was released as a battle cry as he lunged forward.

The guard managed to pull back in time to avoid being skewered, but he still had not yet gotten his weapon free. Unable to back up the stairs, he could not evade the next thrust. It pierced his gut and his hands reflexively went to his stomach.

Reph twisted the blade, pushing it in deeper before extracting it. Involuntarily, the guard relieved himself as gore spilled forth and blood drooled from his mouth.

His body crumpled to the stone stairs while the enraged berserker searched for other adversaries, but none were to be found.

***

In response to the horn, a guard came running from the barracks toward the tower stairs. Ginderbar moved forward to meet him in the archway, which was a far more defensible position. He did not know what had gone wrong, but he figured that they were going to have to fight their way out.

The guard's vision was focused beyond him, so the dwarf braced himself and raised the sword just as the guard reached him. The running guardsman impaled himself. The blade entered just below his sternum and punctured a lung. He gasped and folded up, his knees giving out. The unconscious body fell into the hallway and blood began to coat the polished stone.

Ginderbar noticed that Starspire was behind him and he recognized that the girl coming down the last stairs was Lady Noan. He also saw another guard coming from the hallway, with drawn sword. This time he would not have the advantage of the surprise factor. He therefore turned his full attention to this adversary.

***

Jienna heaved a sigh of relief when her brother appeared.

"Get moving, you two!" Anndimfoss hissed, staring down the hallway.

As they passed her, she saw another guard approaching the stairway. This end of the hallway was still dark, so, as she stepped into the open, she immediately threw her hand ax. It swirled through the air and dug into his chest. Not waiting to see the resulting effects, she took off after the others as fast as her short legs could manage.

At the bottom of the stairs, she saw her husband actively engaging another palace guard, who was bleeding from a gash in his left shoulder. The other four were apprehensively watching the combat. Footsteps rang from above, growing louder as they came closer. At least one more guard could be seen approaching from beyond Ginderbar. Things looked dismal.

"Downstairs!" Jienna ordered. "We have no other choices!"

Starspire led the others down the stairwell, which was familiar to him. Anndimfoss stopped to reclaim Ginderbar's hand ax as he finished off his current foe with a successful parry and thrust. Glancing down, she noted that Pastiffon was still motionless.

The enemy at the archway was attempting to cautiously maneuver his way over the two bodies. Ginderbar made a deep cut into the human's thigh, but he received a blow in return, slicing into his left arm. His wife saw someone else coming into view on the stairs above them and hurled the hand ax. Again, her aim was true. It sank in below his abdomen and his falling body crashed down to the stone floor below.

"Come, Gin!" she shouted. "We have to retreat and join the others!"

No further coaxing was necessary. He turned and followed her, though they knew it would be but a moment or two before other guards were pouring down the stairway in pursuit.

***

"There seem to be two choices," Jienna commented to Noan at the bottom of the stairwell. "We can go down the hallway or try this metal door."

"It isn't really a choice," Starspire said. "The hallway

leads to the wine cellar, which is a dead end. I believe the door enters the dungeon. It is probably also a dead end, but it is defendable."

He turned to the berserker.

"Help me move straw to the bottom of the stairway, Reph. It may help buy us time once the others are down."

They quickly moved much of the straw, which covered the floor, from the region before the dungeon to the base of the tower. As the dwarves passed them, Starspire signaled for everyone to enter the dungeon. Boots could be herd tromping downward.

As Jienna and Ginderbar pushed the door open, the spellcaster recited the incantation for Pyrra's Flame. Just as the first legs came into sight, fire leaped forward from his hands, igniting the pile of straw. Not looking back, he followed the others.

Forcing their way into the stone room, they saw two guards. One drew his broadsword as he stepped away from the table. The other pushed back his chair as he began to get up.

He suddenly was grasping for his throat as his body reeled backwards against the cell gate behind him. Tiniki had reacted instantly to her friends' entry. She had reached through the bars and successfully slipped the garrote around the guard's neck. He was now her prisoner!

Ginderbar and Jienna stepped forward to meet the advancing guard. Meanwhile, Reph, Anndimfoss and Starspire closed the large metal door and slipped the bolt in place, sealing it at least for now. Noan stood to the side, carefully observing the situation.

The dwarf was to the left of their target; the druid was to the right. The guard, holding his sword in his right hand, swung at Ginderbar. Noan watched as the three blades moved quickly toward their intended goals, reflecting the light from the fireplace's flames.

Ginderbar's blade was deflected, and he only received

a surface nick on his cheek as the broadsword completed its movement. Nonetheless, his left arm continued to bleed and this cut just added to the quantity of precious fluid flowing forth. Facing their foe's unguarded side, Jienna's scimitar made a shallow cut below his leather jerkin.

Stepping to the side, the guard directed his next blow at the druid. Neither had expected this sudden change in his position. Ginderbar's metal swished through empty air while Jienna's merely cut a gash in his tunic, just scraping against the leather. His blow, however, sliced through the body of her dress and ran along three of the ribs on her right side. Drops of blood began to trickle out.

This blow surprised Jienna, and adrenalin suddenly coursed through her system, though it did not have the same effect as it did in her brother. Even so, she avoided the next movement of the broadsword, and her scimitar took a deep bite into their adversary's shoulder. Ginderbar, meanwhile, took advantage of the guard's diverted attention. He thrust straight forward, piercing the leather and passing into their opponent's torso. As he pulled the blade back, the body slumped to the ground.

***

While the druid tended to the cuts, cleaning them and applying dressings, with assistance from the spellcaster, Tiniki turned her attention to the dwarf in her custody.

"Whether you continue to breathe will depend upon how well you follow my directions and answer my questions. I hope you understand." She tightened the garrote for a moment and then slackened it just enough to allow him to gasp in some air.

"First, I want you to remove your belt and drop it and your sword off to the side."

As he complied, Noan drew a bit closer, drawing Ginderbar's sword from its sheath. Reph and Anndimfoss had joined the others.

"Are there exits besides the way I was brought in?" She loosened the metal wire enough to allow him to speak, but he was only able to cough at first. A red welt across his throat already marked where the garrote had been biting into his skin.

"I don't think so," he said hoarsely.

"What about the two hallways where you took food earlier...especially the one to the right where you took the large tray of food?"

"It's a dead end. The other guard lives there. The other hall goes to the lower level of the dungeon."

"The other guard..."

"He's a giant!" the only other visible prisoner called out from another cell.

"A giant?" the gnome asked.

"Uh-huh. Seen him a couple a' times. I'd guess he's a dozen feet high or so. They call him with that gong."

"Thanks, friend." Her concentration returned to the guard in her control. "Tell me, does that giant always listen to you?"

"Usually."

"What do you do if he doesn't?"

"Well..."

Tiniki tightened the garrote and held it there. She then released the pressure and he desperately sucked in air. The rest of the party was now paying full attention to the exchange.

"One last time to answer!"

"In case of trouble," he coughed out, "we've got a potion that gives control over a giant."

"And where is it?"

"On a shelf...at the end of the hall near the gong," he gasped. There was a negative tone to his response.

"I'll get it," Ginderbar offered. "Just in case we need it," he added as he strode forward.

He stepped into the hallway and the floor suddenly opened beneath him. He dropped out of sight and the floor slammed shut. The report of stone against stone echoed off the walls and reverberated down the corridors. It was at least as loud as any sound from the gong could have been!

***

Flaying out with his unharmed arm, Ginderbar found himself falling into a pit of darkness as the trapdoor sprang shut above him. One foot struck a solid stone floor and his leg folded under his weight as the rest of his body reached the ground. Excruciating pain surged through his limb. His jaw closed with the momentum of his descent, biting into his lower lip. The piercing pain and the salty taste of blood in his mouth were all that kept him from succumbing to unconsciousness.

The extreme agony in his leg made it impossible for him to rise. He was unable to tell whether it was a broken bone or a sprained muscle, but he could not accept the idea of simply sitting there and waiting for someone to come to his rescue. The strong odor of one or more animals also played on his mind. He could not identify it and, considering his present condition, he did not want to learn by meeting it.

Dragging his body across the floor, he eventually reached a wall. His infravision had come into play and he detected several insects and a couple of rodents, but nothing more. That took the edge off the anxiety caused by the strange odor, but his present problems were still unsolved.

Moving along the wall to the right, he found a door. It had a small, grated window, but the door was locked and the region beyond was just as devoid of light or heat. By continuing the clockwise motion, he rounded a corner and came to another door.

The pain was worsening and he was growing weaker, but Ginderbar persevered. There was no window, and the doorknob turned, but he was unable to open it. Then his hand felt a bar that could be lifted, which would allow him to draw the door open. Shifting to the side, he raised the bolt and pulled back on the door.

At that point, he was blinded by light pouring down from above and to his right. He stumbled through the doorway, losing his balance on his good leg. The door shut behind him and he heard the bolt fall back into place. There was a sound in the room behind him, and an even louder one directly before him. He waited for his infravision to come back into operation, fighting against the extreme pain and the throbbing in his head.

***

A scream escaped from Anndimfoss' lips as she saw her husband suddenly vanish. She turned and stared at the guard. Tiniki could not help but read the anguish in her friend's face.

"What happened?" she demanded. Anger was evident in the tone. "Where is Gin?"

"You better speak!" Tiniki hissed, tightening the wire just a bit.

"Why?"

"Don't you want to live?"

"I can't believe you, and Torg'll be coming now."

The gnome began to tighten the garrote.

"Stop!" Jienna called out. "He may still be of use to us." She hurried over and took control of the wire wound round his neck. Reph moved to stand immediately behind his sister.

Tiniki retrieved her thieves' tools and quickly succeeded at picking the lock to her cell. As she had guessed, it was quite simple. She swung the gate open and stepped out just as a growl issued from the corner of the room.

Turning around, she, Noan and Anndimfoss found a war dog charging toward them, its teeth bared and its ears flattened back. Feeling naked without any weapon, the dwarf desperately scanned the area around her. She saw the guard's short sword lying on the ground and dove for it. This motion immediately attracted the dog's attention and it swerved, moving toward her.

Anndimfoss drew the blade but was only able to rise to her knees before the dog reached her. Holding the hilt against her gut, she aimed the point at the attacking animal.

Once more this evening, a member of the party had fortune favoring them. The dog impaled itself upon the sword, knocking Anndimfoss over. The wind was driven from her and the blow of her head upon the floor dazed her. Shaking her head, she found herself pinned down by the dog's inert body. Noan had been able to finish it off with a coup de grace.

Reph lifted the dog's body and tossed it into the open cell while Noan and Tiniki helped Anndimfoss to her feet. Starspire meanwhile pulled the body of the dead guard toward the cell and Reph helped move it in with the dog.

Jienna had somehow been able to maintain control of her prisoner while this had all been occurring. She lessened the pressure so he was able to stay conscious.

Before they were able to congratulate one another, the tremor of the ground captured their attention. Freezing where they stood, they heard heavy footsteps.

"That's the giant," the other prisoner warned them.

"We must act quickly," Jienna said. "We have to get that potion!"

"But what about the trap door?" Anndimfoss asked.

"I've seen a guard go down that hallway. If only we knew where the edge was," Tiniki muttered.

"Then we'll find it," Jienna said, forcing the guard

before her.

He struggled, but she once again tightened the garrote until he was gurgling in his attempt to breathe. The others followed, their eyes glued to the ground. As the floor opened beneath him, Jienna released her hold. The guard's body plummeted headfirst through the gap. The stone again slammed shut, but they had seen that an eighteen-inch margin existed on the left side.

"I'm going this time," Tiniki asserted as she withdrew her moonstone. She moved into the darkness, turning to the left and disappearing from their field of vision.

Meanwhile, the heavy footsteps slowly but steadily grew closer. Reph moved across the room, drawing his long sword. If need be, even in his weakened, tired state, he would try to defend the others.

***

By the blue light, Tiniki saw a set of shelves just a few feet before her. A stoppered glass vial was alone on the middle shelf. As she grabbed it, she saw her sheathed dagger on the shelf below it. There were other items, and she was sorely tempted to investigate them, but she forced herself to turn and go back to where the others were waiting. She was careful to stay to the side as she covered the last distance.

As Tiniki handed the vial to Jienna, the giant rounded the corner. He was over a dozen feet in height, with a broad chest and muscles rippling on his arms and thighs. All he wore were boots and tight-fitting trousers. His sandy hair and beard were both closely cropped, revealing the angular features of his head. The club he cradled in his two hands was perhaps eight feet in length, and he appeared ready to swing it as he glanced around the room.

As she removed the stopper, the druid wondered if the guard had been honest, but she saw no other acceptable options. Raising the vial to her lips, a strong, pungent odor reached her nose. Closing her eyes, she sucked in and quickly swallowed the rather viscous liquid.

The sweet, syrupy fluid flowed down her throat and images of the giant bowing in subservience before her formed in her mind. Forcing her eyes open, she saw him cautiously moving toward her brother. Reph was partially crouched, ready for both offensive and defensive action.

"Stop, friend!" she called out, holding an open palm toward the giant.

"Friend?" he asked, a quizzical look forming on his face.

"Yes, friend! My name is Jienna. What is yours?"

"Lork..." There was a questioning note in his voice.

"We are all your friends, Lork. We are fleeing from enemies who are on the other side of the doorway. Your job is to stay at this post and prevent their entry."

Lowering his club, he resumed his advance, keeping a careful eye on the berserker. As Reph took a less threatening stance, the giant moved more comfortably.

Jienna knew they had only gained a little breathing time. She did not know how long the effect of the potion would last, nor did she know its limits. What should she do?

Glancing around, the look of anguish on Anndimfoss's face resolved the question. The first order of business was to find Ginderbar. Then they had to find a safe way to get Noan and themselves out of here. They could try to take the route the dwarf had taken, but what of the other two routes?

Lork stood by the metal door, club in hand. His face had a stern, steadfast and distant gaze to it. He understood the duty now assigned to him and, at least for the moment, he accepted it.

In a conversational tone, Jienna asked, "Tell me, Lork, what are down the two hallways?"

"One goes to my home," he responded with possessive pride. "It's a nice, comfortable cave. The other goes to a small stairway."

"Where does the stairway go, Lork?"

"I don't know. Too small for me."

"He's not lying to you," the prisoner called out.

"How do you know?" Tiniki asked.

"I can read people's faces and the tone of their voice. I don't really know just why, but there's something about them that let's me sense when someone is intentionally lying."

"What's your name?" Jienna queried.

"I'm called Jondo. Can I join you in trying to find a way out? I'll offer whatever help I am able in return for being freed from this infernal cage."

Jienna glanced around. The others nodded, so she told Tiniki to open his cell. Turning back to the pressing issue, she decided that the left turn would have to be their choice.

"Listen, Lork, I and the rest of your friends are going to find out where these stairs go. Then we'll let you know."

With that, the remaining members of the Coterie, plus Noan and Jondo, took off toward that hallway.

13 – UNDERGROUND

U hu tensed when he heard the blast of a horn. The people he could see in the distance began to actively move toward the castle. His pessimistic thoughts centered on what could have gone wrong and he was uncertain what he should do. At a gentle pace, he had the horse move the wagon further into the forest's shade. The other steeds obediently followed.

Shortly thereafter, a loud gong sounded. He could see smoke rising from the tower as Swoop sailed in and landed on a neighboring branch.

"What can you tell me?" the elf queried.

"Not enough. A fire is burning somewhere within the structure and everyone is agitated. I did not see any of your friends. What next?"

Thinking briefly, Uhu decided to move down to the forest in the region below the cliff. He would wait there. If the party somehow escaped, the owl was directed to try to lead them to him. If that failed, they would jointly figure what action to take. If any of Blavin's forces began to head south, he would take off on a single steed and the two of them would flee.

That decided, he then began to move toward the descending road while Swoop returned to observing Tiufrann.

***

As Jienna started down the stairway, Starspire asked Jondo why he had been in the cell.

The solidly built young man responded freely.

Avi Ornstein

"Besides being able to tell when someone openly lies, I find I'm not able to lie myself when I choose to talk. I had had too much to drink one afternoon and openly expressed my opinions about Blavin's partner, Esthinpeem. Unfortunately, he was passing behind me and heard it. I was thrown in the dungeon until I choose to publicly state what I said was not true. Problem is, I can't do that. If your small friend hadn't opened my cell, I guess I'd have been there the rest of my life."

He turned and thanked Tiniki, who was right behind them.

Smiling back, she asked what he did for a profession.

"I'm a pretty good horseman and an even better wagoner," he said proudly.

"Them's skills th' Coterie needs," Reph commented.

Jienna had reached the bottom of the stairs. She turned back and hushed the party's discussion.

***

As his infravision came into play, Ginderbar found himself in a large room. The odor was nauseating, but it was the other resident of the chamber that caused fear to chill his body. This level of fear was so intense that he momentarily became unaware of the bodily pain.

A manticore was stalking him! Its scorpion-like stinger was raised over its head and its teeth were bare. A guttural growl issued from its throat. The head and body resembled those of a lion – only larger. It flexed its claws as it slowly advanced.

The dwarf found he was unable to move. His legs throbbed intensely, as did the damaged arm. He was unable to find anything to grab with his good arm other than a few scraps of chewed bone. His mind became disoriented while it uncontrollably painted gory images of where the bones had come from. He screamed as the stinger swiftly descended and struck his chest followed by a sharp, burning pain that surged through his body. As it was withdrawn, he found he could physically do nothing as the manticore's open mouth drew closer. At that point, he went unconscious.

***

Jienna had been studying the hallway when the others joined her. A single candle mounted on the wall opposite the stairs dimly lighted it. There were two options, as it went to the left and the right, perhaps twenty feet in each direction. A closed door was visible at each end of the hall and an additional door was on the same side as the stairs, just prior to each end.

A scream was heard to the left.

"Ginderbar?" Anndimfoss called out. Panic showed on her face and was clearly evident in her voice.

The group took off in that direction, with Jienna and Reph leading the way. Reaching the doorway, Reph pulled it open, but the hallway beyond was dark.

Starspire quickly cast the cantrip of Lamanna's Light and Jondo held the door open as the spellcaster, Jienna, Reph and Anndimfoss rushed through. Tiniki remained behind, restraining Noan from following the others.

The pale blue light only lit a small region. They heard a loud roar from somewhere ahead and Starspire abruptly stopped.

"Give me a moment to cast a spell that will offer more light," he pleaded.

The impatience of Anndimfoss was evident, but the rational need to see where they were going and what lay ahead held her back. As he finished the spell, a bright white light appeared above him, floating in the air. He could move it around as he wished, but he decided to have it stay above him as he moved. The four advanced down the hallway.

They could see a door on the left, followed by four cells. The hallway then ended in cold stone. The door was metal with a thick glass window. As they reached the window, the others were glad that Anndimfoss was too short to see through it. Starspire shuddered and almost lost control of the light, as he abruptly moved away from the window. He felt like retching and was surprised that he was able to control his gut.

Reph began to breathe heavily and reached for the door, but his sister held him back.

"We are too late," she said in a whisper, turning her back on the horrendous sight of the manticore feeding upon their friend. As she forced her brother to step back, she told Anndimfoss what they had seen. The dwarf suddenly collapsed to her knees, failing in the battle to hold back her tears.

Gasping and then slowly standing up, she said, in a steely tone, "We must go on. We have to find a way to take Noan out of this cesspool of a dungeon and thereby justify my husband's death!"

Reph knelt down so his eyes looked directly into hers.

"True 'nuff. We's gonna do that wi' ya' an' we's not gonna fergit Gin – ever!"

***

The four cells were barren and the doorway back in the lit hallway revealed the dead body of the guard who had fallen through after Ginderbar. This left two more possible doors to be investigated.

The doorway beyond the stairway was locked, but Tiniki was able to successfully pick it. As they carefully pulled the door open, they saw that a cell door was just inside it. The light spilled into the room and they saw a body sleeping on a cot. While they watched, it began to move and appeared to be male. As he awakened, he covered his eyes to block the glaring light.

"You won't even let me sleep through the night?" he asked in a deep, raspy voice. "I know we're underground, but this is my domain! I know what time it is! Let me be!" he shouted as he stood and turned to face them.

While the light blinded him, they could clearly see the prisoner. He was shorter than Tiniki, but was unquestionably not a child. He had bright orange skin and his hair and eyes were clearly red. His broad, flat nose and pointed ears could be seen easily. Small, sharp fangs were displayed from his wide mouth as he protested to them. A hobgoblin stood before them!

"What do you want from me?" he roared. "I've told you and your dumb ruler that if you release me, my father will pay a handsome ransom!"

"It seems I wasn't the only card Blavin was keeping up his sleeve," Noan noted.

The hobgoblin's ears turned sharply at hearing her comment.

"Wait! You're not guards! Who are you? Can you help me?"

Eyes flitted back and forth. None had any liking for hobgoblins, but there was a sense that an enemy of their enemy might be able to help them. As he had said, they were in his domain here, deep within the ground.

Jienna ventured a response.

"We are seeking an exit from this dungeon. If you can help us, we may be able to do the same in return."

"There's an ancient tunnel," he replied, an excited tone in his voice. "It supposedly connects our realm to this, but there is a door that won't open from our side. We don't know why. If it isn't collapsed, it will take us out of here!

"I had been exploring the region around the castle, as I sensed an external entry to it, when Blavin took me prisoner. I can sense that natural tunnel is close by."

Starspire turned to Jondo.

"What do you sense?" he whispered.

"As far as I can tell, he's not lying...though I will never fully trust anything a hobgoblin says," he answered, hoping that their exchange was not heard in the cell.

Jienna turned to the others, an unworded query visible in her eyes. There was an evident sense of hesitancy, but no one openly opposed this option. She saw that Starspire gave a quick nod of approval and she decided to accept the venture, as the path behind them clearly would not work.

Turning back to the hobgoblin, she asked what they should call him.

"I am of noble birth," he said rather haughtily, "but you can call me Blag."

"Well, Blag, you can call us the Coterie."

"What is a coat-a-ree?"

"Don't worry. It is our name."

"You all have one name?"

"We's the Coterie an' we don' needs anythin' else," Reph replied proudly, grinning at his sister. "Let's go!"

Saying naught, the hobgoblin pointed at his shackled ankle.

Tiniki took the ring of keys from Jienna. Working quickly, the gnome found the correct item and cautiously opened the clasp. She noticed that Blag eyed the tools she was using, so she carefully handed them to Reph for safekeeping. The hobgoblin's displeasure with that action was palpable.

Everyone moved back as he exited his cell. The bright light that shone above Starspire lit the hallway and clearly bothered the hobgoblin, but no comment was made about it. Shielding his eyes, he slowly scanned the group that had liberated him. His distrust of the four humans was discernable by all, nor did he seem to be especially comfortable with the mountain dwarf. His feelings toward the gnome were at best neutral. Their opinion of him was no better. Nonetheless, they all recognized that they were going to have to work together, trying to achieve a possibly common goal.

Pointing toward the door just beyond his cell, he simply said, "That's the way."

**

The door was heavy, made of oak and reinforced with metal bars. There was no lock, but it appeared to only be able to be opened from this side. Neither the druid nor the spellcaster was able to move it.

"Don' git hurt, Ji an' Star. Lets me try," Reph said.

Straining a bit, he shoved the door open and held it while the others proceeded to investigate the region beyond.

There was a series of six empty cells with an open path between the fourth and fifth, ending in a solid metal door. It proved to be locked, but Tiniki reclaimed the ring of keys from the berserker and found she did not have to test her personal skills, as one of the keys again met their needs.

Placing her arm through the ring, she and Jienna grabbed hold of the metal bar and pulled upon it with their combined force. There was a rusty, grating sound as the heavy metal door was slowly forced open and a thick layer of cobwebs was torn apart. The air beyond was musty and cold. The passage appeared to be a natural fissure in the rock and the bottom of the pathway consisted of a layer of sand and gravel.

"I will go first," Blag asserted.

Jienna had a queer gut feeling, but she was uncertain what it meant so she decided to accept his offer. It was quickly decided that Anndimfoss would be second with Starspire and his light behind her. He was to be followed by Jondo and then Reph. Jienna would be after her brother, with Noan behind her and Tiniki would be last, using her moonstone to let those at the end see their way.

Carelessly sweeping the spiders and their webs aside, the hobgoblin stepped into the tunnel. He walked with a clear sense of confidence, scanning only slightly to the left and right as he strode forward. The dwarf had no trouble following him, but, as they proceeded, the spellcaster found that his height proved to pose a difficulty. The light was not a physical entity, so it was no encumbrance, but he had to be careful that he did not bump or scrape his head on the rough, uneven rocks above him.

The path descended and curved gently, first to the right and then to the left. Small things darted out of the way into cracks before they could be identified. However, some started to peer out of their hiding places once Starspire's bright light had passed. Jienna and Tiniki saw millipedes and mites, plus many spiders and a few scorpions. Fungus also grew on the walls, apparently supplying a source of food for these residents.

While the air got no colder, it did become thicker and breathing became slightly more difficult. Then the crevice suddenly became very narrow.

The hobgoblin took off into the darkness. Everyone other than the gnome had to work slowly to get bodies that were too large through the passageway. Progress became very difficult and they felt that they were advancing at little more than a snail's pace. All questioned what lay ahead and complained how hobgoblins were unable to be trusted. Jondo cursed himself for not discerning any lies, though Blag's statements had probably been too limited.

"That was the warning the ooph gave us!" Jienna declared. She was far enough beyond the light of the moonstone for her voice to be heard by those ahead of her.

"What warning?" Jondo asked.

"Several days ago, we rescued an ooph. She made a prophecy. Part of it said how, underground, we had to beware a 'king uncrowned'."

"That's right," Starspire said. "Blag proudly told us he is nobility. I bet his father is – or was – the king of their tribe. He may have passed away. That would make Blag a king uncrowned."

Agreeing on that perception, they noted that recognizing it after the fact was unfortunately of minimal value. Nonetheless, they persevered and continued to move slowly onward.

Eventually, the crevice in the bedrock finally gained enough width and height to let them proceed unimpaired. Picking up the pace, they saw that the hobgoblin's footprints were very clear and that he had been running. They came to a fork and, thanks to the marks in the sand, had no trouble deciding to follow the trail to the left. As she passed the split in the tunnel, Anndimfoss noticed an isopod as large as her hand moving slowly along one wall, but her attention shifted back to the path.

After a straight length that continued to slope downward, it made a sharp bend to the right. Hearing a mixture of hobgoblin profanity and cries of pain ahead, the dwarf gestured those behind her to stop.

Looking around the corner, she was unable to see anything, due to Starspire's light. Deciding that having him douse the light and then waiting for her eyes to adapt would be counterproductive, she silently urged the group to proceed slowly, drawing Ginderbar's sword as she progressed. The hobgoblin would see the approaching light, so she felt that they had to be ready to deal with him.

After only a few steps, Blag became silent. As they closed the distance, he became visible. He was smiling at them.

They all paused, uncertain of what should be done next.

"I came ahead and found the way!" he called out. "However, there is a rope I am unable to remove and I need your assistance."

"Why should we help you?" Anndimfoss called out.

"As I said before, my father will reward you."

"What type of reward?" Jienna queried.

"He will pay for your valiant assistance in gold and gems."

"He's clearly lying," Jondo whispered to the others at a barely audible level.

Drawing nearer, they discerned that there was an open area with two metal doors. Each had a lock and was structured to open outward. In addition, a glistening rope spanned the area, tautly binding the doors together. The rope appeared to be clean, but there were drops of blood on the sand near the door to the right and pieces of cloth were wrapped around each of the hobgoblin's hands.

"Help me untie or cut this rope and unlock the doorway," he said, a tone of pleading in his voice.

"Where does each door lead?" the druid asked.

"The one to the right leads to my realm. The other is a dead end."

Jondo stared at him and asked "Where does the second actually lead?"

"Nowhere."

"Stop lying!" Jondo shouted.

The hobgoblin began to open his mouth but he closed it as he saw Jienna drawing her scimitar and Reph his long sword.

"Well, I believe it actually leads to the surface. It was the route I was seeking when Blavin took me prisoner. However, we need to go the other way if you are to earn a reward."

"I think not," Jienna said slowly.

Suddenly, a mixture of anger and panic became evident on Blag's face and he started to run toward the druid.

She held up her scimitar in defense, but it did not

come into play. Anndimfoss cracked open his skull with a single downward blow of her husband's sword, venting some of the anger surging inside her due to her intense personal loss. Reph had simultaneously stepped in to protect his sister.

The hobgoblin fell face-first against the ground. A pool of dark blood began forming around his head as the dwarf pulled free her weapon, wiping it off on his clothes.

"At least we know which way we want to go," Noan said, turning toward the left.

Jienna hesitantly touched the rope. She felt nothing, but found she was unable to untie either knot. Her scimitar bounced off it, doing no harm. The same occurred when Reph and Noan each tried to cut it. Tiniki tried to undo the knot but immediately pulled away, placing her fingers in her mouth.

"It burns!" she said in a muffled tone.

Starspire held up an open palm and went to investigate it as the others stayed back. Casting a Detect Magic spell, a smile appeared on his face.

"It is clearly magical," he said. "But that's my last spell until I get a decent sleep. I've depleted my manna. It's fortunate that the light continues until I cancel it."

Carefully touching it with a single finger, he found it did not burn him as it had the thief, or as it previously had done to the hobgoblin. He found he was able to easily untie the rope at each end, relieving the stress exerted on the two doors. He then carefully coiled the rope, which was something over thirty feet in length, and slung it over his shoulder.

***

Swoop landed on a branch above Uhu, who had positioned the wagon and horses to the west of the road just a short distance within the beginning of the forest.

"What can you tell me?" the elf queried.

"I have not yet seen any of your friends, if that is what you are asking," the owl replied. "As far as the fire, it seems to be coming under control, though the people are very agitated and I am guessing it will still be quite a while before the fire is no more. I will hunt for dinner and then resume my observations."

"Good hunting," Uhu called as his friend silently took wing. The elf then settled down to nap, feeling that it would be best to be well rested, no matter what action was to follow.

***

Tiniki found that none of the keys on the ring worked in either door, trying each key twice.

"I guess we're depending on your skills," Jienna ventured.

The gnome motioned for the others to be silent as she moved to the door on the left. Working slowly, listening carefully to the sounds made as her tools were used, her nervousness was replaced by a taut grin as the doorway swung open.

The gust of fresh air coming in was welcome, clearing the stuffiness and lessening the odor emanating from the dead hobgoblin.

"We don' needs th'other door," the berserker noted. Nods and facial expressions made it clear that everyone agreed.

Resuming the order they had used to leave the castle dungeon, they began to ascend this passageway, heading toward their world and whatever awaited them.

***

While both the actual stone and the structure of the crevice were the same as in the region through which they had earlier traveled, other aspects were very different. Rather than a layer of sand and gravel being underfoot, they found they were walking on soil with occasional leaves. A wide variety of insects were moving around, both on the walls and underfoot. There was a somewhat familiar, faint odor, though they found that they were unable to identify it.

The path was narrow, but passage was manageable as long as they progressed in a single file. It stayed rather constant. The direction wavered left and right as it ascended, so the distance they could see at any time was limited. Nonetheless, the overall mood was more confident than when they had been descending behind the hobgoblin.

Anndimfoss proceeded slowly but steadily with her sword drawn, staying within the region made visible by the spellcaster's light. Jondo and Reph followed right behind Starspire. They were ready if danger should appear, but weapons were held down. There was then a slight gap in the group, as Jienna and Noan stayed in the area that received the light from Tiniki's moonstone.

Signaling those immediately behind her to stop, the dwarf waited until the other three had caught up with them and Tiniki had covered the moonstone.

"I recognize the odor," she whispered. "It is the unpleasant smell when dogs are present."

Others quietly agreed, as their minds suddenly were able to associate the aroma with past experiences.

"We don't know just what that means," Jienna commented in a hushed voice, "but we need to advance with caution. Reph, I'd like you to move up behind Anndimfoss. You'll be able to see over her, and whatever we face will have to get past both of you first. Noan, I hope that you understand that our purpose of being here is to bring you out safely. We do not mean to slight you, but your protection is our responsibility."

Noan gave a single nod, signifying both her

understanding and acceptance. Even so, she glanced down at the short sword she held in hand, clearly ready to use it should the need arise.

The dwarf gestured the others to follow and cautiously resumed the upward trek.

***

As they progressed, the odor grew stronger. In addition, scraps of bone began to appear on the bottom of the passageway, becoming more frequent with each turn. The tension increased, as everyone was uncertain just how this should be interpreted.

Finally, a curve let the light fall upon a large cave. The tunnel continued on the opposite side. To the side was a female wolf with two nursing pups. She growled menacingly at the intruders, but she was off to the side so they hoped they would be able to pass through the cave without having to fight her. It was clear that a rather large pack lived here, but the rest were apparently out hunting. They were probably the wolves they had heard when they first reached Tiufrann. Whispered comments exchanged these views and the hopes that there would be no need to confront the pack. They were tired and drained and ill prepared for such an event.

Under Jienna's directions, they quickly and quietly passed through, staying as close as possible to the side opposite the wolf. They avoided making any threatening motions as best they were able. Fortunately, there was nothing they had to deal with other than the growled warning that continued until they were all beyond the cave. Once they were again in the passageway, they picked up their pace while being attentive to the possibility of any sounds, both before and behind them.

The path now leveled off and, after only two more twists, it straightened. They then heard the sound of pouring water ahead and were able to view vines falling across the cave opening, obviously concealing the entrance. Listening carefully, they could just make out distant voices over the noise of the waterfall.

Jienna signaled Tiniki to cover her moonstone so that it would not hamper the necessary conversation they would need to have to be able to decide what to do.

"It is time to extinguish your light, Starspire."

"Are you certain? Once it is gone, I will be unable to replace it."

"Yes," the druid said with confidence. "What light we need will have to be supplied by Tiniki's stone, which will also make it harder for others to hear us."

She turned to Jondo.

"You are most familiar with this area. Carefully look beyond the vines and see if you can tell where we are. We want to move away as quickly as possible, but only in a manner that is safe."

Jondo nodded and moved forward rather slowly. With the spellcaster's light gone, there was only the blue light that was once again being emitted from Tiniki's hand. However, this limited source made safe progress difficult, so he took his time.

He slowly parted the vines just a bit and looked out. He then returned to where the others were waiting.

Tiniki covered the moonstone with her other hand. In the darkness, he quietly explained to the others that they were directly below the eastern side of Castle Tiufrann. The sky was dark, implying that it was still covered by clouds. The waterfall was to their right. There seemed to be about a two-foot drop from the mouth of the cave. If they went to the left, following the narrow gorge, it would lead to the lower level, below the cliff, to the south of the castle.

"Good," Jienna replied. "That is the direction we want to go."

She turned to her brother.

"Reph, Tiniki will hold the moonstone and you will descend and then help her and Anndimfoss down. Everyone else will follow, being as silent as we are able. Hopefully, the waterfall and blue light will hide any sounds and no one will be looking down from the castle walls. We need to move as rapidly as we are able, given the conditions we face. Caution and silence are both critical.

"Does anyone have any questions?"

Seeing that there were none, she told the gnome to expose the stone and they then followed her plan.

Each member was nervous as he or she exited the cave, involuntarily looking up at the castle. Seeing smoke and the light of a fire, they felt reassured by having something else demanding the attention of those above them.

Once everyone was out, they began moving downriver, with Tiniki taking a position in the middle of the line. There was a narrow bank along the river, but it was level and dry close to the cliff, making passage fairly simple. As they exited the gorge, they moved to go around a small hill so it would be between them and the castle. They then headed straight toward the forest to the south and the cover it offered.

As they moved in that direction, an owl passed by close overhead. It looped around again and then took off toward the forest.

***

"Awaken! Awaken!" Swoop called out as he flew over Uhu.

The elf rubbed his eyes as he sat up.

"I have found your friends! They are headed this way!"

"Excellent! I will prepare the mounts and cart. Try to direct them here, but let me know if you are unable."

"I will!" he called out as he flew away, maneuvering between the trees.

***

"D'ya see th' bird?" Reph asked. "I thin' 'twas Uhu's."

The group had just entered the forest and Tiniki had covered her moonstone, which had let him know that he was able to talk. He had been unable to hold back his positive offering. They were far enough that they could not be heard and now they could not be seen. It was not totally dark, and even those without infravision were adjusting to be able to proceed cautiously.

"I thought the same," Starspire responded.

Just at that point, the owl reappeared. He matched his name, swooping in front of them, and then veering slightly to the left. They caught on and turned in that direction.

Shortly thereafter, they came upon Uhu just as he finished preparing for their arrival.

"Introductions will be later," Jienna called out. "Help Noan onto the seat, Starspire, and you will get in behind. Once we're on the road, you will try to sleep to regain your manna. Jondo, you will show your wagoner skills. Tie Ginderbar's pony to the wagon and everyone else get ready to ride. Uhu, you will lead us to the road and then we head for Castle Vork. Reph, you and I will follow behind, in case anyone follows us."

Uhu directed Swoop to patrol behind them and let them know if anyone followed. He shared that information with the others. With that, they all mounted and took off.

***

They traveled at a steady pace, but they chose to not overexert the ponies. When morning came, the sky was clear and sunny. Swoop landed on the wagon and joined the spellcaster in sleeping. The rest had decided to push until early afternoon. They then would move off the road and get the sleep that they were missing. Uhu had agreed that he would stand watch, as he was the only one that had gotten some real sleep during the night.

As the dwarf and gnome rode together, the emotional impact of Ginderbar's death hit Anndimfoss.

"How can that have happened?" she asked herself. She was thinking about the evening's actions without actually seeking anyone else's opinions or input.

"What do you mean?" Tiniki asked.

Anndimfoss looked over at her friend and then realized she had vocalized her question.

"Before we departed to rescue Noan, I went to a seeress. When I asked if we would survive this undertaking, she said we would," she moaned.

"Do you remember just what the seeress said?"

The dwarf was silent as she tried to remember the exact response to her query.

"I asked, 'Will we survive?' and she said, 'You shall survive, but I foresee much suffering.' I'm almost certain those were her words."

Tiniki mulled this over.

"The words of any prophecy are critical. You asked about both of you, but she probably was responding by only telling your future. I'm guessing that she was only foreseeing your survival, replying in the singular. Ginderbar's death was the suffering she foretold."

"Had I known that, I wouldn't have come!" she wailed.

"Perhaps, but the prophecy was fulfilled. Did she answer any other questions?"

"She said I would lose Ginderbar! She was referring to him as something near to me! But she said I'd gain many-fold in return. What could be more valuable than Ginderbar?"

"Did you get the answer to a third question?" Tiniki prodded.

Anndimfoss had a startled look on her face as she recalled the third prophecy. The recollection hit her psychologically and she almost fell off her pony.

"She said Ginderbar and I would have a child that would grow to adulthood! How can that be, now that he is gone?"

"Remember when you were 'tired' at the inn? I'd venture that you are already carrying your child at the earliest stage!"

"Could that be?" Anndimfoss asked.

Tiniki did not respond, but the possibility carried the dwarf beyond the trough of the emotional stress. As they rode, her mood became more neutral as she attempted to sort out all the changes she had just experienced and that now awaited her in the future.

***

In late morning, they heard a horse approaching them at a rapid rate. They moved to the side of the road to let the rider pass, feeling that would be the easiest action.

As he came into sight, it was easy to see that he wore the garb of the royal guard of Glawynia. He was riding rapidly, but he pulled the reins to stop his steed.

"Do you come from Tiufrann?" he asked. Before anyone responded, his face revealed his recognition of Noan.

Dismounting, he knelt on one knee and said, "M'lady!"

Noan looked down at him. A very formal tone suddenly replaced the familiar, friendly voice that the group had grown accustomed to hearing.

"Stand. What is your duty?"

"I precede a larger party. Our role is to assist in your

rescue, though it seems that has already been achieved."
Looking at the others, he bowed in turn to each.

"How far behind you are the others?" Jienna asked.

"Perhaps a quarter hour," he replied.

"Then let us decrease that time," Noan said.

With that note, they resumed their movement, with the royal guard riding aside the wagon, matching pace with the others.

***

As they approached the party of over a score of guards, they slowed down. Both groups stopped and the captain then rode forward to meet them.

Seeing Noan, he dismounted and bowed. The action was followed by all of the other soldiers.

"M'lady," he said, "the king has asked that you be escorted to his castle."

"King Linoan's? Not my father's? Why is that?"

"The king has decided that he needed to take action to prevent a civil war. He has chosen to stop the dispute between your father and uncle by naming you heir to the throne. You are to be our next ruler, m'lady!"

On that statement, the entire royal force officially saluted her.

"This explains her uncle's announcement," Starspire whispered to Jienna, who was on his side of the wagon. "Noan was within Castle Tiufrann when the prophecy was made."

"And she is to have a long and undisturbed dynasty," Jienna added.

Their conversation stopped when the captain turned to address them.

"King Linoan also instructed me to tell you that, if you succeeded in rescuing Lady Noan, that he will match the reward being paid by her father, Lord Pitar."

The members of the Coterie grinned on hearing this.

"You will be included in the reward," Jienna said quietly to Jondo. "And, should you be interested, you can join our unforeseen future. I see us working on other ventures."

He nodded and smiled.

Noan looked at the members of the party.

"I have viewed you as friends rather than mere mercenaries," she said, "and that won't be changed by you receiving what you have earned. I welcome all of you to consider becoming part of my royal force."

Turning around to face Anndimfoss, she continued, "You have suffered an especially costly loss in this venture. Nonetheless, you kept a clear head and stayed on task. I would like to ask you to serve as my personal bodyguard. If you are willing, it will make me feel more comfortable and, at the same time, it may increase the chance of reuniting our kingdom. Do not answer yet, but think about it as we travel onward."

As the steeds resumed moving, flowing as a unit, Tiniki turned to the dwarf.

"Gaining many-fold," she reminded her.

The dwarf smiled back at her friend.

Avi Ornstein

Born in Manhattan, **Avi Ornstein** was raised in New York and spent summers in Pennsylvania. Though he earned a degree in biology at MIT, he followed a path that was not the expected norm. He first made a living as an artist, and then moved into the profession of science and math education where he taught for over forty-six years. He's been writing in a variety of forms for a long time, predominantly dealing with education. For over forty years, he's also been involved in D & D, where he created his own world, which has been visited by his children and their friends, his students in two different school systems, and now his grandchildren and their friends. It is in this world where his fantasy adventure stories are set. In the real world, he lives in Connecticut with his wife.

A list of previous publications is available at www.aviornstein.com.

Avi Ornstein

Enjoy more novels and short stories from

https://www.twbpress.com

**Science Fiction, Supernatural, Horror, Urban Fantasy,
Thrillers, Romance, and more**